Suddenly, strong arms pulled her back, slamming her against a rock-hard chest.

Rhys held her against him, his arms encircling her, as the carriage thundered past, making the ground tremble beneath the horse's powerful hooves.

Helene's senses seemed to come alive at the moment. The fright at almost being run down. The glory of being held by him. "Rhys," she whispered.

He abruptly released her. "Take more care, Helene," he said gruffly.

He blamed her? She had not seen the carriage coming. No one could have.

He seized her arm and led her across the street, letting go of her the minute they were on the pavement again. What? Did he think she could not safely cross a street now?

Madame Desmet was several paces ahead of them. Helene glanced at Rhys, whose expression seemed to have soured.

Had touching her been that abhorrent to him? Even to save her life? Helene felt tears of anger sting her eyes. She blinked them away, determined not to allow his animosity to affect her. She had come to terms with what she had done in _____ him. Why couldn't h

Author Note

One of the joys of writing historical romance is fitting in the real history of the time period. In this book I've tried very hard to be accurate in my historical details, particularly concerning the Duchess of Richmond's ball and the Battle of Waterloo. The Battle of Waterloo continues to captivate me and I never tire of setting books in and around the battle. Perhaps it is because I am the daughter of an army colonel (US Army, that is) that most of my heroes are army men who value duty, honor and country.

To those readers who love this pivotal episode in history, look for those real historical details and forgive me if I've gotten anything wrong. I've tried hard not to. To others, I hope Rhys and Helene's story sparks an interest in the battle and the people and events around it—the real heroes and heroines.

DIANE GASTON

—

Her Gallant Captain at Waterloo

H HARLEQUIN
HISTORICAL

Recycling programs for this product may not exist in your area.

ISBN-13: 978-1-335-50600-9

Her Gallant Captain at Waterloo

Copyright © 2021 by Diane Perkins

All rights reserved. No part of this book may be used or reproduced in any manner whatsoever without written permission except in the case of brief quotations embodied in critical articles and reviews.

This is a work of fiction. Names, characters, places and incidents are either the product of the author's imagination or are used fictitiously. Any resemblance to actual persons, living or dead, businesses, companies, events or locales is entirely coincidental.

This edition published by arrangement with Harlequin Books S.A.

For questions and comments about the quality of this book, please contact us at CustomerService@Harlequin.com.

Harlequin Enterprises ULC
22 Adelaide St. West, 40th Floor
Toronto, Ontario M5H 4E3, Canada
www.Harlequin.com

Printed in U.S.A.

Diane Gaston's dream job was always to write romance novels. One day she dared to pursue that dream and has never looked back. Her books have won romance's highest honors: the RITA® Award, the National Readers' Choice Award, the HOLT Medallion, the Golden Quill and the Golden Heart® Award. She lives in Virginia with her husband and three very ordinary house cats. Diane loves to hear from readers and friends. Visit her website at dianegaston.com.

Books by Diane Gaston

Harlequin Historical

The Lord's Highland Temptation
Her Gallant Captain at Waterloo

The Governess Swap

A Lady Becomes a Governess
Shipwrecked with the Captain

The Society of Wicked Gentlemen

A Pregnant Courtesan for the Rake

The Scandalous Summerfields

Bound by Duty
Bound by One Scandalous Night
Bound by a Scandalous Secret
Bound by Their Secret Passion

Visit the Author Profile page
at Harlequin.com for more titles.

To my longtime good friend Helen,
whose name I borrowed for my heroine and
who first introduced me to Regency romances.
Oh, what she started!

Chapter One

Brussels, Belgium—June 1815

Raucous laughter, loud voices, and the scent of hops and male sweat assaulted Helene Banes as she stood in the threshold of the Brussels tavern. Her mother's voice rang in her ears. *Ladies do not enter such places.* But her mother was not here, was she? And Helene had already visited three other such establishments before this one.

Resolutely she stepped through the doorway, followed by her weary old manservant.

''Tis a bootless errand, Lady Helene,' her servant said. 'We'll never find him.'

The poor man. She'd dragged him from Northamptonshire to Ramsgate, across the Channel to Ostend and Ghent and finally to Brussels, with very little rest.

'This will be the last, Wilson. I promise.' Helene craned her neck to peruse the dark, crowded room. 'If he is not here, we will return to the hotel.'

They were searching for her younger brother, the only family member she had left since her parents died not even six months ago. David, only eighteen years of age, had tricked her, saying he was visiting school friends. In-

stead he ran off to Brussels. His letter, posted from the
Hôtel de Flandre, had reached her six days before, breez-
ily explaining that he refused to miss the event of the
century—the impending battle with Napoleon.

But David was not a soldier. He was little more than a
boy with no ounce of sense!

She pushed her way slowly through the crowd of red,
blue or black-coated soldiers and plain-clothed Belgians,
ignoring the hoots and whistles that had also followed her
at the other establishments. She searched for one scrawny
blond-haired youth, almost impossible to see in the dim
light of the oil lamps and the crowd of larger men. Poor
Wilson. Her servant looked dead on his feet, but he'd refused to let her search alone.

One man's laugh broke through the din. Her head
swung around to the sound and all thoughts of her brother
fled. A red-coated soldier with dark brown hair and a certain air about him sat at a nearby table. He took a swig of
beer and turned his head slightly.

Helene gasped and quickly averted her gaze. Her heart
pounded.

It could not be him.

Could it?

She stole another glance and her chest ached.

He looked older, of course. And thicker—more muscular. Even though she'd only caught a glimpse, that grin
was painfully familiar. It was, though, only a glimpse,
so she could not be certain. It could be him. He'd left for
the army immediately after…after…

After he'd learned she'd changed her mind about marrying him.

Helene closed her eyes and again remembered the
pain—her father informing her that all was settled. Her
father had informed him that the elopement was off and

that he would instead become a lieutenant in the army. She edged away, hiding her face with the hood of her cloak. If it was him, he'd have no wish to lay eyes on her again.

An angry shout and a scraping of chairs made her turn back. A few tables from where *he* sat was her brother, nose to nose with a man twice his size. The man was dressed in town clothes.

'David!' she whispered. Her servant caught up to her.

David swayed on his feet, tankard in hand. 'Napoleon will be defeated!' he shouted. 'He's not half the general Wellington is!'

The man shrugged and responded in French, *'Napoléon pourrait gagner. Wellington ne l'a jamais affronté au combat.'* Napoleon might win. Wellington never faced him in battle.

'Napoleon will not win!' David flung his drink into the man's face.

The room got quiet. Soldiers half rose from their chairs.

The large man's eyes blazed with anger.

'No!' Helene cried.

Suddenly he was there, his hand gripping David's shoulder.

No doubt now. It was Rhys Landon. The man she almost married.

She'd never learned what regiment he'd joined, because no one would speak of him to her. She'd known he was alive, because she'd searched every list of the wounded and killed in every battle and breathed relieved sighs when his name did not appear. She'd realised he might be in Brussels, because many British soldiers were sent here to face Napoleon's army, but what were the chances of encountering him? She'd intended only to find her brother and return to England straight away.

Yet here he was. With her brother.

'Apologise to this man, boy,' Rhys said in that silken voice she remembered so well, only now it was even deeper. 'Before he beats you to a pulp.'

'I'd like to see him try!' David cried.

Rhys laughed. 'No, you would not like to see him try. He will kill you.' He shook David. 'Apologise. You were out of line.'

'No,' growled one of the soldiers. 'Fellow deserved it.'

Rhys glared at the man. 'We do not want a fight.' His voice was firm and commanding and the soldier backed down.

David bowed his head and looked sheepish. 'My apologies, sir. I am sorry I threw my beer in your face.'

'Say it in French,' Rhys demanded.

Since Belgium was annexed by the French Republic in the late 1700s, French had become the dominant language.

David obeyed. '*Je regrette beaucoup, monsieur.*'

The man shrugged again and sat back down in his chair.

A tavern maid appeared with a towel and the man wiped his face. She turned to David with a question on her disapproving face.

He had difficulty meeting her gaze. 'Bring me another.' He sounded sheepish. 'Please.'

David should not have more to drink! But if Helene tried to stop him, Rhys would certainly see her.

David turned and peered into his captor's face. 'Rhys?'

Rhys released him and his brows drew together, an expression so familiar to her that it was like a shaft to her heart. 'Do I know you, pup?'

'I'm David!' her brother answered. 'David Banes! The Earl of Yarford's son.'

No. David *was* Earl of Yarford. When their father died,

David earned the title. He was simply too young and callow to accept the responsibility of it.

Helene watched the look of shock come over Rhys's face, a look he immediately schooled into something devoid of emotion. 'David Banes? What the devil are you doing here?'

The maid handed David another tankard of beer. 'Here for the battle, of course!' He grinned at Rhys. 'Would not miss it for the world.'

'Lady Helene.' Wilson tapped her shoulder and pointed to David. 'There he is. There is your brother. Shall I get him now?'

His voice was loud enough for both Rhys and David to hear. They turned her way. Rhys's expression hardened.

David gaped, then broke into another inebriated grin. 'Helene!'

'Come with me, David,' she said. The sooner she left this place, the better.

David shook his head, 'Too early! Not done drinking.' He took a long swig of his tankard, smirked at her, then suddenly collapsed. Rhys caught him before he touched the floor.

'David!' she cried in alarm.

'Too much drink,' one of the soldiers commented. 'He's had quite a few.'

Wilson rubbed his brow. 'What are we to do now?'

Indeed. What was she to do? She glanced up and caught Rhys's gaze, but it was too painful to hold. 'We take him to the hotel,' she said. 'Somehow.'

Rhys gave a weary-sounding sigh and slung David over his shoulder. 'I'll carry him.'

'Thank you,' she whispered. 'Thank you, Rhys.'

He scowled and retrieved his shako from the table

where he'd been sitting. His companion, a fellow soldier, stood and touched his arm. 'Shall I assist you?'

'No need,' Rhys responded. 'I can do this.'

Rhys started towards the door, still without acknowledging Helene. His companion tossed her a curious glance before she hurried to keep up with Rhys. He carried David out into the street as though he weighed a feather.

'Where do I take him?' Rhys asked, still not looking at her.

'Hôtel de Flandre,' she replied.

Rhys gave a dry laugh.

Wilson caught up to them. 'May I assist you, Rhys?'

Rhys nodded to the man. 'Wilson. It has been a long time.'

Wilson smiled wanly and swayed on his feet.

Rhys noticed. 'I do not need your help.' He glanced at Helene, his expression disapproving, before turning back to the servant. 'You look exhausted, Wilson.'

'Aye,' agreed Wilson. 'I am a bit weary.'

Helene bit her lip. She knew she'd pushed the older man much too far. She'd tried to insist he stay at the hotel, but he'd been adamant about accompanying her. Wilson, always a faithful and caring servant, had been there when she and Rhys played as children. He'd been there when her friendship with Rhys deepened. What he thought of her and Rhys parting ways, he'd never said.

Wilson walked a few steps behind her, and she followed Rhys through winding streets up the hill to the Hôtel de Flandre. David, still flopped over Rhys's shoulder, occasionally mumbled something. How Rhys could so effortlessly carry him this distance astounded her. When they finally reached the hotel, Wilson limped ahead to open the door.

Without looking back at her, Rhys said, 'What room?'

She gave him the room number the hall servant had told her earlier that day was her brother's room. There were several stairs to ascend. Wilson stumbled on the second flight and Helene turned to catch his arm.

'You must go to your room, Wilson,' she said with concern. 'And do not rise until you are well recovered from our journey. David and I will go about quite well without you for however long you need.'

The old man protested, but she insisted and finally he nodded and passed them up the stairs to make what she supposed would be a long walk to the small rooms procured for servants.

Rhys waited for her, but again did not look at her. 'You may go to your room, as well,' he said. 'I will see to David.'

He wished to be rid of her, she suspected. 'I need to see my brother settled first.'

'Very well.' He started up the stairs again.

When they reached the room, Rhys slid David off his shoulder and leaned him up against the wall. 'Search his pockets for the key.'

The key. Of course. They would need the key.

Reaching into David's pockets put her inches from Rhys, so close she could feel the heat of his body and that scent that was so uniquely him. It brought her back to the time she'd been happy. Tears stung her eyes, but she blinked them away.

She found the key and unlocked the door. He brushed against her as he carried David into the room. Her heart beat wildly again, but he seemed unfazed. The room was dark except for a few glowing coals burning in the fireplace.

Rhys dropped David on to the bed. He removed David's boots. David groaned and mumbled, 'Want to sleep.'

'Will he be all right?' she asked.

Rhys removed his shako and held it under his arm. 'He will have a prodigious headache in the morning. Otherwise he will live.'

She hated to ask Rhys questions, presuming he wished she did not exist, but she had never dealt with someone as cup-shot as her brother. She did not know what to do or even what to think.

'Should I stay with him?'

He made a derisive sound. 'I doubt he'd thank you for it.'

David mumbled something and rolled over, curling into a ball the way he'd done when he'd been a mere bantling.

Rhys turned towards the door, still avoiding facing her. 'Stay or go. It is all the same to me.'

'I'll go.' She hurried out of the room behind him, closing the door behind her. 'Thank you, Rhys,' she said again when they were in the hallway.

He did face her finally, but his handsome face was cold. 'Are you here to witness the battle as well?' His grey eyes seemed to glow in the flickering flames of the hallway's wall lights but glowed with disdain.

She bravely met his gaze, although it cost her fresh pain. 'I came only to bring David home. I agree that his desire to witness the battle is a foolish one.'

Two inebriated soldiers stumbled past them and continued down the long hallway.

Rhys's gaze followed them until he turned to her once more. 'I will walk you to your room.'

It was clear to her he would rather not. 'It is not necessary,' she said.

'I will walk you to your room,' he repeated, this time in that commanding voice he'd used in the tavern.

They walked together. She spoke only to provide directions. He spoke not at all. When they reached her room, she wanted to face him, to gaze at those features that were once like manna to her.

But she would not force him to look at her, so she turned her gaze away. 'Goodnight, Rhys,' she whispered before entering her room.

When she was inside, she leaned against the closed door and listened to his footsteps receding down the hallway.

Rhys couldn't shake her presence as he walked slowly away from her room.

Helene Banes. His Helene.

He'd only seen her in lamplight, but she'd looked even more beautiful to him than she had five years before. Her face was as smooth and pale as fine porcelain, but more angular, more haunting. Her lips remained pink and kissably full. One tendril of her mahogany-coloured hair brushed her cheek. It was her eyes, though—her intense blue eyes—that still held the power to ensnare him. He'd longed to stare at her but had not dared.

How was it she was here in the same city, the same hotel, and—God help him—on the same hallway as his own room? He'd not heard a word about her in the five years that passed between now and that day she'd shattered him by breaking her promise to marry him. No one, especially his family, ever mentioned her or her parents to him again. Of course, he would not have asked. He knew nothing about her life since the day her father came to deliver her devastating message.

He assumed she would marry a title, as her father wished, some man with more prestige and money than a mere vicar's son. But if she was married, where was her husband? Surely a husband would not allow her to visit a common tavern with only poor Wilson in tow. Or even to travel to Brussels at such a volatile time.

Rhys turned the corner past the staircase and leaned against the wall for a moment.

Why the devil did he care? He'd long forgotten her—hadn't he? Congratulated himself on losing her. Celebrated the fact that her rebuff led to his commission in the army. The army, after all, was a life that suited him, a place he excelled. He was proud to serve his country and he served it well. Now that Napoleon had escaped Elba and reclaimed himself Emperor, there was more work to be done. Rhys would do his part to rid the world of Napoleon's rule once and for all. He did not need to be distracted by Lady Helene Banes.

Right down the hallway from him.

He pushed away from the wall and made his way to the suite of rooms he shared with his friend Grant. He pulled out the room key and turned it in the lock. He and Grant joined the 44th Regiment, the East Essex, at the same time and saw action together on the Peninsula. They'd become closer than brothers. They'd both risen to the rank of captain. They'd both learned what it meant to lead men in battle. And what it meant to lose them to enemy fire. They also both knew what they were facing. Napoleon had quickly raised an army as soon as he stepped foot back on French soil. He'd once been the conqueror of Europe. Could he do it again?

Grant was seated in their small drawing room, a glass of brandy in his hand. He hadn't stayed at the tavern, apparently. He raised his glass to Rhys. 'Shall I pour one for you?'

Rhys pulled off his gloves and unbuttoned his coat. 'Please.'

He collapsed in the chair next to his friend and took

a sip. The familiar taste and chest-burning heat of the brandy was welcome but did not quite still his unease.

'Care to tell me what that was all about?' Grant asked.

Rhys had witnessed the heartache Grant suffered in Spain, the betrayal by a woman Grant loved. Before then the two of them had done as soldiers do, took pleasure when it was offered to them, women whose faces—and bodies—blurred with time, but Grant had fallen deeply for this woman and had been wounded just as deeply by her betrayal. Such pain Rhys understood, although he'd never told Grant about his own failed love affair—with Helene.

He did not intend to speak of her now.

'People from where I grew up,' he said. 'A foolish lot.'

Grant's brows rose. 'Indeed.'

The two men drank in silence. One thing Rhys could depend upon, Grant would not press him to say more than he wished to say, no matter what Grant might be thinking. Rhys could feel the questions hanging in the air, nonetheless. Who was the woman? What had she been to Rhys?

She had once been everything to him. They'd grown up together, she, the daughter of the local earl, he, the vicar's son. The vicarage was close enough to the earl's country house that they'd played together as children, as inseparable as two playmates could be, exploring the woods and streams, making up games of damsels in distress and valiant knights. He was eventually sent to Cambridge and they were forced to part, but when he returned, she'd become the beautiful young woman with whom he fell hopelessly in love. She became the very air he needed to breathe. He'd thought only of their being together.

He'd fancied she completed him, as if he had no purpose without her at his side. He'd been so untethered then. Too restless to study law, too irreverent to think of the church, too poor for much else. When it came time for him to return to Cambridge, rather than be separated again, he and Helene hatched a plan to run off to Gretna Green, to marry, to be together for ever. All would be well as long as they were together.

Apparently she'd come to her senses. Her father came to tell him she'd realised she, an earl's daughter, could not marry the vicar's son. Her father, the Earl of Yarford, offered Rhys a commission in the army as consolation, an offer the Earl made impossible for Rhys to refuse.

Eventually, the army had been the making of him.

Rhys took the last sip of his brandy and leaned back in his chair, closing his eyes. A vision of her came unbidden, the way she'd been back in those untroubled days. Young, smiling, leaning in for one of their stolen kisses. He shook his head and opened his eyes to find Grant staring at him.

'Merely some people from where you grew up?' Grant asked.

'People I had no wish to see,' he responded. Although he'd just learned what a falsehood that was. A glimpse of her had shown him he'd yearned for her all along.

Well, he'd pushed thoughts of her away once before; he could do it again.

He stood. 'I'm for bed.'

At least she would not be in Brussels long if she merely came to take her brother back home. With any luck he would not see her again.

He reached down to pick up the brandy bottle and his glass. He poured himself another and downed it in one gulp.

Chapter Two

Rhys rose early enough to ride to where his men were billeted, to see to their welfare, dealing with any of the rivalries or resentments that threatened to lead to bigger problems. The post-dawn air was crisp and fresh, and the scent of the wheat fields reminded him of home.

And home reminded him of Helene, sleeping so near to him, in a room steps away.

After she and her father cast him out, Rhys had expected he'd never set eyes on her again. He convinced himself she would marry and leave Northamptonshire. Was it possible she'd done neither of those things? Or perhaps there had been a husband behind the hotel room door. But why would any man allow her to search through taverns with only a servant in tow?

And why was he still asking himself these questions?

When he reached his company, there were enough problems to sort out with his men that he kept her out of his thoughts.

Almost.

By the time he rode back to Brussels, he reminded himself again that he'd been better off without her, had made a life for himself that suited him very well. Fighting in wars. Rhys's company in the regiment was small, merely fifty men counting his lieutenants, but his job was to keep them alive and to vanquish Napoleon once and for all. Rhys was up to the task and so would his men be.

He stabled his horse and made his way back to the hotel. When he returned to his room to wash up, Grant had apparently gone out. Perhaps he'd risen early, as well, or perhaps he was eating breakfast in the dining room. Rhys hurriedly washed off the dirt of the road and made his way downstairs to the dining room.

And straight into the path of the woman he most hoped to avoid—and could not banish from his mind.

Helene sat at a table directly in front of him. Her brother, sitting adjacent to her, looked over and broke into a grin. There was no avoiding them. Rhys straightened and stepped forward.

David sprang from his seat. 'Rhys! It is you, by God! I thought I'd conjured you up.' He gestured with his arm. 'Come! Join us, will you?'

Rhys glanced around the room, hoping Grant would be there to give him an excuse to refuse, but his friend was nowhere to be seen. Helene looked about as pleased at the prospect of his company as Rhys felt about sharing hers. That settled it. He approached the table and sat in the chair across from her brother so he would not be tempted to gaze at her.

'You've recovered I see.' Rhys spoke to David, giving Helene a curt nod.

Her features stiffened and she averted her eyes.

David pressed his fingers to his temple. 'Head hurts like the devil, actually.' The youth grinned again. 'Imagine running into you here in Brussels! Here for the battle that is coming, eh? Heard you joined the army. Capital idea! Wish I could do so.'

Perhaps he would not wish it, not if he'd ever witnessed the horror that was a battle. Rhys had no patience for the numbers of British in Brussels hoping to be spectators of the bloodshed, like Romans at the Colosseum.

'You are better off returning to England,' Rhys said.

David grimaced at Helene. 'That is what Helene insists upon.'

'She is right about that.' He glanced at her and caught her eye momentarily.

The dining room servant appeared at Rhys's side. 'What may I bring you, Captain?' he asked in French.

'Coffee,' Rhys replied.

His request caused Helene's brows to rise an almost imperceptible amount. In their youth he and Helene had turned up their noses at the strong bitter brew, but drinking coffee was only one of the many ways he'd changed since then.

David went on talking about the impending clash with Napoleon. 'I do not understand Helene's objection. It will be like witnessing history. A battle between the two greatest commanders of our age, perhaps the greatest commanders of all time. It is simply not to be missed.'

The servant poured Rhys's coffee, which he drank without milk or sugar. 'A battle is a messy business,' he told David. 'Not at all like watching a boxing match or a horse race or even a cock fight. Cannon and musket balls cannot tell the difference between a spectator and a soldier. And, once witnessed, the carnage of battle can never be unseen.'

Rather than sobering at the warning, David widened his eyes in excitement. 'Have you seen many battles?'

Sabugal, Fuentes de Oñoro, Ciudad Rodrigo, Badajoz,

Salamanca, Burgos…but Rhys was not about to discuss any of them with the boy.

'Enough.' His voice rasped at remembering.

He thought Helene glanced at him again, but he was trying not to look at her, so he was not certain.

David's voice turned dreamy. 'I would so like to be a part of it all.'

'Your duty is at home,' Helene insisted.

Rhys's duty was to stand firm when cannon and musket fire were aimed at him. If he could not exhibit courage, how could he expect his men to do so?

'I know I cannot fight in the battle,' David protested. 'But this is important to me. I cannot miss it!'

Helene's voice turned low and firm. 'I travelled all this way to bring you home and you *will* come home with me.'

'You are not in charge of me!' David cried like a petulant child. 'I will not listen to you!'

Other diners looked over at the disturbance.

David rose from his chair. 'Leave me alone!' He stormed out.

Suddenly Rhys was alone with Helene. There would be no ignoring her now. In fact, his senses filled with her presence. The scent of her. Her posture. Her emotions.

She seemed to grit her teeth and he felt her anger and worry. 'Foolish boy.'

Rhys needed to distract himself from her. 'How old is he now?' he asked.

'Barely eighteen.' She picked up a piece of toasted bread, but put it down again. 'A very foolish eighteen.'

About the age he'd first realised he was in love with her. 'With a foolish sister who visits taverns no lady should enter?' He took a sip of his coffee.

Her eyes flashed. 'What else was I to do? I worried

he would become embroiled in some trouble and I was correct, was I not?'

True. David would have been beaten to a pulp had Rhys not intervened, but he was not about to admit that to her. 'You were at risk yourself, you realise.'

'Wilson was with me.'

'Wilson,' he scoffed. 'The poor old man was so weary he could barely stay on his feet. He ought to have been in bed, not frequenting taverns.'

'So I told him.' She glared at Rhys. 'He refused to let me to go out alone.'

Rhys knew what could happen to a woman walking these streets alone at night. 'At least one of you has some sense.'

She looked away and picked up her toasted bread, barely nibbling on it, her expression somewhere between injured and angry. It had been an unnecessary jab on his part. Striking out at her revealed more emotion than he wished to exhibit, more emotion than he admitted to feeling.

He changed the subject. 'How is Wilson this morning?'

'I do not know,' she responded. 'I told him to sleep as long as he wished. I left a note for him to say we did not need him this morning.'

At least she showed that much consideration.

She directed her gaze at him again and the power of her eyes was like a punch in the gut. 'Do not feel you must share this table with me, Rhys. David gave you no choice, really, but I certainly will not hold you.'

She wished him to leave her? Then he would stay. 'Are you expecting someone?'

She looked puzzled. 'No. Who would I expect?'

He might as well ask her if she had a husband with her. 'Your husband, perhaps? Is he not with you?'

Her eyes flickered. 'I am not married.'

It felt as if his heart stopped, but he recovered. 'Indeed?' He used his most sarcastic tone. 'I assumed you to have married a duke by now, or at least a marquess. Was that not the plan?'

Her gaze caught him again. 'And you? Are *you* married?'

He gave a dry laugh. 'Only to the army, perhaps.' He peered back at her. 'Who came with you, then? Your father?'

Her voice turned brittle. 'My father is dead. My mother, too.'

He glanced away. 'I did not know.'

He had not known of her parents' deaths. What a substantial piece of information for his parents to conceal in their letters. Rhys had plenty of animosity towards Helene's father, but Rhys knew what death looked like and he would wish it on no one. How had they died? he wondered, but he would not ask.

She seemed to recover and shrugged. 'Not even six months ago.'

'I am sorry for it.' Would she believe him? He'd hated her father for a long time, even though the Earl had paid for Rhys's commission and supplied him with enough money to purchase everything he'd needed. The Earl had not done so out of the goodness of his heart, however.

Helene fiddled with her toast and Rhys took another sip of coffee and the silence between them filled with too many unspoken words. He certainly was not going to speak them out loud.

She put down the toasted bread. 'I believe I will go check on Wilson.'

He stood as she rose from her chair and breezed past him. He watched her leave, watched until she reached the staircase they'd walked up together the night before. When he could no longer see her, he sat back down and finished his coffee. There was a serving table filled with cold meats, cooked eggs, cheeses and fruits, but his appetite failed him. Too many questions nagging at him.

Such as, why had she not married?

Helene could feel Rhys's eyes upon her even as she reached the staircase. She gulped in some air. At least she could breathe again. How painful it had been, sitting next to him, feeling his hostility. And yet it took all her strength to seize upon a reason to leave him. She was worried about Wilson, though. Even though he had her permission to sleep as late as he wished, it was not like him to stay abed so late. It was almost time for the clock to strike eleven. A late morning for Wilson would have been eight.

Wilson's room was on an upper floor, down a long, narrow, uncarpeted hallway. The lighting was spare and the hallway dark as a result. She had not realised the servants' rooms were so far and so dim. Poor Wilson! He'd had to climb the extra stairs and walk this long hallway the night before when he'd been so very tired. She could, at least, make certain he'd eaten a meal and had sufficient rest.

She knocked on his door.

'Who?' he asked, his voice gruff and very unlike Wilson.

'It is Lady Helene,' she responded. 'I came to see how you are.'

She heard his footsteps shuffling to the door. He opened it a crack. 'Lady Helene.' He attempted a bow but gripped the door handle as if he had difficulty standing. Through the narrow gap she could see he was dressed in nightclothes and nightcap. Even in the dim light he looked ashen. This was more than fatigue.

'Are you ill, Wilson?' Her voice filled with concern.

He opened his mouth to speak, but staggered back. She pushed open the door and stepped inside his room in time to steady him on his feet.

'You *are* ill.' She seized his arm.

'A bit poorly,' he mumbled.

'Back to bed with you.' She led him to a narrow cot in the corner of the small room. She should never have pushed him so far.

He did not protest. 'Tired, that's all, m'lady.' He lay down on the cot, and she covered him with the blanket.

She felt his forehead. 'You are burning with fever!'

'Be all right.' He smacked his lips together and swallowed. His lips were cracked and their corners red and raw.

She glanced around the room, but there was only a water ewer for bathing, nothing to drink.

'Have you eaten anything?' There were no signs that he'd done so, no plates, no glasses.

They'd only eaten a quick dinner before searching the taverns for David the night before. Helene dampened a towel with the water from the pitcher and placed it on his forehead. She'd never known Wilson to be ill. He'd been one of her rocks throughout her childhood. If she got herself in a scrape—if she and Rhys got themselves in a scrape—Wilson was always there to help.

She was alarmed. 'I will be back directly.'

She rushed out of the room, down the long hallway and the stairs. She reached the lobby just as Rhys was about to climb the staircase.

He caught her arm. 'What is wrong?' His voice was gruff.

She shrugged him off. 'Where is the hall servant?' The man was not at his post. 'I need to speak to him.'

'Tell me what is wrong,' he insisted.

His hand gripped her arm again. She ought to be angry at his heavy-handed interference, but she was too concerned about Wilson. 'Wilson is burning with fever. I must get help. He needs a doctor.'

'Wait here,' he commanded.

But she followed him back to the dining hall where he commandeered the help of one of the servants, instructing him in French.

The man nodded and cried, *'Tout de suite, Capitaine.'* He dashed off.

Rhys turned to her. 'He will bring the doctor. Where is Wilson? I will attend to him.'

'He needs something to drink.' She looked around the dining room for another servant. When one appeared, Rhys took charge again, instructing the man to prepare a tray with small beer, bread, tea and some kind of broth. When the man returned with the tray, Rhys took it from him. *'Je vais le porter.'*

'Oui, Capitaine.' The servant bowed.

Helene reached for the tray. 'I'll bring it to him, Rhys.' He was so brusque, so unlike the Rhys she used to know.

He held on to the tray and his voice turned firm. 'I will carry it.'

She was too worried about Wilson to argue. She led Rhys up the stairs and down the long hallway to Wilson's room, knocking briefly before opening the door.

'It is Lady Helene again, Wilson,' she said.

The older man tried to rise.

Rhys set the tray down on a table beside the cot and came to Wilson's side. 'I am here, as well, Wilson,' he said in a caring voice more like she remembered. 'Rhys Landon. Remember me?' He urged the man back into bed.

'Rhys, my boy. You are back.' The old servant attempted a smile. 'Back with m'lady.'

Wilson was a little delirious. Rhys *was* here, but not *back* with her.

She, too, approached the bed. 'We've sent for a doctor for you. But you must drink something.' She glanced at Rhys. 'Can you help him to sit up?'

'No need to fuss over me, Lady Helene,' Wilson protested.

Rhys eased Wilson to a sitting position with a gentleness that reminded Helene of the old Rhys, the boy who rescued injured birds and rabbits and once even a hedgehog they'd named Henry. Helene had helped Rhys collect insects and berries to feed him.

But Rhys now was a man commanding enough to control a tavern full of rowdy soldiers and strong enough to carry David through the streets of Brussels and up the stairway to his room. She'd once seen this harder, tougher Rhys long ago when they'd been children. Some village boys pushed her around and pulled her hair. Rhys ran in and fought them all, even though it was three against one. After that he taught her how to fight like a boy, in case he wasn't around to come to her aid.

Helene stuffed the pillow and an extra blanket behind Wilson to help him sit, vowing to bring him more pillows so that he might sleep upright and breathe better. Rhys brought the one wooden chair in the room next to the bed and gestured for her to sit.

She pulled the tray closer. 'I am going to feed you some broth, Wilson.' She spooned the liquid into his mouth.

The old man cooperated, swallowing the broth and

making satisfied, but unintelligible sounds. She got him to consume the whole bowl and a few sips of the small beer, as well. The man's eyes grew heavy then and he dropped off to sleep.

She placed her palm against Wilson's forehead and glanced at Rhys. 'He still is very hot.'

He nodded. 'He has aged these five years, but I can only see him as he was, strong as an oak.

'Scolding us half the time.' She smiled inwardly at the memory.

An ache of nostalgia filled her chest. When she'd been with Rhys, she'd really had an idyllic childhood. It was only after he left her that life became bleak.

Rhys presumed she would be married by now, but how could she have married? True, her father had financed a couple of Seasons, but the young—and not so young—men who'd been thrown in her path could never compare to Rhys. She'd rebuffed any of their attempts to court her. Her father had been livid. He'd threatened to disown her and toss her out on the streets, but she knew he would never risk the censure of his peers if he'd done so. Instead he put all his hopes and energies in poor young David, hammering lessons on his role as Earl some day. Who knew David would need those lessons so soon?

But David had shown no signs he was ready to grow up. She needed to help her brother accept his role or their family estate, their workers, their village, would all suffer.

She slid a glance towards Rhys, his expression full of concern for Wilson. 'Are you at liberty to stay with him for a few minutes? I should not like him to be alone if the doctor arrives, and I want to let David know Wilson is ill.'

His eyes hardened again when answering her. 'I will stay with him.'

She nodded in acknowledgement. Could he not at least be civil?

She left the room and made her way to David's room. She knocked.

'Who is it?' he said from behind the closed door.

'Helene.' She half feared he would not open it for her.

But he did open it and she entered the room, which was a great deal messier than the previous night. Clothes were strewn on chairs. His stockings were scattered on the floor.

She held her tongue about the mess. 'I came to tell you that Wilson is very ill.' She gave him the directions to Wilson's room and his room number. 'I will be with him at least until he is seen by the doctor, who has been sent for.'

'Does that mean you are not going to try to make me travel back to England today?' he grumbled.

Her brows rose at her brother's lack of concern and her tone turned sharp. 'No, we will not be leaving today.' Wilson must be completely well before they travel home.

To his credit, David looked chagrined. 'Oh, that sounded churlish, did it not? Do I need to do anything to assist?'

'No.' She was about to add that Rhys was helping her, but she did not expect Rhys to stay.

'Then I will go out, if you do not mind?' The petulance returned to his voice. 'I will not drink, if that is what you fear.'

She ignored his infantile temperament. 'I hope to see you at dinner.'

'Dinner,' he repeated. 'If I must.'

Her gaze swept the room again and landed back on him. 'Do not forget. Dinner.'

She walked back to Wilson's room. She was probably

keeping Rhys from whatever soldierly duties were required of him.

She reached Wilson's door and knocked but did not wait for permission to enter. 'I am back,' she said unnecessarily.

He rose from the chair next to the bed. 'As I see.'

She walked closer to the bed. Closer to Rhys, she was struck by how tall he was. So often she remembered him as a boy, only two years older than she and not too much larger.

'How is he?' she asked, although she could see for herself Wilson's breathing was laboured.

'The same.' Rhys's voice softened a bit.

As if catching himself, he stepped away from the chair and inclined his head for her to sit. Self-conscious again, she avoided looking at him when she lowered herself into the chair.

'I am quite able to stay by his side now,' she assured Rhys. 'No need for you to stay.'

His direct stare was his only reply.

She held his gaze. 'I am very grateful for the assistance you've provided for me, both last night and today, but I will ask no more of you.'

'I helped your brother and your servant.'

Not her, he meant. Fair enough.

He leaned against the wall and crossed his arms over his muscular chest. 'I will stay for Wilson's sake. He was always very kind to me. If I do not stay, and you have an urgent need for assistance, you will have to leave him. I will stay at least until the doctor arrives.'

She turned back to Wilson. 'So be it.' He was right. Until they knew if Wilson could be left alone, it was better for them both to be there.

Once being together would have felt as natural as

breathing. Now she felt all the tension that crackled between them. Her heart pounded faster because of it. Her nerves were as taut as the highest note on a harp.

Chapter Three

David strode through the Parc de Bruxelles, oblivious of the carefully tended lawns, lush trees and classic statues he passed by. He supposed Helene wished him to hide away in his hotel room, but he had no intention of listening to her. How dare she come to fetch him home as if he were some recalcitrant schoolboy ditching his classes. He was eighteen, after all. A man.

Or practically a man.

If he were only a few years older, no one could stop him from purchasing a commission in the army. First his father; now Helene. All because he was the heir. Did they not understand that there was no glory in running an estate or listening to boring speeches in the Lords? He wanted to be *doing* something important! Like his schoolmate, William Lennox. William had been allowed to join the army. He had a cornetcy in the Royal Horse Guards and even had been an attaché for Wellington in Paris. How exciting was that? Most recently he'd been General Maitland's aide-de-camp and he was David's age.

Of course, William was a younger son and had the advantage of his father, the Duke of Richmond, being a great friend of Wellington's.

The Duke and Duchess of Richmond had moved their family to Brussels earlier this year and David had written to his friend when he'd arrived in the city. William invited him to call. William would know the latest news from the Duke of Wellington. At least David would be that close to events he was certain would take place soon.

A battle between Napoleon and Wellington!

He made his way through the streets of Brussels. It seemed everywhere there were soldiers. Some in red coats, some blue or black. How unfair that he was dressed merely as a gentleman. He'd been exploring these streets for over a week and had learned where the Duke of Richmond lived on Rue de la Blanchisserie. He reached the door and sounded the knocker. The Duke's butler answered the door and escorted him to a drawing room. A few minutes later William Lennox entered the room.

William was not dressed in the finery of the Royal Horse Guards, though, but in clothes more suited for a day in the country. And he wore a patch over one eye.

'Good God, William!' David cried. 'What happened to you?' Had he been injured in a battle? Had he even fought in a battle? As far as David knew William had purchased his commission after the peace, but would not it be glorious to be injured fighting for his country?

William walked towards him. 'A riding injury. I consider it a trifle, but General Maitland won't have me on his staff because of it.'

What a dreadful business. 'You are not his aide-de-camp?'

'No, and my father refuses to speak to Wellington about it. Says His Grace despises such interference.'

'But is there not to be a battle soon? Will you not be needed?' Would not every man be needed?

William frowned. 'I hope old Boney will wait until my

eye heals. It would the outside of enough to be cheated out of doing my duty.' He shook his head as if driving out such thoughts and clapped David on the shoulder. 'But what a surprise to see you in Brussels. Good to see you.'

David grinned. 'Is this not where every man wishes to be? I would not be anywhere else for the world.' He did not want to mention that his sister had chased after him, although he'd probably wind up telling the whole story eventually. 'I, too, am eager to see the great battle between Napoleon and Wellington. I am determined to at least be a witness to it.'

'So you understand my sentiments. To defeat Napoleon is the opportunity of a lifetime.' William gestured for David to sit. 'But I am delighted you are here. I have been trapped here with my sisters and little brothers and am about to go mad. You are just the companion I need.' He sighed, then smiled. 'Shall I order us some tea?'

David's return smile was conspiratorial. 'Tell you what I would like better. Let us get out of here. The taverns serve the best beer and some potatoes they call *frites*. Surely we can find some excitement here in Brussels.'

William laughed. 'I see why I am so glad to see you. Let me grab my hat and gloves and we'll be off.'

Helene and Rhys waited over two excruciating hours, rarely speaking to each other. As the minutes ticked by, Helene's mind raced with questions she wished to ask him about his life these past five years. One thing she would never ask him was if he'd understood why she broke their engagement.

But she did not speak, and he asked nothing more about her than he'd discovered already.

Finally a knock on Wilson's door announced the arrival of the doctor.

'I am Dr Carlier.' The doctor spoke French, like most Belgians.

Rhys responded before Helene could open her mouth. 'This is Lady Helene Banes.' He gestured to Helene. 'And the patient is Mr Wilson, her servant.'

The doctor looked curiously from Helene to Rhys.

Rhys added, 'I am Captain Landon.' He paused. 'A friend of the family.'

Helene ignored his hint of sarcasm in the word *friend* and leaned down to Wilson, 'The doctor is here to see you, Wilson.'

'Oh, no doctor,' the old man said. 'No fuss.'

'Nonsense. You need a doctor. You are ill.' She addressed the doctor in French. 'He started feeling poorly yesterday and when I checked on him this morning he was burning with fever.'

Carlier shooed her away. 'Sit up, *monsieur*,' he said to Wilson, still in French.

To her surprise, Wilson understood the instruction, although he struggled to sit in his weakened state. She'd not known he understood French.

The doctor felt Wilson's forehead, nodding as if he'd doubted her description. He leaned down and put his ear to Wilson's chest, frowning as he listened.

'Bad lungs.' The doctor picked up the empty glass from the side table and held it under Wilson's mouth. 'Cough and spit into the glass.'

Wilson obeyed.

The doctor examined the sputum and placed the glass back on the table. He addressed Helene. 'Your servant has an infection of the lungs.' He took paper and pencil from his bag, wrote on it, and handed it to Helene. 'Take this to an apothecary. Give it three times a day. It may help with the fever.'

'Should I not make him drink? What do you recommend?' She was accustomed to more recommendations from doctors. 'Broth?'

He appeared faintly annoyed at her question. 'He should drink as much as you can make him drink. Broth or beer. Tea, if that is what you English like.' He shook his finger at her. 'He must not leave this room. We do not wish to spread this English fever throughout Brussels.'

Helene straightened. 'I have no intention of allowing him—'

Dr Carlier interrupted her, his voice rising. 'He may become more ill before he recovers. *If* he recovers. But he must not leave this room until he is free from fever for two days.'

'He will need someone to attend him,' Rhys broke in. 'Can a nurse be hired?'

Helene whipped around to face him. 'I will tend him!'

'No, Helene,' Rhys countered. 'You will not.'

The doctor gave a weary sigh. 'It is of no importance to me who tends to the man. If you want a nurse, the hotel will find one for you.' He closed his bag. 'If he is not better in two days, I should be summoned. Otherwise, I must go. I have many patients to see.' He extended his hand for payment.

Before Helene could reach in her reticule, Rhys handed the man some coin. 'Enough?' Rhys asked.

The doctor nodded and pocketed the money as he left, clearly glad to have no more to do with the *English* and an *English* fever.

The door closed as Helene pulled her coins from her reticule. 'Here, Rhys.'

He held up a hand. 'Do not insult me. I can afford to pay this for Wilson.'

Her cheeks burned at his assumption. She'd meant no

insult, only that Wilson was her servant and her responsibility. It was probably useless to explain that to him, though.

Instead she lifted her chin. 'I will care for Wilson, not a nurse. I will not leave him in the care of a stranger in a foreign land.' Especially because too many Belgians seemed to have no taste for the English who'd suddenly flooded their city.

Rhys scowled. 'What can you know about nursing?'

'I nursed my mother and father.'

'With the support of your many servants, no doubt,' he responded sarcastically.

No, she'd kept the servants away as best as she could. Wilson had helped and Mrs Wood, the housekeeper. First her mother, then her father succumbed to a terrible fever and Helene had worked tirelessly, bathing them with cool cloths, spoon-feeding them broth. She'd spent a month tending to them, first one, then the other. She caught the fever, too, but she lived; they had not.

Rhys continued. 'Here you would be caring for Wilson alone. How would you summon help if you needed it?'

Once she would have assumed he would help her.

'I would manage,' she said.

Helene feared it was her fault Wilson was ill. She never should have allowed him to travel with her. Rhys's disapproval merely increased her guilt. Oh, she supposed some wild, improbable part of her wished he would help her. Foolish notion. She could manage. She was used to managing hard tasks alone.

She'd felt herself alone ever since Rhys left the village five years ago. Could watching him walk away from her again be any more painful?

Rhys's voice softened. 'Hire a nurse, Helene. Hire two or more. You cannot do this all on your own.'

* * *

Rhys shook his head. Did Helene not realise she could catch this fever? What good would it do her to be ill when she and David needed to leave Brussels?

His more conciliatory tone seemed to have little effect on her. She crossed her arms over her chest. 'I assure you I am entirely capable, even of hiring a nurse, if that is what I wish to do.'

He spoke firmly again and extended his hand. 'Give me the paper for the apothecary. I will see that it is prepared for you. And I *will* speak to the hall servant about sending a nurse. Do with that what you will.'

Rhys knew how to command and was not hesitant to impose his will on her. Wilson's condition distressed him. The old servant was dear to Rhys. When Rhys was growing up, his father and mother were often preoccupied with the needs of the parishioners and Rhys was left to his own devices. Wilson always seemed nearby when he or Helene needed help or a firm scolding. Even when Rhys was not with Helene, he would seek out Wilson and help him at his tasks. Rhys credited Wilson with teaching him how to take care of himself, his clothes and his gear. Rhys had a batman to assist him while the regiment was on the march, but he was spared the expense of a personal servant otherwise.

Helene handed him the paper with the doctor's instructions on it and turned away, returning to her seat next to Wilson's cot. Rhys put the paper in his pocket.

'No quarrelling, children,' Wilson muttered. 'I'll tell your fathers.'

Wilson's delirium worried him. But how many times had Rhys heard Wilson speak those same words when they were young? Like the time they argued about who threw a stone the farthest. Or who could climb a tree the highest. Or who caught the bigger fish.

Wilson never told their fathers anything they'd done.

He walked back to Wilson. 'We are not quarrelling, I assure you. Take a nap now. Rest.'

Together he and Helene adjusted the pillows and blankets to make the ill man as comfortable as possible. She was close enough that he could inhale that familiar sweet scent of her, lavender and lemon, and was instantly transformed to his youth, to the sweet kisses they'd once shared.

She looked directly into his eyes for a moment before averting her gaze. 'Ask about a nurse,' she said quietly. 'I will at least meet her before deciding.'

'Very well.' He stepped back, fighting the impulse to lean in closer to her. 'I will go now.' He touched his pocket where he'd put the instructions to the apothecary. 'I'll see this is delivered to you.'

'Thank you, Rhys.' Her voice was little more than a whisper.

Rhys watched her for a moment as she fussed with Wilson's blanket. Collecting himself, he walked out the door and made his way through the hallway and down the stairs to the hall. Best he stay away from her and simply arrange for the hotel servants to deliver the medicine and send a nurse.

The hall servant was nowhere to be found, however. Rather than wait for him, Rhys decided to go to the apothecary himself. He returned to his room for his hat and gloves. On the street, he asked a passer-by where to find the shop. The man directed him to a street nearby.

Rhys opened the door and stepped inside, the fragrance of herbs and spices enveloping him. The walls of the shop were filled with floor-to-ceiling shelves of countless white jars with blue lettering. Words like *mercure*, *centaurée* and *absinthe*. A man wearing a white apron stood behind a long wooden counter. The apothecary, Rhys presumed.

Rhys removed his hat. *'Bonjour, monsieur.'*

The apothecary nodded in return, raising his brows in question.

Rhys pulled the doctor's paper from his pocket and handed it to the apothecary. *'S'il vous plaît.'*

The man read the instructions and turned to his wall of ingredients, pulling several down, grinding some with his mortar and pestle, mixing those with a liquid, and decanting the whole into a round brown bottle sealed with a cork.

'Two teaspoons, three times a day,' the apothecary explained in French and handed Rhys the medicine.

'Merci, monsieur,' Rhys responded as he placed the proper coins in the man's hand.

When he returned to the hotel, the same servant who'd procured the doctor for him was attending the hall.

'How is Mr Wilson, Captain?' the man asked. 'Was the doctor of assistance?'

'Yes. I thank you,' Rhys replied. 'Mr Wilson is to stay in his room until he recovers. He is, I fear, in need of nursing. Do you know any capable women we might hire to tend to him?'

The servant frowned. 'I will send for someone.'

'Have the woman come to his room. Lady Helene or I will be with him.' Why had he said he would be there? He'd done enough, had he not?

Rhys started to walk away, but the servant called him back. 'Captain! I forgot. A letter was delivered for Mr Wilson this morning. Would you like to bring it to him?'

A letter? 'Of course,' he replied. 'Happy to.' But who would write to Wilson? Someone from Yarford House, no doubt, but why not send to Helene, or even David?

The hall servant gave the letter to Rhys. Wilson's name was written on it, but no indication of where it was from.

Rhys looked up at the servant. 'This came with the mail?'

'No,' the man said. 'A boy delivered it.'

The only person he could think of who might send Wilson a message was David, but the writing seemed distinctly feminine.

He nodded thanks and made his way to Wilson's room, forgetting that he'd intended to have one of the hotel servants deliver the medicine to Helene. When she opened the door to him, her eyes blinked in surprise.

'I have the medicine.' He handed her the bottle and gave her the apothecary's instructions for its use.

'I will give him some right away.' Her skirts rustled as she returned to Wilson's cot and coaxed him awake. Carefully she poured the liquid into a spoon and held it to his lips. 'Medicine, Wilson. It will make you feel better.'

He obligingly opened his mouth and she fed him the medicine.

'Another spoonful,' she said.

As she was placing the cork back on the bottle, Rhys pulled the letter from his pocket. 'Wilson received a letter.'

Her brows rose. 'A letter?'

He handed it to her. 'Does the hand look familiar?'

She stared at the letter and shook her head.

'Does he know someone in Brussels?'

'No,' she said, adding uncertainly, 'at least no one I know of.'

They exchanged glances, the kind of silent communication that had been so common between them at one time, both questioning what to do. Rhys inclined his head towards Wilson and Helene nodded in agreement.

She roused Wilson again. 'You have a letter, Wilson.'

'From someone here in Brussels, I think,' Rhys added.

The old man sat up, gaining an alertness they'd not witnessed before. 'Louise?'

Rhys exchanged another glance with Helene.

She showed Wilson the letter. 'Open for me,' he murmured. 'Read.'

She broke the wafer and read aloud in French.

My dearest Samuel,
Imagine my pleasure to learn you are in Brussels.
Yes. You may call upon me. Do so as soon as you
are able. I will be waiting in great anticipation.
Yours,
Louise

Wilson rose from the bed, his unsteady legs barely able to support him. 'Must go to her. Louise.'

'No!' Helene cried.

Both Rhys and Helene rushed to his side and helped him back on to the cot. He struggled against them, but wore himself out in an instant. He lay back against the pillows again.

'You must not get out of bed,' Helene scolded. 'You are very ill.'

'Must see Louise,' Wilson said weakly. 'Must see her.'

'Not today.' Helene's voice was gentle. 'Today you rest.'

He fell asleep or perhaps fell into a stupor.

Rhys gestured for Helene to step away from the bed. 'Do you know this Louise?'

She shook her head. 'I have never heard him speak of knowing anyone in Brussels. Or anyone anywhere else besides at Yarford.' She glanced back at the old man's fitful rest. 'She seems important to him.'

'Indeed.' Rhys knew he would be unable to ignore this latest drama. He might as well be caught in a web, the threads holding him becoming thicker as he tried to free himself.

He could simply walk away. Helene. Wilson. David. None of them were any of his concern. His only concern was his regiment and their readiness for battle. The time waiting weighed heavily on him. On all his men. To fill time, Rhys's soldiers got embroiled in all sorts of mischief, but even sorting them out was not enough to keep him occupied. Rhys had time to tend to Wilson.

He simply should not let old memories distract him, memories of how it once was with Helene.

He returned to the hotel's hall and the servant attending it. 'I have a question, sir,' he asked the man. 'I want to assist Mr Wilson in every way I can—'

The servant cut him off. 'I have sent for a nurse, Captain. I assure you.'

'I am obliged. But it is not about the nurse. The letter that arrived for Mr Wilson. Do you know who sent it?'

The servant frowned. 'I was not told who sent it.'

Rhys persisted. 'Do you know the boy who delivered it?'

'I am sorry, Captain. I do not.' He bowed and stepped away.

Damnation! Rhys should simply shrug his shoulders and let it go, but the mystery nagged at him. Who was this Louise? Why was she so important that Wilson would attempt to rise from his sickbed for her?

Chapter Four

That evening Rhys and his friend Grant returned to the same tavern where he'd encountered Helene. Had it merely been the night before? The place was now haunted by the memory of the first vision of her after so many years, like a dream materialising in the dim light. Also like a cannonball to the chest. What sense had he to return here?

But why not? The beer and the food were excellent, and he rather had a craving for the tavern's cooked mussels and *frites*.

He'd not returned to Wilson's room after delivering the medicine, not wanting to encounter Helene again. When Rhys and Grant were leaving the hotel to come here, the hall servant informed Rhys that a competent nurse had been sent to the elderly man's room. Rhys would check on this nurse later. He'd stop by Wilson's room before retiring. Surely Helene would not be there then.

He and Grant settled at a table near the one they'd shared the night before. Grant had spent most of his day with officers from other regiments, all comparing rumours of how long they would have to wait for marching orders.

Grant took a swig of his beer. 'There is considerable gathering of French troops on the border and Wellington believes the French will attack soon. It seems clear that Brussels will be Napoleon's aim, but there are three possible routes. Tournai seems most likely, but Boney could well come through Mons or even Charleroi.'

It was as Rhys feared. 'The battle could be days away, no matter his choice of route.'

'That seems the right of it,' Grant responded.

This was not new information, but mere confirmation of what intelligence had supposed for some time as Wellington's spies reported on the troop movement inside France. Rhys's first thought, though, was of Helene. It was madness she had travelled here at this dangerous time and even more madness that David considered the whole thing one great lark. They needed to leave Brussels right away.

At that moment Rhys looked up to find David approaching their table. Rhys was not happy to see him. David was accompanied by another youth remarkable only because of an eyepatch on one eye.

'Rhys! How grand to find you here!' David cried. 'May we join you?'

Rhys glanced at Grant, who, returning Rhys an inquisitive look, inclined his head in agreement.

David happily pulled up a chair and signalled the tavern maid to bring them some beer. His friend sat next to him. 'May I present my friend, William Lennox? William, this is Rhys. Captain Landon, I mean. I've known him my whole life! He's the vicar's son and a great childhood friend of my sister's.'

Grant seemed to be raptly interested in this information.

Rhys introduced him. 'This is Captain Grantwell.'

'Captain.' The young man nodded politely. 'I am David Banes.'

Curious. David's father was dead. David would be Lord Yarford now. Why had he introduced himself with his given name? On the other hand, did Rhys care what the boy called himself?

Rhys turned towards David's companion as he lifted his tankard of beer to his lips. 'Do you have a notion to witness the coming battle as well, Lennox?'

The young man frowned. 'I hope to recover in time. I am—or rather was—attached to General Maitland's staff. Before this.' He pointed to his bandaged eye. 'A riding accident,' he explained. Rhys doubted he or Grant would have had any inclination to ask.

David puffed up his chest proudly. 'William is the Duke of Richmond's son and His Grace is excellent friends with Wellington, so I have no doubt William will be part of the action.'

Wellington, the Field Marshal of the Allied Forces, was also a duke. This pretentious reference to two dukes in one sentence reminded Rhys of Helene and David's father. Now there was a man who revered titles. No surprise David was cut from the same cloth.

Rhys took a sip of his beer. 'David, I do not think it at all wise that you returned to this tavern, not after last night.'

The youth looked mystified. 'Why not? The food is good here.'

'You nearly provoked a townsman to fisticuffs.'

'Oh, that.' David waved a dismissive hand. 'I do not credit that.'

Rhys glanced around the room. The man from the previous night did not appear to be present. Perhaps he would not have to rescue David again from being beaten to a pulp.

He changed the subject. 'How is Wilson?'

'Wilson?' David looked puzzled, but then his expression cleared. 'Oh, yes. Wilson. He is ill, Helene said.'

'I know he is ill.' Rhys leaned forward. 'Did you not check on him, to see how he fared?'

'Me? What could I do?' David replied. 'I've been out all day.'

Rhys felt his anger rise. 'Out all day and not once checking on your servant?'

The boy puffed up his chest. 'Helene is the one who brought him here. Let her check on him.'

Rhys turned away in disgust. David should be offering both Wilson and his sister his assistance. If David stepped up to his responsibility, Rhys could walk away with a clear conscience.

The maid came and took their food orders and soon the food arrived. Grant and young Lennox struck up a conversation about possible battle strategies, with David inserting his unschooled opinion. Rhys tried to follow the conversation, but his traitorous thoughts kept returning to Helene, alone and worried about Wilson.

When they finished, Lennox rose. 'I must return home. This has been capital, Captains!' He picked up his hat. 'No need to come with me, David. I will see you tomorrow morning for our ride.'

'We are riding into the countryside tomorrow,' David explained happily.

Lennox started to walk away but turned back. 'Oh, my mother is planning to give a ball on Thursday. I will see that you all receive invitations.' He bowed.

A ball only three days away? A ball was the last thing that could interest Rhys with a French attack so imminent.

'Shall we order another round?' David asked after his friend left.

Rhys stood this time. 'I think not. Time for you to return to the hotel, David. Report to your sister.'

David laughed. 'Oh, I forgot. I was supposed to meet her for dinner. Oh, well, she won't mind. Let's have another round. The night is just beginning!'

Rhys leaned into the young man's face. 'Last night you were so cup-shot you were nearly beaten to a pulp and I needed to carry you to the hotel. Your night is over.'

David's lower lip jutted out, but he did as Rhys commanded.

Grant lifted his still full tankard. 'I'll stay.'

Rhys spoke few words to David as they walked back to the hotel, although the boy kept up a steady stream of cheerful, inane conversation. The boy needed a proper dressing down in Rhys's opinion, but David was not his concern.

When they walked through the hotel doors into the hall, though, Rhys could keep quiet no longer. 'Go straight to your sister's room and let her know you are still alive. After what you've put her through, she probably fears the worst.'

David scowled. 'What room is she in? I did not attend when she told me.'

Rhys gave him the room number. His room was, of course, on the same floor, but he'd had enough of David's company for one night. He took a different stairway to Wilson's room instead.

He knocked on the door, expecting the nurse to answer.

The door opened and Helene appeared instead.

Rhys took an involuntary step back. 'I thought the nurse would be here.'

Helene stepped aside. 'She is here.'

Rhys entered the room and saw a simply dressed plump woman at least two decades older than Helene.

Helene extended her hand towards the woman and said in French, 'This is Mrs Jacobs.' She turned back to Rhys. 'Captain Landon. He is an old friend…' she paused '…of Wilson's.'

'Captain.' The woman nodded to him. She had one of those faces that seemed to smile even when at rest.

'How is he?' Rhys kept his attention on the nurse.

'Feverish.' Mrs Jacobs's brow furrowed in worry. She turned back to Wilson and placed a cloth on his forehead.

'He is no better,' Helene said in a worried voice.

Rhys turned to her. 'What are you still doing here?'

Mrs Jacobs answered for her. '*Mademoiselle* insists upon staying. Although if you ask me, she looks in great need of a rest. I told her I am quite capable—'

Helene broke in. 'It is not that. I know you are capable. It's that I left my brother a note that I was here. I am waiting for him. We are to eat dinner together.'

'Did you eat dinner?' Rhys asked the nurse.

The woman nodded. '*Mademoiselle* sent for food for me and for our patient.'

Rhys extended his hand to Helene. 'Come,' he ordered. 'David is in the hotel. I'll take you to him.'

He fixed her with a determined glare. After a pause, she obeyed.

Helene disliked this change in Rhys—ordering her about as if she were one of his soldiers. The only time she caught glimpses of her once kind and attentive friend was when he spoke to Wilson. Why did he insist upon taking her to David? Why not simply tell her where to find her brother? She was so worn out from worry and too little rest, though, that she went along with him without protest.

'I will take you to David's room,' he intoned in that dictatorial voice. 'He likely is there by now.'

He led her to David's room. David did not answer their knock.

'Perhaps he is waiting for you in the dining room,' Rhys said.

She was too tired to tell Rhys she knew the way to the dining room.

After they descended the steps and reached the hall, Rhys asked the hall servant. 'That young fellow I walked in with, have you seen him again?'

'Non, Capitaine,' the man said.

Rhys had walked in with David? From where?

Rhys faced her. 'He could still be in the dining room.'

She finally found her voice. 'Thank you, Rhys. I will look for him in the dining room. Whether he is there or not, I am going to eat. I'm too tired and hungry to chase him all around the hotel.'

To her surprise, he followed her.

'You do not have to accompany me,' she said.

'I will see if David is there,' he responded.

It was nearly nine o'clock and the dining room was full. Several tables were filled with officers enjoying their food and drink, their voices loud, their laughter louder. Helene looked over the room but did not see David anywhere.

'He is not here,' she said.

The dining room servant approached them. 'Shall I show you to a table?'

'Yes, please,' Helene responded, her empty stomach responding to the smell of the food.

To her surprise Rhys also followed the servant, who led them across the room.

'Really, Rhys,' she said to him. 'Do not feel obligated to stay. I can dine alone.'

His gaze swept the crowd. 'I fancy a glass of wine.'

The servant showed them to a small table in a discreet corner. It was the sort of table she once would have relished sharing with Rhys, private enough to pretend they were utterly alone. What cruel jokes fate was playing on her, giving her what she'd once most yearned for, reminding her again of what she'd given up.

They sat across from each other.

Another servant approached their table.

'You should try the cooked mussels,' Rhys said to her. 'If they have them. It is a Brussels specialty.'

'We have mussels,' the servant said.

'And *frites*,' Rhys added.

This time she was grateful he was telling her what to do. She had no energy to make a decision. 'Very well.'

He ordered wine for them both, but nothing else for him.

'Are you not eating, Rhys?' she asked.

'I ate earlier.' He nodded for the servant to leave.

Suddenly she pictured him separate from her company, doing things. Soldier things? Dining, where? With whom? Who peopled his life? Friends...? Women?

But his life was none of her affair.

'Is the nurse satisfactory?' His gaze just missed meeting hers.

She fiddled with the silver fork set before her. 'She seems so.'

He lowered his gaze to the table, giving her a view of his thick dark lashes. His chin was shaded with a dusting of beard at this late hour. So much of her memory of him was as a smooth-faced youth. This very masculine image made him appear almost like a different person. Someone she no longer knew at all.

After the food arrived he watched her eat while he sipped his wine, his full lips moistened by the burgundy-coloured liquid. Hungry though she was, it made it difficult to swallow.

As she was forcing another bite of mussel, he suddenly said, 'You and David must leave Brussels as soon as possible.'

This latest command took her aback. 'As soon as Wilson is well enough to travel.'

His gaze bore into her. 'That could be days. Weeks, even. Leave tomorrow.'

Tomorrow? Impossible. 'I cannot leave Wilson!'

He lowered his voice. 'Heed me. Napoleon plans a march on Brussels. Any day now.'

She understood then. He was warning her. 'This is certain?'

He looked away. 'Almost certain.'

Helene certainly did not want to be in Brussels when Napoleon tried to breach its walls, but Wilson's illness changed things. 'I really must stay in Brussels until Wilson is well.'

'I will see he is looked after,' Rhys said.

She raised her eyes and her gaze locked with his. 'How? You will be fighting in the battle.'

Rhys would be in the thick of it, with cannonballs and musket balls and swords and lances all flying towards him, trying to kill him. And, even though he'd changed, even though he might wish to never see her again, that thought was like a knife piercing her heart.

As it had been every time news reached England of

another battle, until she read through the casualty list and his name did not appear.

Her gaze did not waver. 'I promise you, David, Wilson and I will leave as soon as Wilson can travel.'

Rhys took another sip of wine. Her blue eyes had a powerful effect on him, pulling him back to those old halcyon days they'd shared together. He ought to have known better than to accompany her to dinner, but if he had not, she'd have been a woman dining alone, one small lamb amid a room full of hungry wolves in army uniforms.

He tried to thrust his thoughts away from what might have been between them. The truth was, he ought to thank her for spurning him. If she had not, he would never have had the opportunity to join the army. He valued being an officer in the East Essex regiment. Valued leading his men. He even relished the excitement of battle—almost as much as he hated its carnage. If he'd not become an officer in the army, what would he be?

He'd never been given the chance to find out.

She broke the silence between them. 'Tell me. How will this battle happen?'

He could talk about this. 'No one knows for certain what route Napoleon will take, but he will come. He will want to take Brussels. He will want to face Wellington.'

Rhys would feel more secure about this impending battle if the Allied army under Wellington consisted of more seasoned British troops and if enough time passed for the Prussians to provide support. If the Russian troops had time to arrive, Napoleon would be vastly outnumbered, but, of course, Napoleon realised this. That was why he would strike quickly. Napoleon was known for splitting forces and emerging victorious.

Napoleon was also capable of spectacular defeats, though. Like in Egypt. And Russia.

None of this would be helpful for her to know, however. Better she and her brother—and Wilson—be safely away.

A line of worry formed between her dark perfectly arched brows. 'So is there a danger we won't win?'

Could she still read his mind? When they were young, they often knew what the other was thinking. 'I would rather march under Wellington's command than any other. And I have done so many times.'

She expelled a breath and her forehead relaxed a bit. Rhys continued to sip his wine, trying not to watch her eat.

When she'd finished not even half of what was on her plate, she placed her fork down. 'That was delicious, Rhys,' she said. 'Thank you for suggesting it.'

Then why had she eaten so little of it?

She stood, as did he. 'I will just check on Wilson one more time, I believe.'

He escorted her out of the dining room, stopping to arrange the meal to be charged to him.

'No, Rhys,' she protested. 'I will pay.'

He bristled at this reminder of her wealth. He was no longer penniless. 'No,' he commanded the servant. 'Charge it to me.'

She started walking to the staircase. He caught up with her.

'You should allow me to pay,' she said.

'No,' he said firmly. 'I will come with you to Wilson's room. I, too, wish to check on him.'

They walked together in silence, up the stairs and down the dimly lit hallways to the servants' rooms. The oil lamps illuminating their way were smaller and much further between than in the hallways of the more expensive rooms. When they reached Wilson's door, Rhys knocked lightly.

The nurse opened it.

'I just wanted to see how he is, Mrs Jacobs.' Helene stepped inside. 'Is he any better?'

The nurse smiled benevolently. 'There has been no change in the last hour, *mademoiselle*. It is too soon for improvement in my experience. Let us see how he does by morning.'

Helene walked over to Wilson's bed and felt his forehead. She adjusted his covers and swept his damp hair off his face. Her gentle gesture made Rhys's throat tighten with an emotion he did not wish to feel.

Mrs Jacobs stepped closer to her and put her hand on Helene's shoulder. '*Mademoiselle*, I will take good care of him. You get your rest. Go with your handsome captain here and do not fret over our patient.'

Helene shot a glance at Rhys when the nurse said '*your handsome captain*'.

'Check on him in the morning, Helene,' Rhys said.

She reluctantly backed away from the bed but turned to Mrs Jacobs. 'You will send for me if he takes a turn for the worse?'

The nurse patted her hand. 'I will. *Certainement.*'

'Do you need anything?' Rhys asked the woman.

She shook her head. 'There is a nice footman in the room next to this who has agreed to summon help for me, if needed. He does not mind if I have to wake him, but I do not expect that to be necessary. You may both rest easy.'

Rhys nodded to her and opened the door. Helene reluctantly followed him into the dark hallway. Walking in the dark reminded him of once when he and Helene both sneaked out of their houses and met in the garden at Yarford House. They'd walked hand in hand down the paths and shared a secret kiss behind the hedges. She must have been sixteen and he, eighteen.

When they reached the main staircase, she said, 'Good-night, Rhys. I believe I will try one more time to see if David is in his room, before I retire.'

What would she do if David was not there? Go out searching for him like the night before? Only this time there would be no Wilson to accompany her and offer her his meagre protection.

'I'll go with you,' Rhys said.

Chapter Five

At least Helene did not argue with him for accompanying her. Rhys told himself he was only remaining with her because the hotel was filled with officers and other men in town who did not have enough to entertain them and plenty of opportunity to consume a lot of Belgian beer.

When they neared David's room, the boy had just stepped out into the hallway, humming a tune.

His cheerful expression drooped when he spied his sister. 'Oh. Helene.' He gave Rhys a more cordial look. 'Rhys.'

Helene faced her brother, elbows akimbo. 'Where are you going, David? It must be after ten o'clock.'

'I am going out.' He jutted out his chin. 'It is not so very late.'

She glared at him. 'Where have you been all day? I left you so many messages. About Wilson—'

'I know. I know,' he interrupted. 'Wilson is sick. I am sorry for it, but you already told me there was nothing I could do.'

Her voice rose. 'You might at least have sent me a note informing me as to your whereabouts. And that you would not meet me for dinner.'

He looked chagrined. 'Yes. Dinner. So sorry about that. Slipped my mind.'

Rhys thought again that it should be David who acted as Helene's escort, not him.

'So where were you all day?' Helene demanded.

David pursed his lips. 'Not that it is any of your affair, I'll have you know that I was with William Lennox. He is here with his parents, the Duke and Duchess, and he will likely have an important role in the battle—if his eye heals quickly enough.' He puffed out his chest. 'And if you do not believe me, ask Rhys, because William and I had dinner with Rhys and another captain in the army.'

She shot Rhys a severe glance.

'I told you I saw him,' Rhys said.

'Not that you had dinner with him.'

David ranted on. 'You are not my keeper, Helene. You cannot tell me what I may and may not do. With whom I may and may not dine. I want to go out now and you cannot stop me.' His voice turned shrill, like a child having a tantrum.

Rhys stepped forward, looming over the boy. 'Mind your tongue, David.'

David shrugged his shoulders. 'She's only my sister. She has no business trying to manage my life.'

'I came because it is not safe for you to be in Brussels, David,' Helene said. 'You should not have come. You need to be home.'

'Well, as Wilson is *ill*, we are staying, are we not? I am going out!' David pushed past them and strode swiftly down the hall.

'David—' Rhys started after him, but Helene seized his arm.

'Let him go,' she said. 'I am too angry at him to have more words with him tonight.'

Her touch flooded Rhys with memories.

And temptation.

She looked surprised at herself and abruptly released him. She glanced down the hall where David disappeared. 'I do hope he will not drink too much again.'

'After last night, he should have learned his lesson.' Although did Rhys know any young man who remembered a morning headache when night-time fell? 'You will not go after him,' he insisted in as firm a voice as he could muster.

'No.' Her voice sounded both stressed and weary. 'I will not go after him.'

Rhys walked by her side to her room. His arm still felt the pressure of her slender fingers and he remembered, a long time ago, twining her fingers through his and admiring their graceful beauty.

'Goodnight, Rhys,' she said as soon as they reached her room. 'Thank you again.'

She unlocked the door and disappeared inside.

Rhys stepped back and stared at the closed door, then he turned away and started towards his room. After passing the stairway, he stopped and reversed direction.

'Cursed boy!' he said aloud.

He descended the stairs and made his way to the outside, feeling obligated to make certain David Banes returned to this hotel without doing a thing to worry his sister.

Helene rang for a maid to attend her and crawled into bed as soon as the woman left, but she tangled herself in her bed linens trying to quiet her racing mind and restless emotions.

She wished she could say her struggle was due to her anger at David or her worry over Wilson. Those concerns certainly were not conducive to sleep, but, if honest with herself, it was Rhys who kept Morpheus at bay.

She had to admit she loved seeing him again. His handsome face. His deepened voice moved her, even when his imperious tone grated at her nerves. She did not understand why he insisted upon being in her company when he obviously derived no pleasure from it. Especially because it had been she who sent him away. It had taken her a long time to accept that she would never see him again. Now, after accepting it, here he was.

A different person.

In the morning she woke still thinking of him. The maid arrived to help her dress. Afterward she left her room to check on Wilson.

The nurse answered her knock. 'Good morning, *mademoiselle*.'

'Good morning, Mrs Jacobs.' She entered the room. 'How is he?'

'No worse.' Mrs Jacobs moved away so Helene could approach the bed. 'He has been sleeping these last two hours, more quietly, I think.'

The room was tidy, and Wilson was comfortably propped up on pillows, the bed covers neatly over him. His breathing was ragged, but he was still.

That might be a good sign, although her parents had moved in and out of delirium before their fevers robbed them of life. She remembered some moments of rest, too, before her own fever deprived her of her senses. At least she had awakened from the fever and survived.

'What of you?' she asked the nurse. 'Were you able to rest?'

'*Oui, mademoiselle,*' she responded cheerfully. 'He slept. I slept. We got on very well.'

'Has he spoken to you at all?' Helene asked.

Mrs Jacobs nodded. 'Nothing that had meaning. He speaks the name Louise a great deal.'

Yes. Who was Louise? 'We know nothing of Louise. Did he say anything that would tell us more about her?

'Only the name.' The nurse tilted her head apologetically.

Helene glanced over at Wilson, now murmuring in his sleep.

She turned back to the nurse. 'May I do something for you, Mrs Jacobs? I am at liberty to perform some errand or to sit with him if need be.'

Mrs Jacobs laughed. '*Mon Dieu!* It is I who am hired to help you, not you to help me.'

'But you will need some relief, surely.' Helene remembered how much she needed the respite the servants offered her after she'd spent hours with her ill mother or father.

Mrs Jacobs looked thoughtful. 'Perhaps you would not mind sitting with him for an hour or two? I would like to go home. Check on—check on something. And to gather some necessities for our patient.'

'Of course,' Helene readily agreed. 'Do you need any money? I must pay for whatever Wilson needs.' She took a purse from her pocket and handed the woman some coins.

Mrs Jacobs looked at the coins in her palm and smiled. 'That will do nicely, *mademoiselle. Merci.*'

Helene thought she might have breakfast with David again, but she would leave him a note instead. He'd probably like that better.

'Would you bring a note to the hall servant for me?' she asked the nurse.

'Of course, *mademoiselle.*' Mrs Jacobs wrapped a shawl around her shoulders.

Helene crossed to the table where Wilson had placed pen and paper—to write to the mysterious Louise, no doubt. She penned a quick note, folded the paper and wrote David's name on it. She handed it to Mrs Jacobs.

The older woman grinned. 'Is this for your handsome captain?'

Helene felt her face flush. 'No. No. For my brother. He is also a guest here.'

Mrs Jacobs shook her head in mock disappointment. 'A brother? Not nearly as nice as a note to the captain.' She gestured to a table near the small fireplace where sat a teapot and a plate covered by a cloche. 'The footman next door brought me some food a moment ago. Bread and cheese and tea, of course. I've not touched any of it, so you must have my share.'

Helene was hungry, she realised.

'I will return before two hours have passed,' Mrs Jacobs promised as she walked out the door.

Helene poured herself a cup of tea and placed both it and the plate of bread and cheese on the table near Wilson's bed. She tore off a piece of bread and nibbled on it, the silence broken only by her chewing and Wilson's raspy breathing.

Her handsome captain. He'd once been her handsome Rhys. Helene felt a wave of loss.

She must have dozed a little after eating, because a knock on the door roused her. Was it already time for Mrs Jacobs to return? She rose and opened the door.

Her heart skipped a beat.

Rhys.

'Rhys! It is you.' She clamped her mouth shut, vexed at herself for stating what was so obvious.

He strode right past her, eyes flaring. 'Where is the nurse? Did she desert her post?'

'No. No.' Helene closed the door behind him. 'She was here the night. I offered to stay with Wilson while she went for some necessities.'

He straightened. 'I see.' He glanced towards the bed. 'How is he?'

'Resting more quietly than yesterday, I believe, although Mrs Jacobs said he was still delirious some of the time.' Her heart was still pounding. She'd not expected to see him.

A groan came from the old servant's bed. 'Lady Helene? Is that you?'

She rushed over to the bedside. Rhys followed her. 'Yes, Wilson. It is Helene. And Rhys.'

'Rhys?' The older man tried to sit up, but it was too much effort. 'Ah, yes. I remember. Rhys was here. We are in Brussels.'

'Yes,' Helene said. 'But you have been very ill with fever. Do not exert yourself. You need to rest.'

'No.' Wilson tried to rise again. 'I have somewhere I must go. I must.'

Rhys stepped forward. 'You need to stay in bed, Wilson. You are too ill to go anywhere.' His voice was firm but...gentle.

Like the old Rhys.

Wilson lay back against the pillows again, but he looked quite distraught.

'You should drink something, Wilson,' Helene said. 'Some tea. I'll get it for you.'

Rhys had already walked over to the teapot and poured Wilson a cup. She took the cup from Rhys's hand and spoke quietly. 'Do you think his agitation is about the letter?'

Wilson heard her. 'A letter?'

'Do you remember, Wilson?' Rhys asked him. 'The letter from Louise.'

Wilson extended his arm. 'Let me see!'

She put down the teacup and reached into her pocket for the letter. She handed it to Wilson.

He held it in a trembling hand and put it close to his face, then dropped it on to the bed. 'My eyes will not focus.'

Helene picked up the single sheet of paper. 'Louise wishes you to call upon her.'

'Louise.' Tears filled the old man's eyes. 'Louise.'

Helene glanced at Rhys again, sharing her worry with him. In his delirium Wilson had forgotten the letter.

Rhys put a gentle hand on Wilson's shoulder. 'Do not upset yourself. You need to get well.'

'I need to see her!' Wilson cried.

'Perhaps we can get a message to her.' Rhys's voice was calm and reasonable. 'Can you give us her direction?'

'Rue de l'Evêque. Near the theatre,' Wilson managed. 'Louise Desmet.'

'We will get a message to her,' Helene assured him. 'We will tell her you are ill and cannot call upon her now.'

Wilson nodded, but tears rolled down his cheeks. His tears distressed her. Wilson had often been the one to dry her tears.

She brought him the cup of tea. 'Come. Drink some tea.' It was tepid by now.

Rhys helped him sit up in bed. Helene put the cup to Wilson's lips. He drank the whole.

'Are you hungry?' She held up the plate of bread and cheese.

Wilson grimaced and shook his head vehemently.

She turned to Rhys. 'He needs some broth or porridge.

And something more to drink. He must have some nour-ishment.'

Rhys nodded in agreement. 'I will bring something from the dining room. I can do so right away.'

Helene was glad for his help. At least when it con-cerned Wilson, Rhys was the Rhys with whom she'd fallen in love.

'Message!' Wilson cried. 'Message to Louise.'

Helene turned back to her old servant. 'We will send your message, Wilson. I promise you. Now rest, will you?' She felt his forehead. He was still very hot to the touch.

Rhys stepped away. 'I'll bring some food.'

She saw the concern in his eyes, a concern that matched her own. They were both afraid Wilson would not recover.

Rhys hurried down to the dining room. If only he'd had more sleep, his emotions might not be firing in all directions like Congreve rockets, but he'd risen very early that morning to visit his company and he'd been out quite late the night before.

Rhys hadn't expected to see Helene when he knocked on Wilson's door. When she opened it he'd been momen-tarily struck dumb. She wore a plain striped blue dress and had taken little care with her hair, but her loveliness cut into him like the slash of a sabre. Then to see the nurse was not there—he'd immediately thought the woman had deserted and his agitation had flared. He was accustomed to keeping a cooler head.

He'd even lost his temper at David. The night before it had taken Rhys some time to find the hare-brained boy and, when he did, David was already as drunk as a wheel-barrow and about to engage in fisticuffs with some sol-diers from the Dutch light cavalry. Rhys had rung a peal over David's head for that folly, but he doubted David would even remember it this morning.

Rhys was done, though. This would be the last time he'd put himself in the path of Helene and David Bane—as soon as he made certain Wilson had what he needed.

The dining room servant promised to have a tray delivered to Wilson's room within the half-hour. As Rhys walked back to the hall, Mrs Jacobs, hands full of a large bundle and a basket dangling from one arm, had just reached the stairway.

He caught up to her. 'Mrs Jacobs, may I assist you?'

She smiled at him and handed him the bundle. 'Ah, Captain. You are a most welcome sight.' They walked up the stairs together. 'I brought some clean nightclothes for Mr Wilson. And some food and some things for me.' She lifted the basket, then inclined her head towards the bundle he carried. 'The hotel gave me these clean linens. I do not know how I would have managed had you not come along. You do not mind carrying these to Mr Wilson's room, do you?'

'Not at all.' Even though Rhys had not intended to return to the room.

'You truly will not mind when you see who is there with him.' She grinned at him. 'Your lovely *mademoiselle*!'

He was about to tell her Helene was not *his*, but she interrupted him, her expression sobering.

'She did not mind me leaving her with Mr Wilson. I had her permission. I had to go to my home. I—I needed to check on…' Her voice trailed off but the distress in it did not escape him.

'Is something amiss at home?' Rhys asked.

'Oh.' She sighed. 'My husband is a bit poorly, that is all.'

'I am sorry to hear that,' he responded.

'It was not the best time for me to leave him, you see, but we do need the money.' She seemed to force a smile. 'And I like to be of service when the hotel calls upon me.'

'Is there anything we can do?' he asked, catching himself saying *we* as if Helene and he really were together and as if he was not adding Mrs Jacobs to his list of people with whom to become embroiled.

She shook her head. 'All is in hand. My husband will be able to care for himself.' She glanced at him. 'I should like to check on him once a day, if possible.'

'We will arrange that, then.' He said *we* again.

They reached Wilson's door.

'Ah, Mrs Jacobs,' Helene said as they entered. 'You are back.'

'With clean linens and nightclothes for Mr Wilson. Food for me, and—' the nurse smiled cheerfully 'your handsome captain.'

A nerve twitched in Rhys's jaw. Helene's smile froze.

Helene recovered. 'You did not have to bring your own food. I will happily pay for you to eat. Whatever you wish to have.'

Mrs Jacobs grinned. 'Thank you, *mademoiselle*.'

Rhys spoke up. 'The hotel will deliver some broth, porridge and beer for Wilson. You can ask them then for whatever you want.' He again sounded as though he and Helene were acting in concert.

'Louise?' Wilson called from the bed. 'Louise? Is that you?' His voice was a painful rasp.

Helene hurried over to him. 'Not Louise, Wilson.' She brushed the damp hair from his face and Rhys felt her tenderness as if her gentle fingers had touched him. 'Your nurse is here. Her name is Mrs Jacobs.'

'Nurse?' Wilson murmured. 'Too much fuss. Too much money.'

'Not too much fuss,' Helene assured him. 'And you know I can well afford it. You need a nurse. You should not be alone while you are so ill.'

He grasped her hand. 'You will send the message to Louise?'

'Yes. I will do that right away.' She squeezed his hand and brought it to her cheek. The loving gesture pierced Rhys's heart.

Mrs Jacobs shooed her away from the bedside. 'Now you go off with your handsome captain, *mademoiselle*,' she said. 'I will take good care of Mr Wilson.'

Rhys once again grimaced at Mrs Jacobs's words, but, at the same time, it seemed so familiar for Helene and him to be seen as one. He shook himself. He must not be seduced into again thinking their inseparable childhood had ever been intended to last.

He walked out of the room with Helene at his side, exactly as they might have done had they been together.

As soon as they stepped out in the hall, she said, 'I am not sending a message to Louise Desmet. I am going there myself.'

Good idea, he thought. 'No,' he said. 'I will go.'

She whirled on him. 'No, Rhys. It must be me. Wilson is my responsibility. I need to deliver his message.'

'You can trust me with the errand,' he countered, his tone sharp.

'What does trust have to do with it?' She sounded exasperated. 'I want to meet this Louise.'

Rhys hardened his voice. 'You cannot go alone.'

She glared at him. 'Of course I can go alone. Or I can arrange a servant to attend me. You do not need to go!'

She did not want his company? That decided the matter. He would go, no matter what. 'I know Brussels. You do not.'

She put her hands on her hips. 'Someone will direct me. No matter what you do, I am going to call upon Louise Desmet.'

He held her gaze. 'Then we go together.'

She stared back at him. 'I will need my hat.'

He continued to look her in the eye. 'I will meet you in the hall, then.' He needed his hat and gloves, as well.

They resumed walking again. When they reached her floor, he parted from her, but turned to say, 'Do not set out on your own.'

'What?' she responded in a mocking tone. 'You do not trust me?'

He almost laughed. She always could give as well as take.

Chapter Six

As Helene descended the stairway to the hall, Rhys was waiting at the bottom, looking resplendent in his red coat and sash and gold epaulet on his shoulder. He stood more erect than in his youth, taller, but stiffer, as she expected an army officer must stand. A sight more intimidating than the welcoming young man of her past.

As she neared him, his stony expression did not change. 'I have directions to Rue de l'Evêque.'

She merely nodded and fell into step beside him.

They walked out of the hotel into a lovely summer day. The sun shone in blue skies dotted with puffy white clouds that looked like cotton wool. They were the sort of clouds she and Rhys used to gaze at on summer days, lying on their backs in the grass. *Oh, I found a cat*, she would say, pointing to the sky. *I see a knight*, he would add. Sometimes they could even find what the other pictured, but, in those days, they often saw eye to eye.

This day she walked silently at his side, feeling more like a stranger. He led her up some stairs and through an iron gate. Suddenly they stood in a huge garden laid out in every direction with white gravel paths, plots of green grass and an abundance of flowers, trees and fountains.

The garden was surrounded by magnificent houses, public buildings and the Place Royale where the Prince of Orange lived. The park was filled with officers wearing every type of uniform, many with elegant women on their arms. Some sat in the grass under the trees or clustered in small groups, conversing animatedly.

Helene gasped at the sight. She'd only really seen Brussels at dusk and night, when she and Wilson entered the city through crowded narrow streets and wound up a hill that brought them to the hotel. When searching for David they returned to those lower streets whose shops and taverns looked much like those in London, except their signs were in French. She'd not guessed how beautiful Brussels could be—a city of grace and grandeur and opulence.

She'd almost taken his arm as they joined the other promenaders on the paths, the gravel crunching beneath their shoes. 'What is this place?' she asked.

'The Parc de Bruxelles,' Rhys answered. 'It will be faster if we cut through here.'

He set a brisk pace.

Did he not notice the beauty of this place? Everywhere were sights that delighted. From the colourful flowers, to the lush green trees, the white statues of gods and goddesses, the magnificent buildings.

Up ahead a group of officers chatted with some fashionably dressed ladies. As they neared the group, one of the men in a uniform like Rhys's gazed curiously at them and nodded to Rhys. She recognised the man as Rhys's companion in the tavern that first night in Brussels when she'd finally found David. Rhys acknowledged his friend's silent greeting but did not stop to speak to him.

They left the garden and soon the Gothic towers of a cathedral filled her vision, its stone shining golden in the sunlight and its stained-glass windows sparkling with reds and blues and greens.

She could not help but pause to gaze at it.

Rhys walked on a few steps, then turned and walked back to her, standing at some distance.

'It is so magnificent, is it not, Rhys?' She forgot for the moment that they were estranged.

Rhys hesitated, caught by the vision of her in the sunlight, her lovely face filled with awe. He stepped closer to stand at her side.

'It is a beautiful cathedral,' he admitted.

She turned, surveying all that surrounded them, then smiled at him. 'This is my first real sight of the city.'

That made sense. She'd either been searching for David or caring for Wilson.

'I have been in Brussels for some time,' he responded. 'I am used to it.' Not used to the power of her smile, though. He should not have accompanied her. She opened old wounds by reminding him of how it had once been between them.

He gazed at the cathedral. 'This is the Cathedral of St Michael and St Gudula, a Roman Catholic church.'

'Oh?' She gazed at it again. 'I have never been in such a church.'

He and Grant had visited the sights of the city when they'd first arrived. It had been a pleasure to visit the churches and other fine structures, as well as the Grand Place with its old Gothic guild buildings. What would Helene think of the Manneken Pis, he wondered, whose water poured out from a singular place in a statue of a small boy?

She stepped back. 'Forgive me, Rhys. I am acting like a tourist. We should go.'

He did not offer his arm. After all, they were not strolling together as companions or lovers, like other couples they passed.

They turned left on the Rue de la Montagne and took the first right which led to the Theatre Royale. Once there Rhys asked a man for directions to Rue de l'Evêque. It was not far. Just a little way beyond the theatre and past the Hotel de Monnaies. They entered a street lined with modest grey or white stone buildings at least three storeys high. Most housed shops on the lower floors. Rhys asked several people where to find Louise Desmet, and they were finally directed to a thin building wedged between two larger ones with shops underneath.

The door was directly on the street. He knocked.

A slim woman with grey hair peeking out from a plain white cap opened the door a crack. Her plain dress was covered by an apron, like clothes worn by so many of the ordinary women of Brussels. She looked to be about Wilson's age, although Rhys could not guess how old that might be.

Helene spoke first, in French. '*Pardon, madame*, we are looking for Louise Desmet.'

The woman eyed her with some suspicion. 'I am Madame Desmet.'

Helene expelled a relieved breath. 'I am so glad we have found you! We come with a message from Wilson—from Samuel Wilson.'

The woman's eyes darted from Helene to Rhys and back again. 'Samuel?'

Helene continued. 'He wanted you to know he cannot call upon you.'

Madame Desmet's features drooped in disappointment, but her expression changed quickly to one of mistrust. 'And who are you to deliver me such a message?'

Rhys spoke. 'This is Lady Helene Banes. Wilson—Mr Wilson—is in her family's employ.'

Comprehension dawned on Madame Desmet's face.

He went on. 'I am Captain Landon, a...family friend.'

Madame Desmet opened the door wider. 'Please, come in,' she said in perfect, lightly accented English.

'You speak English?' Helene said in surprise.

Madame Desmet did not respond, but simply waited for them to enter a small hall. There were stairs to an upper floor directly in front of them and a small hallway to the right. She led them up the stairs which opened to a tidy sitting room with two upholstered chairs facing a small fireplace. On the chair closest to the single narrow window lay some sewing which Madame Desmet quickly snatched up. She moved the sewing to a table upon which was a small wooden sewing box. Its open lid revealed scissors and some spools of thread.

She gestured to the chairs. 'Please sit down. May I offer refreshment?'

'Oh, no,' Helene said as she sat. 'We will not trouble you.'

Rhys had been in houses similar to this. He imagined the kitchen was on the floor below with a table and chairs to eat upon instead of a dining room. Above would be one or two bedchambers. There might be an attic room for a servant, if she had one. This was not poverty, but a comfortable existence. He was fairly certain Helene had never been in such a modest house. Even the vicarage where he'd grown up was spacious compared to this.

He watched Helene's reaction, but she seemed to take no notice. Her eyes remained fixed on their hostess.

Madame Desmet picked up a wooden chair from a corner of the room. Rhys moved quickly to take it from her.

'Allow me,' he said, placing it near where Helene sat.

He lowered himself into it, leaving the upholstered chair for Madame Desmet.

She looked uncertain for a moment before accepting the more comfortable chair. 'May I ask why you have come and not Samuel? Did he change his mind about seeing me? Why send you and not simply write another letter?'

Helene bit her lip and glanced at Rhys.

He leaned forward. 'He is ill, *madame*. Too ill to write.'

'Ill?' Her voice rose.

'He has a fever,' Helene explained. 'He's very weak, but he insisted we get a message to you.'

Rhys added, 'We decided to do so in person, rather than engage a messenger.' They were talking as they used to do, he realised, as if speaking with one voice.

Madame Desmet stared past them. 'How ill is he?'

Helene gave her a wan smile. 'We have every hope of his recovery.'

The older woman closed her eyes and looked as if someone had stabbed her in the heart. She stood abruptly, making both Rhys and Helene jump.

'I must see him!' she cried.

'He may be contagious,' Helene warned.

'I do not care if he is. Please, Lady Helene, I must see him!' she cried.

Rhys stood and turned to Helene. 'We should take her to him.'

Helene attempted a reassuring smile for the woman. 'Of course we will take you to him.'

'Let us go now,' Madame Desmet said, her tone frantic. She removed her apron and descended the stairs, grabbing a shawl and bonnet from pegs on the wall next to the door.

Helene and Rhys exchanged a glance, a silent communication that her urgency had surprised them both. They'd so often not needed words to know what the other was thinking. In the past, that was.

They followed Madame Desmet out the door.

Once outside the older woman walked swiftly, knowing, of course, the way to the hotel. Helene skipped hurriedly to catch up to her.

'May I ask how you know Wilson?' Helene asked,

'We met years ago,' Madame Desmet said.

'In Brussels?'

'Oui.'

'Wilson was in Brussels?' Helene was nearly out of breath at the older woman's fast pace.

'Long ago,' Madame Desmet replied. 'Before the war.'

And the occupation by the French, Helene presumed. She still thought of Wilson as a child might, that his existence began and continued with her life, not that he'd had a life before coming to Yarford House.

'He never spoke of it,' Helene said.

Madame Desmet looked at her as if she were a simpleton. 'He is a servant, no?'

Of course. What servant ever spoke of their own life?

Rhys, with his long legs, had no difficulty keeping up. 'What brought Wilson to Brussels, then?'

'He served a young gentleman on his grand tour,' Madame explained.

Before the war with Napoleon, a trip to the Continent had been customary for wealthy young gentlemen, who were accompanied by a tutor and a servant to tend to their needs. The young gentleman was expected to expand his knowledge by visiting the major sights and cities of the various countries, to immerse himself in their art and architecture. Helene was not such a green girl to fail knowing that a young gentleman's education might also include brothels and gaming rooms for an entirely different sort of education.

What an adventure it must have been for Wilson, as well.

Helene had a dozen more questions, but it was too difficult to walk this briskly and carry on a conversation at the same time.

As they passed the cathedral, Madame Desmet dashed across the street ahead of Rhys and Helene. Helene, trying to keep up with her, stepped into the street. At the same time, a speeding carriage came around the corner. Its two horses, sweat gleaming on their coats, headed straight for her. She froze in alarm.

Suddenly strong arms pulled her back, slamming her against a rock-hard chest. Rhys held her there, his arms encircling her, as the carriage thundered past making the ground tremble beneath the horses' powerful hooves.

Helene's senses burst into life. The fright at almost being run down. The glory of being held by him.

'Rhys,' she whispered.

He abruptly released her. 'Take more care, Helene,' he said gruffly.

He seized her arm and led her across the street, releasing her the minute they were on the pavement again.

Madame Desmet was several paces ahead of them and apparently had not seen her close call. Helene glanced at Rhys whose expression turned to stone.

Helene felt tears sting her eyes—of anger and perhaps relief. She might have been killed! Rhys saved her, but in such an unfeeling, gruff way that she felt trampled upon, nonetheless.

She caught up with Madame Desmet at the door of the hotel. Helene swallowed her own feelings and turned her attention to the older woman. 'Do you need a moment or shall we take you to his room directly?'

'Take me to his room,' Madame Desmet said, her voice trembling.

Rhys offered Madame Desmet his arm. 'Come,' he said gently.

Madame Desmet was offered kindness and Helene received a mere scolding? She trailed behind them, watching Rhys climb the stairs slowly, knowing he was doing so to help Madame Desmet compose herself before entering Wilson's room. Knowing, too, that he did not care a fig if Helene followed or not. It seemed he had not changed quite as much as she thought. He'd merely changed towards her.

Rhys and Madame Desmet had already gained entry to Wilson's room when Helene stepped through the doorway.

'He is dozing,' Mrs Jacobs was telling them.

Rhys held Madame Desmet back from rushing to the bedside. 'Mrs Jacobs, this is Madame Desmet. She is the Louise Wilson has been calling for.' He turned to Madame Desmet. 'Mrs Jacobs is his nurse.'

Mrs Jacobs, certainly unable to miss the distress and worry in Madame Desmet's face, took her in hand, and placed a comforting arm around her. 'I am certain you will be like a tonic to him.' She squeezed her a little, like one might do a child. 'We will wake him. Tell him you are here.'

'I'll wake him,' Rhys said. He quietly approached the bed and gently touched Wilson on the shoulder. 'Wilson. Wilson. You have a visitor.'

The older man's eyes fluttered open and he smiled faintly at Rhys. Rhys stepped aside and gestured for Madame Desmet to approach.

'Samuel?' Her voice cracked. 'Samuel.' She flew to his side.

Wilson's face beamed as if lit by the sun. 'Louise,' he whispered, reaching for her hand.

She grasped it and, lowering herself into the chair, placed his hand against her cheek. 'I am here, Samuel.'

Tears again stung Helene's eyes, but this time due to this tender scene.

Mrs Jacobs, her arms crossing her chest, nodded her head. 'They were lovers, you can bet upon it. I can always tell.'

Rhys, who had paid Helene no attention at all since her close encounter with the carriage, now turned to her, but his expression remained grim. To her dismay, her insides fluttered in response to his gaze. She supposed she would always react to his eyes upon her, even when he hurt her.

Helene walked past him to Wilson's bedside. She squatted down so that she could be almost at eye level with him. 'See, Wilson? We have brought your Louise to you. She may remain at your side for as long as you and she wish. I am going to leave you now, but I will return later to check on you.'

With his free hand, Wilson reached for hers, clasping it firmly. 'Thank you, m'lady. Thank you.'

She did not deserve all his credit. 'Rhys accompanied me. I could not have found your Louise without his help.'

'Rhys?' the old man cried. 'Rhys is here?'

Helene frowned. He'd not remembered it was Rhys who had awakened him?

Rhys came to Helene's side. 'I am here, Wilson. Here to help in whatever way I can.'

'With Lady Helene again!' Wilson turned to Madame Desmet. 'Is that not delightful?'

She gave Helene a worried glance. She, too, had noticed his mind was still addled. She smiled down at Wilson, though. 'Very delightful.'

Helene patted Wilson's hand and pulled hers out of his grip. 'I am leaving now. I will be back.'

He paid no heed, simply gazed at Madame Desmet.

Helene walked over to Mrs Jacobs whose smile could not have been wider. She inclined her head towards her patient and his visitor. 'Isn't that a pretty sight? Reminds me of me and my Hulbert.' Her smile drooped for a moment but a poor replica of it returned when she faced Helene. 'And you and your captain.'

Rhys walked over before Helene could correct her about Rhys. 'I will leave, as well.' He walked to the door.

'Are you comfortable with having Madame Desmet stay?' Helene asked Mrs Jacobs.

The woman laughed. 'I think she is just the medicine he needs.' She shooed Helene towards Rhys. 'Do not worry over a thing. Enjoy this pretty day, you two.'

Mrs Jacobs closed the door behind them and Helene and Rhys stood in the dimly lit hallway, facing each other. The silence between them stretched to an unbearable length. What had happened to the days where they had much to say to the other?

She could not stand there another second. 'I shall go to my room,' she stated. She turned away from him and hurried down the hallway.

Rhys kept pace with her, searching for something to say, anything but what was in his heart—that he was so grateful she was alive, so thankful he had been there to pull her out of the path of the speeding carriage. What would have happened had he not been there? That was all he'd thought of since he'd held her close.

He could say none of that to her.

'What did you think of Louise Desmet?' he asked instead.

She looked surprised at his question or perhaps surprised that he spoke at all after he'd been silent for so long. 'They seem devoted to each other,' she finally said.

He agreed.

Rhys saw himself in Wilson, even though Wilson was so much older. How Wilson looked at his Louise? That was how Rhys once felt to be with Helene. Full of joy and relief. As if his world was finally complete.

Something else he could not tell Helene, not after Helene scraped him raw that day when he learned she would not marry him, and her father sent him away. He'd learned to bury that pain.

'Are you not checking on your brother today?' His tone turned disdainful.

'I left him a note,' she said.

Rhys decided not to tell her he'd dragged her brother out of yet another tavern the night before. Why worry her more?

They reached her floor. 'No need to walk me to my room,' she said. 'I will bid you good day here.'

'As you wish.' He turned to leave her.

'Rhys?'

He turned back to her.

'Thank you for coming with me to find Madame Desmet. You were correct. It would have been difficult for me to find her alone.' Her lovely face had a ghost of a smile. 'And I am for ever in your debt for pulling me out of the way of the carriage.' Her voice wobbled.

His carefully banked emotions threatened to spill over, but he kept his voice even. 'I would have done so for anyone.'

She smiled wistfully. 'Yes, I suppose you would.'

She turned and walked down the hallway to her room. Rhys watched her until she turned the corner. He remained there for a moment not quite knowing what to do. Clearing his throat, he descended the stairs.

He had a sudden thirst for a very large tankard of beer.

Chapter Seven

David sat on horseback as he and William Lennox rode on a country lane past fields of barley and wheat, edged with hedgerows. The sun was high in the blue sky and the horse he rode was a fine one. What could be better?

William had lent David this fine horse. The mare belonged to William's father, the Duke of Richmond. He was actually riding a horse owned by the Duke of Richmond. Wellington's friend. It was almost like being in Wellington's circle, was it not?

David's morning had not begun on a high note. He'd woken with a ponderous headache from the previous night's carousing, but it had completely gone away after his breakfast of eggs and beer. He wished he and William could ride like the wind! He was bursting with excitement.

'So, this is one of the roads Wellington believes the French will use to reach Brussels?' he asked, somewhat rhetorically.

'As my father says,' William responded in a weary tone. 'One of three possible routes, but we have spoken of this before.'

William was in a bit of ill humour this day, but that was due to his eye injury, David believed. The injury might keep him out of the battle. What could be worse? David refused to give in to William's blue devils, though. Nothing would ruin David's good cheer.

'I have, by the way, spoken to my mother,' William went on. 'You, your sister, and Captains Landon and Grantwell will all receive invitations to the ball.'

'I am very grateful!' David cried. 'And it certainly will impress Rhys and his friend that I have procured invitations for them!'

'*I* have procured the invitations, David,' William said testily.

David gave an embarrassed laugh. 'Of course you have! I meant only that I am lucky enough to be your friend.' The ball was another event David greatly anticipated. The Duke of Wellington, the Prince of Orange, and all sorts of important people would be there.

David would not miss a moment of it. 'Perhaps I can come early to the ball. Help you out in some way.' It would not hurt to be considered a close friend of the family. He might even get to meet Wellington.

William glanced over at him. 'Do you not have to escort your sister?'

Helene. What a trial it was to have her chase after him here, thinking she could bully him into doing as she wished.

'I'll get Rhys to escort her. He was our vicar's son and they used to be chums. He won't mind.' David had no intention of being tied to Helene's apron strings at a ball where every important military officer was to be present. He planned to avoid her at all costs, like he'd done that morning, escaping before she came looking for him.

He refused to have Helene dampen his spirits. Even more than the ball, he was about to be part of the most exciting battle of the whole war. Napoleon versus Wellington! What could be more grand?

The road was empty for the moment, but David could just see some movement in the distance, too far to tell if it was a carriage or a wagon or someone on horseback.

His imagination flared. 'Would it not be astonishing if we came upon the French marching on this very road at his very time!'

William responded, 'If the French were this close, Wellington would know of it. He has exploring officers all over the Continent, you may depend upon it.'

'I know.' David sighed. 'But it would be such a coup if you and I discovered the French advance and brought the intelligence to Wellington.'

'At least I would have some role in the battle, then,' William grumbled.

David was riding close enough to reach out and thump William on his shoulder. 'Come now! Your eye will heal! You must be a part of it!'

They rode on, reaching the crest of the gently sloping hill. Below them a small village lay.

'I wonder if there is a tavern in this village,' David said. 'We could stop for some beer. I am prodigiously fond of Belgian beer.'

As they neared the village they came upon a sign giving its name.

Mont Saint Jean.

Helene paced the hotel room. It was comfortable enough, spacious enough for a sitting area near the fire and a table for dining, but, in her restless state, the room seemed like a prison cell. She had nothing to do, none of the distractions of home, the minor tasks, the mending, meeting with the housekeeper, seeing that all ran smoothly. She did not even have a book to read.

She greatly needed distraction. From thinking about Rhys. No matter how she tried, her thoughts returned to him.

She stopped pacing and tightly closed her eyes, remembering how incredible it felt to have his arms encircle her and hold her tight when he rescued her from the speeding carriage. And how bereft when he just as quickly released her.

She clenched her fists and stifled a frustrated cry. She wanted to be gone from this place! She wanted to be home where there were endless chores to do.

She'd planned to be on the journey home by now, she, David and Wilson. She'd not even packed for more than a few days. But how long would it be before Wilson could be well enough to travel—that is, if his fever did not take a turn for the worse, like the fever had done for her father?

Wilson could still die from the fever.

Rhys could die in the battle.

Even David could die, if she did not succeed in keeping him from the battle.

She walked to the window, which faced the street in front of the hotel. Carriages rolled by, men rode on horseback, and all sorts of people dashed about as if life was proceeding normally. She wanted to scream a warning at them. All could be lost. In one day, in one moment, all could be lost.

Like that day her father told Rhys she would not marry him and sent him to join the army.

She groaned aloud.

It did her no good to dwell on that. Better to be busy at something. Anything.

She spun around and strode to the writing desk, removing paper, ink and a pen. She wrote a note, blew on it so the ink dried quickly and folded it. She picked up her bonnet, shawl and gloves and walked out the door and through the hallways and stairs to David's room.

She knocked, not really expecting an answer. She slid the note under the door.

The note asked David to seek her out that day, that she needed to speak to him and hoped he would agree to dine with her that evening. She did not add that she hoped again to reason with him, to secure his agreement to leave as soon as Wilson was well and to promise not to put himself in harm's way in the meantime. What more could she do?

She donned her hat and gloves and walked down the stairs to the hall, stopping by where the hall servant stood.

'May I assist you, my lady?' he asked.

'*Oui, merci,*' she responded. 'If you see my brother, David Banes, would you tell him I wish to speak with him? I have also left him a note in his room.'

'With pleasure, my lady.' He bowed.

She left the hotel and took the route to the Parc she and Rhys had taken that morning. At home when she needed to clear her mind or settle her nerves, she'd take a walk, often returning to where she and Rhys had fished in the stream, picked berries or played knights and damsels in distress, although she'd sometimes complained of always having to be the damsel.

Even with those bittersweet memories, a brisk walk always restored her and today she greatly needed her spirits restored.

She passed through the iron gate and entered the Parc, deciding to first walk its perimeter. The Parc was so large that a stroll around it might be all she needed. If not, she could crisscross all the other paths and see how many fountains and statues she could discover.

It was mid-afternoon and the Parc was every bit as crowded as it had been earlier when she and Rhys had passed through. The perimeter, though, was somewhat sparse of promenaders. That suited Helene as she could examine the various trees and plants at her leisure. Those people she did pass, men in uniform mostly, gave her curious looks that made her uncomfortable in ways she'd never felt walking through the busy streets of London. Of course, she'd mostly had a maid or footman with her on those occasions.

She reached the far end of the Parc where she could see the spout of a fountain rise high in the middle of a circular pool. She walked closer to the fountain where groups of people sat on the grass nearby and others rested at the water's edge, dipping their fingers in the water. The sight of others enjoying the park did not delight her as much as it had that morning. A wave of loneliness washed over her, not unfamiliar. Loneliness often struck her, ever since Rhys had left.

A woman's laugh caught her attention. An elegantly dressed young lady stood flirting with two officers in blue coats; an older woman—her mother, maid or chaperon—stood nearby. The young lady seemed to delight in her suitors. Helene remembered many a ride through Hyde Park when she'd pretended to enjoy a suitor's company when all the time thinking the gentleman was not Rhys.

Better to *be* alone than pretend you are not.

Her gaze was caught by two red-coated uniforms, this time conversing with three women too gaily dressed for midday. One of the men stepped into better view and she gasped.

It was Rhys.

She quickly whirled away, hoping he had not seen her.

Such a simple thing to see him conversing with other people. Why should it pain her so? Of course he had a life separate from her, a life that included other women. Logically she'd always known this to be true; she even told herself he would marry someone else some day. Still, seeing him with other women made that knowledge painfully real.

Helene headed back to the perimeter path, passing three soldiers who talked loud enough for her to hear, in the language she'd heard so many people speak on her trip from Ghent. Flemish or Dutch, she did not know which. These men's uniforms were a dark green with yellow-striped epaulets on their shoulders. They had a rougher look about them than some of the soldiers she'd passed by. She quickened her step to get away from them.

Rhys was not surprised to have encountered Grant in the Parc, surrounded by three townswomen of questionable reputation. Grant had a way of attracting women. He was charming to them, but Rhys knew Grant guarded his heart even more strictly than Rhys did. It made Grant a challenge few women could resist.

Bored by their conversation, Rhys had been about to excuse himself when he glimpsed a woman in a blue dress standing alone.

Helene.

'What the devil?' he said aloud.

She must have seen him, because she turned and fled. He watched her disappear on to the outer path. Debating with himself whether to follow her, he spied three Dutch soldiers nudge each other and head for the same path.

'Damned woman!' Rhys took off after them.

'What?' called Grant after him.

Rhys heard Grant behind him, the protests of his three admirers ringing in Rhys's ears. When Rhys reached the outer path, he slid to a stop. No one was in sight and he was unsure in which direction she'd gone.

Grant caught up to him. 'What is it?'

Rhys lifted a hand. 'Shh!'

He heard a man's cry and he sprinted in that direction. Around the corner one of the Dutch soldiers fell on to the path from a space between the trees. He rose to his feet and brushed himself off but lifted his head to see Rhys and Grant advancing on him. The soldier shouted something and took off.

When Rhys reached the opening in the trees, he found Helene wielding a fallen tree branch, thick as a club, swinging full force at one of the soldiers. There was a loud crack when the branch hit the man in the chest. He tumbled back in pain. The other soldier grabbed for her, but she recovered quickly enough to bring the stick up right between the man's legs. His scream was as high as a girl's. He clutched his privates. The first man scrambled to his feet, fury on his face. He came at her again.

'Stop!' Rhys bellowed. 'Stop!'

The two soldiers gaped at him.

'Officieren!' one cried and the two took off running through the trees.

Helene still held the stick, panting and wild-eyed. Her shawl was caught on a nearby bush and her bonnet was dangling from her neck. When she saw it was Rhys, her shoulders slumped and she let her weapon fall.

'What the devil are you doing in this park alone?' Rhys snapped at her.

She straightened, sparks still flashing from her eyes. 'Fighting off attackers, obviously.' She untied the strings of her bonnet and placed it back on her head.

Grant walked up to stand beside him. 'Oh, the lady of the tavern and this morning's promenade.' He looked at Rhys expectantly.

Rhys extended his arm towards Grant. 'Lady Helene, may I present Captain Grantwell.' He turned to Helene. 'Lady Helene Banes.'

'Banes?' Recognition dawned on Grant's face. 'David Banes's sister! I have heard almost nothing about you.' He bowed.

'A pleasure to meet you, Captain.' Her words sounded automatic. 'We saw you this morning in the Parc.'

Grant grinned. 'I have not been here all day, I assure you, although it must appear so.' He gave her an appraising look. 'I must confess, I am all admiration, Lady Helene. I hope my soldiers fight half as well as you.'

'I had a good teacher.' She glanced at Rhys and walked over to retrieve her shawl.

Rhys seized her arm. 'What possessed you to walk in this Parc alone? Do you not have any sense at all?'

She shrugged him off. 'Enough sense to arm myself when the need arose.' She looked at him with defiance. 'The Parc was filled with people. As no one saw fit to warn me otherwise, I suspected no danger.'

He glared at her. 'Did you fail to notice the whole city teeming with soldiers? Idle ones at that?' In a secluded spot like this one, who would see her in danger or heed her cries?

She brushed off her skirt and pulled up her gloves, one ripped, most likely from rubbing across the branch. 'Well. I thank you, Rhys, for coming again to my aid, unnecessary though it was.' She turned to Grant. 'Thank you, as well, Captain Grantwell. I will continue my walk now.' She glanced towards the interior of the Parc. 'In the more public areas where I am certain I shall be perfectly safe.'

'You will go back to the hotel,' Rhys ordered. 'I will take you there.' He reached for her arm again.

She backed away. 'I am not returning to the hotel. The day is too fine to be cooped up inside.'

'I have an idea,' Grant said cheerfully. 'We can all walk together. I would greatly enjoy your company, Lady Helene, if you will permit me?'

She pressed her lips together before answering, 'Very well.'

It rankled that she so easily accepted Grant's invitation but refused to heed his order.

She also accepted Grant's arm.

Rhys followed a step behind them as they took a path leading back to the fountain and the interior of the Parc. While Grant was acting his charming self, Rhys was regretting his outburst.

'So, tell me, Lady Helene,' Rhys heard Grant say. 'How do you know my friend Rhys?'

She darted a glance back at him. 'As children. We grew up together.'

'Indeed?' Grant responded, also glancing back at Rhys.

'Yes,' Rhys piped up. 'I was the vicar's son. She was the Earl's daughter. You may guess how it was.'

Grant's brows rose. 'I confess I cannot at all guess how it was.' He looked from one to the other.

Rhys assumed his own expression was grim. Helene's, on the other hand, was in high colour, her eyes bright, as if her encounter with the Dutch soldiers had awakened something primal in her. She quite took his breath away.

Grant, ever attuned to unspoken emotions, changed the subject. He began commenting on the people they saw, pointing out to Helene some noteworthy figures. An aide-de-camp of the Prince of Orange. Their regimental Colonel, General John Howard, who acknowledged them with a nod. A very pregnant Lady Frances Webster, rumoured to be the Duke of Wellington's latest paramour, but not the father of her unborn child. Rhys followed silently.

Eventually Rhys noticed Helene falter. 'She is fatigued,' he said. 'Enough walking.'

Grant turned to her. 'Are you fatigued, my lady?'

She glared back at Rhys. 'I am not fatigued.' She turned her attention to Grant. 'I confess I am a little thirsty, though.'

Grant smiled. 'Let us return to the hotel and have some tea.'

Tea? He and Grant had been headed for the taverns.

'A lovely idea,' agreed Helene.

They left the Parc through the same gate Helene had entered, the one Rhys led her to that morning. Rhys's friend Grantwell held her elbow protectively as they descended the stairs leading to the Hotêl de Flandre. Her heart was still pounding from what nearly happened to her. How could Rhys think she would be fatigued? She felt as if she could run straight to Antwerp.

She was proud of fighting off those horrible men. She'd heard them behind her and she'd searched for a weapon. If she had not found one, she'd have done the job with kicks and fists. Just as Rhys had taught her.

As they entered the hotel, Rhys and Grantwell removed their shakos. They made an impressive pair, these two tall British officers walking at her side. She'd noticed the admiring glances from other women in the Parc. They'd even passed by the three women with whom Rhys and his friend had been conversing. Three sets of eyes shot daggers at her.

The hall servant greeted them as they walked through the hotel.

Helene stopped to speak with him. 'Have you seen my brother, by any chance?'

The man looked regretful. 'No, my lady. But I have not forgotten your message.'

'I will be in the dining room, if he happens by,' she said.

'Very good, my lady.'

Rhys spoke up. 'You have not seen David today?'

'No,' she admitted. 'But I left him a note. I've asked him to have dinner with me.'

He returned a sceptical look.

She so needed to have a very frank talk with David. He was the Earl of Yarford now and it was time he accepted the role. He had a duty to keep himself safe. He needed to be home.

They entered the dining room where there were a few other people lounging at other tables. Helene had eaten nothing since the bread and cheese in Wilson's room that morning. She was glad Captain Grantwell suggested tea.

Rhys did not seem at all happy about it, though. She looked into his unsmiling face. 'Rhys, you can leave if staying is so unpleasant.'

He frowned at her. 'Who said it was unpleasant?'

'Shall we sit?' Grantwell asked.

They found a table and ordered their tea. Helene removed her gloves. Both needed washing and one might be too far gone to mend.

Captain Grantwell turned to her. 'And how do you like Brussels, Lady Helene?'

She glanced at Rhys who was seated to her left and seemingly paying no attention to her. 'From what I have seen, its buildings are magnificent.'

'From what you have seen?' Grantwell repeated. 'Have you not had a proper tour of the city?'

'No.' She'd had Wilson to tend to and David to worry about. 'I've not had the time.'

She could sense the Captain's curiosity about her—about her and Rhys—but it seemed nothing more than that. He was not flirting with her, of that she was certain. She'd had enough experience during her Seasons in London to tell if a man was trying to gain her interest.

'No time?' She noticed Grantwell dart a quick look at Rhys.

Helene explained. 'The manservant who accompanied me here became ill. I have been seeing he gets the care he needs.' She added. 'With Rhys's help.'

'I've known the man since I was a boy,' Rhys said. 'He was always good to me.'

'And how is your servant?' Grantwell seemed genuinely concerned.

'Somewhat better,' Helene said.

The servant brought the tea and Helene poured. She asked Grantwell how he took his tea. His brows rose when she fixed Rhys's tea without asking. She knew just how much milk, how much sugar. The servant also brought a plate of biscuits which she passed to the men.

She feared Grantwell's questions about her—and Rhys—would continue. Certainly Rhys would no more want his friend to continue in that vein than she did.

She turned tables on the gentlemen. 'How long have you known each other?' she asked.

'Since right before the second battalion landed in Portugal,' Grantwell said.

'The second battalion?' she asked.

Grantwell answered, 'Second battalion of the East Essex—the 44th Regiment of Foot.'

At least she now knew what regiment was Rhys's.

'When did the battalion land in Portugal?' she asked.

Grantwell turned to Rhys. 'What has it been? Five years?'

'Five years,' Rhys repeated.

Right after leaving her.

'A lot happened in those five years,' Rhys commented.

A bleak look crossed Grantwell's face.

Rhys spoke up quickly. 'But you won't wish to know any of that, Helene. War is not for teatime conversation with a lady.'

She had a pretty good idea of what some of it was like. She'd read every account of every battle she could find.

Grantwell seemed to force a smile. 'We should make a plan to give you a tour of the city.'

Rhys glowered at this suggestion.

'How nice of you to offer, Captain,' she said in her best drawing room voice.

Mrs Jacobs appeared at the dining room doorway, saying something to the servant. Helene seized the chance to get away from Rhys for the moment.

'I see Wilson's nurse. I need to speak to her.' The two officers rose when she stood.

Mrs Jacobs grinned when Helene approached her. 'Now you have a second admirer, *mademoiselle*? Your Captain will be jealous, no?'

Mrs Jacobs was almost as exasperating as Rhys. 'He is *not* my Captain,' she protested.

The woman gave her a sympathetic look. 'Ah, you have had a spat, have you? Never you mind, I am sure all will be well by the morrow.'

Helene shook her head. There was no talking sense to this woman. 'How is Wilson?' she asked instead.

The nurse shrugged. 'Sometimes he seems to rest peacefully. Sometimes he does not.'

Helene's spirits dipped. 'No better? That is not good.'

The nurse patted her arm. 'He is a mite better. I think he rests easier with Louise sitting at his side.'

Louise? Apparently Mrs Jacobs and Madame Desmet were getting along well. 'She is still there?'

Mrs Jacobs threw up her hands. 'I cannot convince her to leave. But she is a great help and I am able to come to order food without worrying about leaving Mr Wilson alone.'

'Order whatever you need,' Helene told her. 'A meal for you and Madame Desmet, as well.'

'Merci, mademoiselle,' she responded. 'Louise promised to go home to rest after she feeds Mr Wilson some dinner.'

'Is he eating?' That would be a good sign.

The nurse shrugged. 'Some broth. A few spoons of porridge.'

'Please get word to me if his fever worsens,' Helene told her. 'But I will stop by before I retire.'

The nurse patted her hand again. 'Now don't you worry, *mademoiselle*. You go back to your Captain and the other fellow. Make him jealous—' She laughed as she walked away. 'That will do nicely!'

Helene returned to the table. Rhys watched her approach. How surprised Mrs Jacobs would be if she knew how things really stood between her and Rhys.

'Helene!' a voice sounded from behind her.

She turned to see David hurrying her way.

He was nearly breathless when he caught up to her. 'The hall servant stopped me! Insisted I speak with you. What the devil is so important?'

Chapter Eight

It was about time David showed up, Rhys thought. Better he see to his sister than spend another night in the taverns.

David stood with her a little distance from their table in the hotel's dining room, but Rhys and Grant, still drinking their tea, could hear every word of their conversation.

'Tell me what you want to say and let me be on my way.' David looked about to bolt at any moment.

'On your way?' Helene glared at her brother. 'Where are you off to?'

'To my room, if you must know,' he retorted. 'To change for dinner.'

'I want you to have dinner with me,' Helene said. 'I want to talk to you—'

David raised his hands in frustration. 'Lecture me, you mean. I do not want to hear it!'

Rhys was beginning to think David needed a good paddling, like a naughty schoolboy. He was certainly acting like one.

'*Talk* to you,' she repeated. 'Not lecture. There are things you should know—'

'I know already!' David cried. 'Wilson is sick. Nothing I can do about that! You brought him here. I did not want either of you to come. I'm a man now and I can take care of myself!'

Rhys started to rise.

'Oh?' Her brows rose. 'Did not Rhys have to carry you out of a tavern two nights ago?'

He relaxed in his chair. Helene was holding her own.

'I could have walked!' David raised his voice and other people in the dining room looked his way.

Helene leaned towards him and spoke in a low, firm voice. 'You passed out, David.'

And David had nearly done the same the next night, Rhys wanted to add.

The boy looked momentarily chagrined, but he soon raised his chin. 'That's all well and good, but no matter, I cannot dine with you tonight. I am expected at the Duke of Richmond's for dinner. I'm to dine with the Duke.'

More likely with the Duke's son, the other young fellow Rhys and Grant had met.

'You could send your regrets,' Rhys called over from his seat at the table.

David glanced over at Rhys and Grant, seeming to notice them for the first time. He greeted them cheerfully. 'Oh, hello, Rhys. Grantwell.' He sobered again and gave Rhys an imploring look. 'I cannot send regrets for dinner, Rhys! I am to dine with the *Duke*!'

'Oh, go off to your duke.' Helene waved an impatient hand at him. 'But tell me now when you *will* meet with me. I am tired of chasing after you!'

'Then don't!' David spun on his heel and started to walk away. He stopped and turned back, speaking loud enough for others to hear. 'By the way, you will receive invitations to the Duchess of Richmond's ball two days hence. They will be delivered to the hotel. I arranged it for you!' He puffed up with self-importance before dashing away.

Helene made a frustrated sound and returned to her seat, a thunderous look on her face.

Rhys rose. Helene probably would not want him to interfere, but he didn't care. He'd had enough of David.

He caught up to David in the hall. 'David!'

The boy turned to face him.

Rhys leaned down to him. 'You are behaving like an insufferable brat to your sister. Stop it at once.'

David threw up his hands. 'You know how she is, Rhys. So bossy. Been like that since I was a child.'

'You are acting like a child now,' Rhys pointed out.

'I am not!' he whined. 'Besides, you and Helene always gang up on me!'

Rhys spoke in a firm voice. 'You owe your sister some courtesy, whether you wish to or not. A gentleman treats a lady with respect. A man faces unpleasantries like a man.'

David released a breath. 'You do understand. She can be damned unpleasant!' He backed away. 'I must hurry. I cannot be late!'

Before Rhys could say another word, David took off and bounded up the stairs.

Rhys returned to the dining room.

He flopped into his chair, disgusted with David and bracing for Helene to upbraid him for interfering. 'I cannot talk any sense into him.'

'Thank you for trying, Rhys,' Helene said in a low voice.

He'd not been prepared for her gratitude. 'Least I could do,' he mumbled.

Their table lapsed into silence, each of them covering the quiet by sipping tea or eating biscuits.

Grant eyed both Helene and him. Rhys could almost

feel the questions brimming inside his friend. He supposed he must tell Grant something, but if Grant had never encountered Helene or David, Rhys would not have mentioned a word about them.

Predictably it was Grant who broke the silence. 'Lady Helene, am I correct in assuming that you now have no dinner plans?'

'No, I do not,' she said.

Grant turned to Rhys. 'Let us take Lady Helene to the Grand Place, since she has seen so little of Brussels. After that we could go to the Roi de Pologne for dinner. The restaurant on the Rue de la Montagne, remember it? We have no other plans.'

It was not good at all for Rhys to spend that much time with Helene, to see her face enchanted by new sights, like the Parc and the cathedral. But somehow he also could not bear the idea of leaving her alone, not after the altercation with the Dutch soldiers and David refusing to deal with her.

Rhys turned to her. 'Would you like that, Helene?'

She stared at him a long time before answering. 'That would be lovely.' She turned to Grant. 'But I would like to freshen up a bit first, if you meant to leave right away.'

Grant smiled. In satisfaction, Rhys thought. 'Take whatever time you require.'

She finished her tea and stood. Rhys and Grant rose, as well, and Rhys took a step forward.

She lifted a hand. 'No need to take me to my room, Rhys. I am perfectly capable of making it on my own.'

Grant spoke. 'We will wait here for you, then.'

She turned in a swirl of skirts and walked away. Both he and Grant watched her until she disappeared through the doorway.

Grant immediately signalled for the servant. 'Some beer, if you please.' He glanced at Rhys. 'Beer, Rhys?'

'Yes,' Rhys agreed.

Afternoon beer had been a lot more typical of their stay in Brussels than afternoon tea.

Finally Grant fixed his gaze on Rhys and Rhys knew what was coming. 'Well, are you going to tell me about her?'

Rhys stared back. 'As I said before, she's an earl's daughter and I'm the son of the Earl's vicar.'

Could Grant not guess? Grant had been through a devastating heartbreak. A true betrayal. He never spoke about it. Could he not figure it out that Rhys did not wish to speak of his relationship with Helene?

But he supposed he owed Grant some explanation. 'We were playmates as children, but things changed as we grew up.'

Let Grant read between the lines as Rhys had done when Grant had been betrayed.

Grant took another gulp of his beer, but perused Rhys at the same time. Finally, in a more subdued tone he asked, 'Should I not have made the invitation to dinner?'

Rhys lifted his tankard to his lips. He put it down again. 'After her brother refused to dine with her, we could not simply leave her, could we?'

Grant's eyes filled with amusement. 'No. We could not.'

Once in her room, Helene paced as restlessly as she had before escaping to the Parc. This time it was David who plagued her. What was she to do about him?

Why he was acting so irresponsibly? Why was he denying his title? Their parents were not long in their graves. Was she denying his grief for them, too?

She groaned in frustration.

She walked over to the dressing table and leaned down to look in the mirror. Goodness! She looked wild. Her face was flushed and her hair was actively escaping its pins. Her dress was not damaged, but it definitely looked jostled.

More than jostled.

She closed her eyes and remembered the Dutch soldier seizing the front of her dress. She'd used his momentum to swing around so that he lost his grip and tumbled on to the ground. How many times had Rhys made her practise that move? So many that even after all these years, she'd performed it by reflex. She was proud of how she fought off her attackers. And all Rhys had done was scold her! She'd wanted him to say, *Well done! I knew you could do it!* Rhys used to compliment her in that very way, with those very words.

After he left so quickly for the army, she'd hoped he would write to her. Or at least send some message through his parents. They denied he ever mentioned her. Had he not understood why she'd changed her mind about eloping with him?

She sat at the dressing table and peered in the mirror again. What a fright she must have appeared to him. She pulled the pins from her hair and brushed it smooth before twisting it back into a knot high on the back of her head and replacing the pins. She rose and washed her face at the basin on the dresser. There was no full-length mirror in the room, but she stepped back far enough to see most of herself in the dressing table mirror. She ought to change her dress, but she only had three with her and one of those was for travel. She straightened her dress instead and brushed it with the clothes brush, tidying it as best she could. She tidied her bonnet and shook out her shawl, draping it over her arm. She automatically picked up her gloves but stared at them. They needed mending.

She put them down again. She would not wear them. She'd need to remove them before eating anyway and who did she know in Brussels who might criticise her for not wearing gloves? Once Rhys would have scoffed at her for even worrying about it. Now she seemed no more to him than an unwanted duty.

'You could have declined dinner, Rhys,' she said aloud to no one but herself. 'If you did not wish to be with me.'

She checked that her purse and handkerchief were still in the pocket of her dress and, key in hand, reached for the latch of the door, but stopped a moment, glancing around the room.

How glad she was that she would not have to spend her evening alone here. She was so grateful to Rhys's friend Grantwell for rescuing her from that fate.

And grudgingly grateful to Rhys for not preventing it.

It would be a pleasure to see more of the city and to eat in a restaurant. She'd eaten in inns and taverns while travelling in England, but never a restaurant. It seemed a very French thing to do.

She hurried down the hallway, but when reaching the stairs, decided to check on Wilson now in case she was back at the hotel too late to stop by later. She would not stay long, knowing Captain Grantwell—and Rhys—were waiting for her.

She made her way up the stairs and down the hallways to Wilson's room. Mrs Jacobs answered her knock.

'*Mademoiselle!* What are you doing here?' Mrs Jacobs peered out of the doorway. 'Where is your handsome captain?'

Oh, dear. What would the nurse do with the information she would be spending the evening with Rhys?

'He is waiting with his friend,' she said.

Mrs Jacobs grinned. 'The *other* handsome one!'

Helene walked past her into the small room.

Madame Desmet sat in the chair next to Wilson. '*Bonjour,* my lady.'

'Madame Desmet, you are still here,' she responded in a friendly tone. 'How is he?' she asked them both.

'Calmer,' Madame Desmet said.

'Yes, much calmer,' Mrs Jacobs agreed. 'He sleeps, but we've been able to give him broth and tea and even some porridge when he is awake.'

Helene noticed that Mrs Jacobs had somehow procured another chair and small table, so the room was more crowded than ever. She walked closer to Wilson and Madame Desmet.

The woman's brow furrowed. 'I hope you do not mind me staying.'

'Not at all.' Helene glanced to the nurse. 'That is, if Mrs Jacobs does not mind.'

'Mind?' Mrs Jacobs laughed. 'She is good company and such a help.'

Madame Desmet gazed at Wilson. 'I must be here,' she said earnestly.

'You should tell *mademoiselle* your story.' Mrs Jacobs said. She turned to Helene. 'It was as I guessed. A love story.'

'I should like to hear of it,' Helene responded. More likely she was dying to know it.

'We met years ago,' Madame said. 'Before the French came, as I told you.'

'They fell in love,' Mrs Jacobs explained helpfully.

'And he offered to stay,' Madame Desmet said. 'But I was promised to another. It was impossible! We were so young. We could not see how we could be together.'

A familiar ache touched Helene's heart. She and Rhys had been young, too, when—when— She could not even finish her thought.

Madame Desmet went on. 'Then Samuel wrote that he was here in Brussels—' Her voice cracked with emotion. 'Well, you can imagine how I felt.' She gazed down at the ill man. 'I am a widow now, so I am free. I cannot lose Samuel again. I cannot!'

Helene leaned down and put her arm around the woman. 'He must recover then.' Tears stung her eyes and she desperately needed to be gone from there, away from the emotions Madame Desmet's story aroused in her.

Mrs Jacobs actually came to her aid, firmly walking her to the door. 'You run off now to your Captain! I expect he is pining for your return. And if he has not come up to snuff yet, keep him on his toes with the other officer.' She playfully pushed Helene out the door.

Helene returned to the dining room where Rhys and Grantwell remained seated. This time there were tankards on the table in front of them, not teacups. Grantwell engaged in some animated discussion with Rhys and did not catch her entrance. Rhys saw her, though. His eyes never left her, but his expression remained stony.

Eventually his friend noticed her, too, and smiled. 'Ah, you are back already.'

They both stood as she reached the table.

'Do not say already, Captain,' she responded. 'I took a frightfully long time.' She glanced at Rhys. 'I stopped to check on Wilson.'

'How is he?' Rhys asked, though his expression did not change.

'Sleeping mostly. But calmer, they said,' she told them. 'Madame Desmet is still with him.'

Rhys simply nodded.

'Well.' Grantwell clapped his hands. 'Shall we be off, then?'

He offered Helene his arm and she accepted it. Rhys followed behind them.

Captain Grantwell led Helene through a maze of city streets, each as charming as those she and Rhys had passed that morning. They soon reached their destination, a large square surrounded by buildings of an architecture she'd never seen before. Many of the buildings were adorned by statues—or rather, remnants of statues. It appeared there had been an effort to destroy them all.

She took them all in, turning slowly to see everything. 'Who built such buildings?'

'They are an unusual mixture of Moorish and Gothic,' Rhys responded.

She was surprised that he spoke. Captain Grantwell had been providing the lively conversation up until now.

'We saw similar buildings in Spain,' Rhys said. 'Plenty of Moorish influence there.'

Helene and Rhys used to pore through her father's books, especially the Annual Registers that often included illustrations of what they called *faraway places*. Rhys especially liked to read about the buildings. It got so he could talk about Doric columns and flying buttresses as if they walked by them every day in the village.

The memory warmed her. She gazed at him. 'You have seen many faraway places, then.'

His eyes caught hers for a moment before he answered, 'More than I ever thought.'

She'd once dreamed that she and Rhys would travel together to faraway places. Perhaps that was what she'd do with her life, once David was settled. Perhaps she would travel. If she could sort out how she might do so alone, that was.

Grantwell had moved a few steps away from them, his interest caught by something in the square.

Rhys turned his gaze back to the buildings. 'This part of Brussels has long been the city centre. The whole square was burned down by the French in the 1600s, but the powerful guilds rebuilt it.'

'But it has been damaged,' she said. 'Look at all the broken statues.'

They were conversing almost like they used to do, Helene realised.

He explained, 'There were uprisings around the same time as the revolution in France. A lot of rioting and fighting in this part of the country. The buildings were defaced then.'

She smiled at him. At that moment he looked so much like that boy who pored through her father's books.

He glanced away. 'I was curious enough to read about this place.'

Once she would have teased him about sounding so bookish, but that had been when they were closer than brother and sister. Not this distance, this estrangement.

'I am glad to know about it,' she said.

Grantwell walked back to them. 'Be careful, Lady Helene. Or he will start talking about military tactics next, another passion of his.'

The warm moment cooled with this reminder that he had a life apart from her.

They crossed the square to look at a church at its far end and strolled through streets, gazing in shop windows. When they reached the restaurant on Rue de la Montagne, Helene was ready to sit and enjoy a meal. And she did enjoy it. Both Captain Grantwell and Rhys were pleasant companions and they seemed to find much to entertain her.

She and Rhys told Grantwell about Madame Desmet, Wilson's Louise. Helene filled Rhys in on the newly learned details of Wilson's ill-fated romance.

Rhys's eyes seemed to bore into her at the telling. She glanced back down to her plate. Had he also felt the parallels?

Grantwell filled the resulting silence with conversation, but she was not attending and could not tell what he'd said.

The restaurant tables were mostly filled with the colourful uniforms of the Allied army, mostly red coats, but also some blue and black. Even two men all in dark green.

'What uniform is the green one?' she asked.

'95th Rifles,' Rhys answered curtly. The camaraderie they'd briefly shared a moment ago had disappeared again.

'Rifle companies are attached to other regiments,' Grantwell explained. 'They carry Baker rifles and are used mainly as sharpshooters, picking off snipers and such.'

'So the green helps them blend in,' she said.

'Yes!' Grantwell was obviously impressed.

Helene even thought she saw the same emotion flicker in Rhys's eyes, but perhaps that was only because she wished it. He would be surprised how much she knew about the army and the war. It had been the only way she could feel connected to him.

Grantwell expanded on his discussion of the Rifles. Helene thought she detected some weariness in the young captain. What a strain to carry the conversational weight in the company of two people who left more unspoken than spoken.

They had finished their coffee, the last serving of the meal, when two men in red coats with the same gold ribbons and cuffs as Rhys and Grantwell approached. 'Grantwell! Landon!'

One clapped Grantwell on his shoulder. 'Are you done with the meal? Come with us! We are off to La Cloche. The night is still young.' He noticed Helene then and bowed. 'Beg pardon, miss. I did not see you there.'

Grantwell made introductions. The men bid Helene goodnight and said they would be on their way. Grantwell gazed at their retreating figures, looking as if he were watching the last coach leaving for London.

'Did you want to go with them?' Rhys asked.

'Another time, perhaps,' Grantwell said, clearly disappointed.

'Go on, then,' Rhys said. 'I'll see Helene back to the hotel.'

Helene blinked in surprise. Was Rhys choosing her company? She quickly added, 'You have devoted most of your day to me, Captain. Please go with your friends, if you wish.'

'What about paying for the meal?' Grantwell asked.

'We'll settle it later,' Rhys said.

Grantwell looked convinced. 'Very well, then.' He stood. 'I greatly enjoyed your company, Lady Helene. I hope we meet again.'

She liked this man. 'As do I, Captain.'

He glanced at both Helene and Rhys. 'Goodnight, then.'

Helene's heart pounded. She and Rhys were alone.

Chapter Nine

It was a cool and clear night as Rhys walked side by side with Helene, as fine a night as he might have wished— if he and Helene were still betrothed. The streets were filled with other couples and plenty of soldiers, but the atmosphere was gay, not at all as if an enemy might soon be on their doorstep.

Helene, of course, looked lovely in the light of the street lamps, even though her dress and bonnet were more practical than opulently adorned. She adjusted her shawl.

'Are you warm enough?' he asked.

'Oh, yes,' she responded, a bit breathless. 'I enjoy the brisk air.'

Rhys kicked himself for being unable to resist his desire to be alone with her, for being lulled into believing he could do so without reliving the pain of the past.

He felt her muscles tense where his arm brushed hers. She straightened. 'I am glad of this evening, Rhys. I am glad we are able to spend this time as friends.'

His guard went up. He had no intention of discussing their relationship—or lack of one. He ought to ignore her comment.

Instead he said, 'Friends? Is that what we are?' He could never think of her as a mere friend.

She blinked. 'I mean, can we not put the past behind us? It was so long ago and we were so young then.'

This time it was his muscles that tensed. When he was with her the past came rushing back and the bad memories overshadowed the good ones. There was no putting the past behind him. At best he could bury it and push it down again if it burst through. He would not discuss this.

She faltered but went on. 'I—I can see how suited to the army you are. It has turned out to be a good thing for you, has it not?'

Rhys kept his voice even. 'All's well that ends well?'

She released a long breath. 'Perhaps.'

'Ease your conscience then, Helene, if it troubles you. You did right to send your father to me that day.' Rhys's bitterness broke through his resolve not to speak of this. 'I *am* well-suited for the army. I am a good officer. I have every expectation of advancing in rank, although I suspect that was not your father's intention when he paid for my commission. I suspect he hoped I would become fodder for cannon.'

'No!' She stopped in the middle of the pavement. 'You are wrong.'

They'd reached the cathedral. The distress in her face was such a contrast to her delight upon seeing the structure for the first time, he almost felt sorry for her.

'My father wanted to help you!' she insisted. 'He didn't want you to die!'

He led her closer to the cathedral and out of the way of other people more happily walking by. It seemed a conversation about the past was impossible to avoid.

'Then why the army, Helene?' Her father's face came back to Rhys, precisely how he'd looked that day. 'He wanted me gone. He offered me the one way I might be gone for ever. After all, a mere vicar's son was not good enough to marry *his* daughter. He told me so. He told me you agreed that I had nothing to offer you. You sent him to deliver your message to me. I should leave the village and never see you again.'

'No!' Her voice rose. 'I never said that—I didn't mean that. Nothing so harsh. My father cared about you. He only wished to do well by you!'

'Do well by me? Cared about me?' He laughed again. 'When he so helpfully met with me to tell me I must leave, my father was present, too, looking panic-stricken. It was clear my father's position as vicar was also at stake. That seemed pretty harsh to me.'

That day the Earl of Yarford forced Rhys to leave behind everything dear to him. His home. His family. *Helene*. Rhys fought hard over the years to make the army compensate for that loss and he was proud to have largely succeeded.

Her eyes narrowed in pain. 'My father forced you to go into the army? He threatened your father?' She shook her head. 'No. I cannot believe it.'

He raised his brows. 'Then you think I am lying?'

Helene leaned her back against the cool stone of the cathedral as the past came rushing back.

Her father had not been a warm man. In fact, he'd never much bothered with Helene until he discovered she planned to elope with Rhys. After Rhys left, her father did press her to make a suitable marriage, but she'd thought he'd merely wanted to see her happy. He had become disgusted with her when she failed to accept any other proposals of marriage, but he'd turned his attention towards David and pretty much ignored her again.

Was it possible her father could have been so cruel to Rhys? To say such things to him and to threaten his father's position?

Why would Rhys say so, if it were not true? Rhys never had lied to her before. He'd also never contacted her after the conversation with her father, as she'd felt sure he would. Suddenly it all made a sickening sort of sense. Rhys hadn't contacted her, because he'd believed she never wanted to see him again. She almost crumbled to her knees. Rhys was telling the truth about what her father said to him. What could she do now to make things right between them? She wanted desperately for Rhys to believe she'd not known her father would be so cruel to him.

She lowered her head, searching for the words to make him understand how her father had twisted her good intentions.

'My father did convince me to break our engagement,' she admitted. 'I did not want to listen to him but eventually he convinced me. He said you had no means of supporting me—or children, when it came to that. He said that you would be forced to live only on my dowry or depend upon my father for support—'

Rhys broke in. 'He told me there would be no dowry if we married.'

Her father had threatened to withhold her dowry? That was another blow.

But she had no choice but to go on. To explain. 'My father said a young man of your character would despise being kept by his wife or supported by her father. I knew you. I knew that would kill your spirit.' She remembered how her father's words had crushed her own spirit and how hard it had been to do what she thought was best for Rhys. She raised her eyes to him. 'I could not do that to you.'

His eyes flashed. 'Did it not occur to you that paying for my commission was precisely that? Supporting me? Making me dependent? Only he gave me no other alternative. Ruin my father or leave.'

She took in a breath. Yes. She could see that now, but back then she'd been convinced marriage to her would ruin *him*. *She'd* been left with no other choice.

The ache inside her grew unbearable.

His voice deepened. 'What little faith you had in me, Helene.'

She met his eye again and spoke the truth. Please let him believe it. 'I sent my father to tell you something entirely different than what you heard. I sent him to give you a future, not to be cruel to you.'

'But you sent him all the same,' Rhys countered.

He was twisting her words. Yes, she knew now it was a mistake for her father to speak to him, but her father had fooled her. She was desperate for Rhys to understand.

Her gaze held. 'Can you not see, though, that we were wrong to plan an elopement, Rhys? No matter how we loved each other. We were not prepared. You could not have supported me.'

'I would have found a way.'

'How?' She persisted. 'Would you have gone into the Church? Studied law or medicine? Entered into banking or civil service? How could you have done any of those things without being supported by my father or dependent upon his help?'

Rhys's face took on its hard edges again. 'We will never know, will we? I had no opportunity to try.' He stepped closer to her. 'If you believed all your father said to you, why send him? Why did you not come to me? We could have made a different plan. Not marry until I could support you.'

She felt tears sting her eyes. This was what she could not forgive herself. At the time, she'd thought she'd have a chance to see Rhys again, to talk about the future, but she'd allowed her father to convince her he must speak to Rhys first. By the time she went in search of Rhys, he'd already gone.

Rhys pinned her against the stone of the cathedral, caging her between his arms. 'Never mind, Helene. There is no going back. I have found my place in the army. Return to Yarford. Find some marquess to marry.' His face was inches from hers, close enough for her to feel his warm breath against her lips, close enough for his masculine scent to envelop her and cause her senses to flare into awareness.

He took a breath and pushed away from her as he released it. 'We should return to the hotel.'

She wrapped her shawl more tightly around her shoulders. They walked in a tense silence.

Helene's senses still flared with need. He'd been about to kiss her, she was almost sure. And she'd wanted his kiss as acutely as a starving child wants a scrap of bread. His physical closeness drove every other thought from her mind and her mind had been spinning.

There was no way to undo the damage her father had done. Or the mistakes she had made. The past was lost to them. How hopeless it was.

How strange to feel hopeless when all hope had been gone for so long. Rhys's life had moved on, even if hers had not. She'd merely filled her days.

They crossed the street in front of the cathedral where the carriage had nearly run her over and where he'd held her in his arms after rescuing her.

When they reached the other side, he stopped again. 'I have one question.'

'What is it?' What more could possibly be said?

'Why did you confess to your father that we were planning to elope?'

He thought she'd told her father? 'I did not tell him!' she protested. 'He discovered it. He learned you'd hired a carriage and guessed the reason.'

'And when he guessed, you admitted it.' He crossed his arms over his chest.

Yes, she had admitted it! 'Rhys! He tricked me. I was only eighteen!'

He said nothing more.

It was another shard from that time that had shattered her. She felt like a broken vase without any glue to fix her.

Well, she'd have to pick up the pieces like she'd done five years before and, painful as it was, she would manage to put herself together again.

Rhys left Helene at the front door of the hotel, not trusting himself to walk her to her room, not after he'd almost kissed her. From where had that impulse risen? It would have been more sensible for him to have walked away from her. Not that he could abandon her on a Brussels street at night.

He returned to those streets, walking as quickly as if being pursued.

He'd never intended to talk to her about the past. Why had he taken her bait? What good had it done? It altered nothing. Even if her father had been honest with her about what he'd intended to say to Rhys, the chance for them to carve out a life together had long disappeared, if it ever existed at all. The army was where Rhys belonged now. The army fulfilled him. Gave him great pride. He wanted no other life. He'd thwarted Helene's father. The army had not killed him. It had enabled him to thrive.

Rhys found himself on the Rue d'Anderlecht near La Cloche, where Grant had been headed with Treadway and Strutton. Knowing those two, they would not stay long in one place, but Rhys could use a drink. Not beer. A real drink.

He entered the place, crowded with other soldiers, smelling of sweat and hops. Through the din he heard his name. 'Rhys! Over here.'

Grant was seated at a table alone. Well, not quite alone. There was a gaudily dressed Belgian woman Grant unceremoniously pushed off his lap.

Rhys raised his brows as he reached the table. 'Am I intruding?'

Grant waved an impatient hand. 'Not at all. She'll recover. Plenty of men to choose from.' He directed Rhys to sit. The woman shrugged and walked away.

Rhys looked around before lowering himself into the chair. 'Where are Treadway and Strutton?'

Grant took a sip of a large stein of beer. 'They've departed. With female company.'

'Whisky,' Rhys called to the tavern maid. 'Bring the bottle.'

Grant's eyes widened and he raised two fingers to the tavern maid. 'Two glasses.' He leaned his elbows on the table, giving Rhys a direct look. 'So. What happened?'

'What do you mean *what happened*?' Rhys settled in his chair.

'What happened that you are asking for whisky?' Grant persisted.

The tavern maid placed a whisky bottle and two glasses on the table. Rhys handed her some coins and poured a glassful.

He drank half the glass at once but still did not speak.

Grant poured a glassful for himself. He lowered his voice. 'Should I not have left you two alone at the restaurant?'

Rhys regarded his friend, who he knew would not press him further. 'Maybe some day I will tell you the whole, but not tonight.'

'I comprehend completely.' Grant, experienced in being betrayed, lifted his glass. 'Well, who knows? Maybe a French cannonball will hit us both in a few days' time. Then none of this will mean anything at all.'

Helene woke early the next day, thinking of Rhys, as she had on and off throughout the night. That she'd slept at all was a surprise. He'd aroused a yearning in her, one that she thought she'd succeeded in burying. At the same time, he'd thrust her away.

She felt unsettled, too, about her father. How could he have lied to her and been so cruel to Rhys? She was surprised Rhys had not cut her completely at that first sight of her in that tavern. How he must have despised her all these years.

What was she to do now? Weeping into her pillow would do no good. She must merely put one foot in front of the other and do whatever needed doing in the moment.

She pulled the bell rope for a maid to attend her. She poured water from the pitcher into the basin on the bureau and washed herself. By the time the maid arrived she had fixed her hair and dressed herself as far as she could without assistance. The girl helped her with her stays and tightened the laces on her dress.

'*Merci,*' Helene said, putting a coin in the maid's hand.

The girl beamed. '*Merci beaucoup, mademoiselle.*'

Helene made her way to David's room. He would not

be out this early. He could at least have breakfast with her. She'd try to have a civil conversation with him. Her heart jumped at the idea that Rhys might appear in the dining room, as he had that first morning. She gave herself a mental shake. It would be better not to see him.

She knocked on David's door. 'David? David? Wake up. It is Helene.' There was no answer. She knocked again and called louder. 'David!'

Finally, she heard the shuffling of feet. She stepped back, expecting him to open the door.

Instead David's voice came from the other side of the closed door. 'Go away, Helene.'

She bent close to the door's crack. 'Please get dressed and have breakfast with me.'

'Give me one good reason why I should.' David's voice was muffled by the door.

'I need to talk to you,' she implored. 'It is important.'

'I am not going back to England!' he cried. 'You waste your breath trying to convince me. Nothing will keep me from the Duchess of Richmond's ball and nothing will keep me away from the battle!'

But she needed to explain to him why she wanted him to come home with her. About him accepting his title and his responsibilities. Or about why he was running away from them.

'You need to go home to Yarford,' she said through the door. 'You have responsibilities there.'

'*You* go back, Helene!' he retorted. 'Nobody wants you here. It would be like you to miss a duke's ball, because you need to make lavender water or something. And if you think you can make me escort you to the ball, you have another thing coming. I am invited for the whole evening and I'm not going to dance attendance on you!'

She held her breath for a moment lest her temper burst.

'Come to breakfast with me,' she tried again. 'We can discuss this.'

'I don't want to discuss it,' he whined. 'I want to sleep. You can bang at the door all you like. Yell loud enough to wake everyone on this hallway, but I won't open the door and I won't talk to you.'

'David,' she cried in exasperation.

She lifted her fist to pound on the door but stopped herself. What was the use of making an even bigger scene? She was sure everyone on that hallway had already heard David's petulant cries and her pleading with him. Coming to Brussels had been another of her mistakes. All she succeeded in doing here was create more pain.

She spun on her heel and made her way to the hall where the hotel's attending servant greeted her by name. 'How are you, Lady Helene? And how is your manservant today?'

So kind of him to remember and to ask about Wilson. 'I have not seen him this morning, but he was a little better yesterday.'

'I am glad to hear it,' he responded.

It was on the tip of her tongue to ask if he'd seen Captain Landon that morning. She resisted the impulse. There was no reason for her to know anything about Rhys's whereabouts. Still, as she walked to the dining room, she wondered if he would be there.

But he was not. She chose a table in a corner where she might not be noticed. She ate her breakfast alone.

As she finished, a wave of loneliness washed over her, but she shook it off, resolving to press on, no matter what. No matter how alone. She stood and walked out of the dining room.

Chapter Ten

Helene met Madame Desmet in the hall. 'Madame Desmet. Good morning.'

Madame Desmet was very stylishly dressed this morning. She'd obviously taken great care with her appearance.

The older woman smiled. 'I am here to visit Samuel. Have you seen him this morning? Do you know if he is improving?' Her expression filled with concern.

Helene shook her head. 'I have not seen him yet. I'll go up with you, if you do not mind? We may visit him together.'

Madame Desmet looked abashed. 'I do not mind. How could I? But, please, call me Louise. Desmet was my husband's name.'

'As you wish… Louise.'

The day before, Madame Desmet—Louise—had left her house in a hurry with no more than her hat and shawl, but today she carried a large cloth bag hung over her arm.

She lifted the bag. 'I have brought some clean nightclothes for Samuel and a tin of biscuits I thought he might fancy. And some sewing. I might as well keep busy when he is sleeping.'

'You will spend a lot of time with him, then?' Helene said.

Louise's brows knitted. 'I do hope you understand. I must spend as much time as I am able. I do not wish to miss a moment with him.'

Helene's heart warmed to her. 'Stay as long as you like. It can only do him good.'

She smiled again. 'You understand how it is. How it is also with you and Captain Landon.'

Helene frowned. 'I fear matters are much more complicated between Captain Landon and me. We are not together, as Mrs Jacobs believes.'

The look Louise returned to her was sceptical.

When they reached Wilson's room, Mrs Jacobs answered their knock with a cheery demeanour. 'Both of you! Now will that not be a treat for our patient. Come in. Come in.' She stepped aside. 'We are just finishing breakfast.'

Wilson, to Helene's surprise, was seated in a chair at a table with a teapot, cup and a bowl of porridge.

His face beamed with pleasure, no doubt due to Louise's arrival. 'Louise!' he cried joyfully.

She rushed to his side. 'Samuel! Look at you.'

Mrs Jacobs laughed. 'Oh, we've been washed and combed and bedclothes changed. And our appetite is better, as well.'

Helene was so glad to hear it.

Mrs Jacobs continued her report. 'We had a fairly restful night. He coughs a great deal. I believe I shall stop at the apothecary and ask for something to ease the cough.' She turned to Helene, a line of worry creasing her forehead. 'I hope you do not mind if I leave again? I will return in no more than two hours, but I would greatly like to check on my dear husband.'

Helene nodded. 'Of course you may go.'

Louise turned her head. 'I will stay with Samuel. I plan to stay the whole day.'

Mrs Jacobs laughed again. 'I rather thought you would.' The nurse walked about the room gathering her items.

Helene would have been happy to sit with Wilson while Mrs Jacobs was away, like she had before. It would have given her a useful means of passing the time, but how could she spoil Wilson's chance to be truly alone with his Louise?

'I will go with you, Mrs Jacobs.' She stepped towards Wilson and Louise. 'Is there anything I might bring you? Anything you need?'

Louise only had eyes for Wilson. 'I cannot think of anything else I need.'

Wilson noticed Helene then. 'Lady Helene. You are here, as well.'

'Only for a moment, Wilson.' She smiled at him. 'But I will check on you later. I am very happy to see you looking better.'

'He is still quite weak.' Mrs Jacobs had her hand on the door latch. 'I will be back in two hours, I promise,' she called to Louise.

Louise did not take her eyes off Wilson. 'I will tend him while you are gone.'

The nurse laughed. 'I wager you will!'

Helene followed her out of the room and through the hallways.

'And how is your Captain this morning?' Mrs Jacobs asked.

Helene sighed. She'd try once more to set the woman straight. 'Mrs Jacobs, you are mistaken about Captain Landon and me. We grew up together. That is why he knows Wilson and is fond of him. But we do not have any attachment.'

Mrs Jacobs gave her an even more sceptical look than Louise had earlier. 'You cannot fool me, Lady Helene. I have eyes in my head.'

Helene did not know precisely what the woman meant, but if she thought she saw loving glances between Helene and Rhys, her eyes must be covered with rose-coloured glasses.

Helene changed the subject. 'You are worried about your husband. Is he ill?'

Mrs Jacobs sobered. 'He is poorly, that is a fact. Otherwise I would not leave my post. Dear Hulbert. He had the grippe, not unlike Mr Wilson, and it has laid him flat even two weeks later. He cannot work so I am very grateful to have employment.'

'What work does he do?' she asked.

'Hulbert?' Mrs Jacobs smiled. 'He is a wicker merchant. He's earned nothing for a fortnight and it might take another fortnight for him to return to working.'

Four weeks? Would Helene have to stay four weeks until Wilson was well enough to travel again? Rhys made it sound like the battle was coming in days, not weeks.

'How difficult for you.' Helene made a mental note to pay the woman very well.

The nurse kept up her chatter until they reached the hall. Helene really had no reason to walk down to the hall, but no reason to return to her room either. Perhaps she would go in search of that glove shop which must be open by now.

'Lady Helene,' the hall servant called out to her. 'I have something for you.'

'For me?' She crossed the floor to him.

Mrs Jacobs waited, nearly bursting with curiosity.

The servant handed her a card. 'An invitation,' he said helpfully. 'To the ball.'

'The ball?' Mrs Jacobs's eyes danced with excitement.

'The event of the season,' the hall servant said. 'The Duchess of Richmond's ball. Invitations also came for Captain Landon and Captain Grantwell.'

She took the card. 'Thank you, sir.'

Mrs Jacobs stepped over to her. 'The event of the season, he says. This is something, is it not? When is it?'

Helene glanced at the card. 'Tomorrow night.'

'Tomorrow? Ooh!' She clapped.

Helene put the invitation in the pocket of her dress. 'It does not matter. My brother refuses to escort me, so I could not attend even if I wished to.'

At that moment Captain Grantwell descended the stairway. 'Lady Helene,' he called. 'Good morning.'

Her heart jumped a little, but only because this was Rhys's friend, one person removed from being Rhys himself. 'Good morning, sir.'

He joined them.

Helene introduced Mrs Jacobs to him.

'I remember seeing you yesterday,' the nurse said. 'With Captain Landon. And I understand you are receiving an invitation to the ball as well as our *mademoiselle* here.'

'Invitation? They have come?' He looked pleased.

The hall servant walked over and handed him two invitations. 'Perhaps you will see that Captain Landon receives his?'

'I will indeed.' Grantwell turned to Helene. 'Your brother came through after all.'

'Yes, but she will not go to the ball she says,' Mrs Jacobs piped up.

Mrs Jacobs! Helene wanted to yell. *Do be quiet.*

'Not go to the ball?' Grantwell looked at her quizzi-
cally.

Helene tried to give Mrs Jacobs a quelling glance. The
woman was completely oblivious.

'Her brother will not escort her,' Mrs Jacobs explained.

Grantwell frowned. 'Then you must come with us.'

'I cannot do that,' she said quietly. 'Rhys—'

'Hang Rhys,' he countered. 'If he objects, I shall escort you myself.'

'See?' Mrs Jacobs chirped. 'It is all settled.'

'Would you care to dine first?' Grantwell asked. 'I
could meet you in this hall at, say, seven o'clock. The ball
starts at ten. We will have time to eat and time to dress
for the ball after.'

'Seven o'clock,' Mrs Jacobs repeated. 'For dinner. Excellent.'

'Lady Helene?' He waited for her answer.

'Yes, I suppose that would do.' Helene agreed simply
to stop this discussion in the hall in the presence of Mrs
Jacobs, the hall servant and anyone else passing by.

'Excellent.' Grantwell bowed. 'Forgive me. I must beg
your leave. Regimental business.'

Helene curtsied. 'Good day, Captain.'

As he strode towards the door, Mrs Jacobs crossed her
arms over her ample chest. 'There. I told you all will turn
to rights. And this is very well, too. It is bound to make
Captain Landon jealous.'

Helene thought her head would explode. 'It will not
matter to him, believe me, Mrs Jacobs.'

The nurse gave her a very patient smile.

'Besides,' Helene said. 'I shall have to send my regrets to Captain Grantwell. I cannot attend a ball. I have
no dress.'

Mrs Jacobs's face fell, but she quickly recovered. 'We

will have to do something about that, will we not? Come
by Mr Wilson's room after I return. You, Louise and I
will put our heads together.'

'Very well.' Helene sighed. She had planned to check
on Wilson later in the day anyway. Perhaps then she could
convince Mrs Jacobs that a ball gown could not be created in a day.

Helene asked Mrs Jacobs to direct her to a glove shop
and the nurse was only too happy to walk her to the *best*
glove shop where Helene purchased a pair of gloves to
replace her damaged ones and, on a whim, a lovely pair
of opera-length gloves at a good price.

Next to the glove shop was a shop displaying beautiful
pieces of lace. Who could visit Belgium without at least
looking in a lace shop?

When she walked out, she'd purchased three new lace
fichus, a lace reticule and a totally impractical lace shawl
dyed a beautiful shade of gold. She had no use for it, but
it was so beautiful she could not resist.

They would be mementos of Brussels, she told herself.
As if she could ever forget this place.

She started back to the hotel carrying her two packages
containing her purchases. The streets of Brussels around
the Parc and the hotel felt more familiar now and she
could fix them in her memory. More people were about,
as well, and whenever she saw a tall man in a red coat
her heart skipped a beat—until she saw the man was not
Rhys. As she neared the hotel door, it opened and David
burst forth in a towering hurry.

Helene was quick enough to seize his arm. 'David!
Where are you going?'

He grinned at her as if he'd not been beastly towards
her earlier in the morning. 'Can't talk, Helene! I'm late.

William and I are going to ride out and watch the regiments drilling.'

She released him.

David's moods went up and down like a seesaw. He would never listen to her.

But she refused to let David—or Rhys—ruin her day. She went up to her room and unwrapped her packages. She draped one of the fichus over her shoulders and sat back and admired it in the dressing table mirror.

'Congratulations,' Helene said aloud. 'You indulged yourself.' It was scant consolation.

She rose and put her other new purchases away. The clock on the mantel struck twelve. Was it that late? She should go to Wilson's room. Mrs Jacobs would have returned by now and she could settle the issue of the ball and the ball gown once and for all.

On her way, though, she decided to visit the dining room to arrange for some tea and biscuits and fruit to be delivered to Wilson's room. Was she hoping she'd run into Rhys? If so, she was disappointed, and she resisted the impulse to ask the hall servant if he'd seen him.

Afterwards, as she approached Wilson's door, she could hear Mrs Jacobs's laughter through the doorway.

She knocked.

'Come in,' Mrs Jacobs called out.

She opened the door and entered the room.

'Ah, *mademoiselle*!' Mrs Jacobs said cheerily. 'I told Mr Wilson and Louise you would come.'

'I ordered tea to be brought up for all of you.' Helene peeked around the woman to see that Wilson now sat up in bed and Louise was in the chair by his side, holding his hand.

'How nice of you!' The nurse clapped her hands. 'I was about to go down for food, now I do not have to.'

Helene approached Wilson's cot, but did not come so close she would intrude on the reunited couple. 'How do you feel, Wilson?'

He gazed lovingly at Louise. 'Happy. Fortunate. Very grateful.'

'Yes, well, he still has a fever, Lady Helene.' Mrs Jacobs clucked her tongue. 'No frolicking for him.'

There was a knock on the door. Not Rhys. The tea arrived and they moved things around to make room for it. Louise assisted Wilson. She sat on the edge of the cot so that Mrs Jacobs and Helene could have the chairs.

Mrs Jacobs swallowed her biscuit and took a sip of tea, then leaned over to Helene. 'I have told Mr Wilson and Louise all about the Duchess's Ball and about Captain Landon and that your brother refused to escort you, so Captain Grantwell offered—'

Helene held up a hand. 'Yes, but I am not attending the ball. I have no dress.'

Mrs Jacobs tossed Louise a conspiratorial look. 'We have that all settled, as well.'

'How?' There was no way to sew a gown in only one day.

Mrs Jacobs gave Helene a smug grin.

Louise spoke. 'For many years I have sewn the costumes for the theatre. I do not sew as much lately, but I am certain the theatre will have a suitable dress among the costumes that they will be willing to lend me.'

'Louise will get your dress from the theatre,' Mrs Jacobs said excitedly. 'And she can make any alterations tomorrow. Very simple, is it not?'

Helene laughed in surprise. How dear of them to plot a way for her to attend a ball she had no desire to attend. 'I hardly know what to say.' She could think of no way to refuse. She looked at Louise. 'You will not get yourself in trouble for this, will you?'

'Oh, no. No one will mind,' Louise assured her. 'You will be wearing a dress that has been worn before. After we return it, no one will mind it has been worn one extra time.' She gave Helene a serious look. 'Besides, you have brought my Samuel back to me. There is nothing I would not do for you.'

Mrs Jacobs shook a finger at Helene. 'Listen to Louise and to me. You will go to this ball that everyone talks about and you will look so beautiful your Captain Landon will beg you to come back to him.'

Chapter Eleven

Rhys's regiment engaged in drills all morning and it was not until well after the noon hour that the troops were dismissed. Word had reached the regiment that Wellington wanted all troops in readiness in case deployment was necessary. Rhys had done what he could to ensure his company could march at a moment's notice, but, riding back to Brussels, he could not shake his concerns.

Grant's horse caught up to Rhys's. 'That went fairly well, I thought.'

'We've been too idle.' Rhys frowned. 'They've been sharper.'

'Come on, man! Why the glum mood?' Grant exclaimed. 'They did well. They will be ready.'

Rhys shook his head. 'They will have to be.'

They rode side by side without speaking.

Grant broke the silence. 'Oh, I have some good news. Our invitations arrived.'

Rhys's thoughts were still on his men and what else he might do to bring them up to snuff. 'What invitations?'

'What invitations!' Grant laughed. 'The invitation to the Duchess of Richmond's Ball. Your friend Banes came through. I have the invitations in my pocket.'

'Banes is not precisely a friend,' Rhys said.

'Whatever you wish to call him.' They rode on for a while, then Grant suddenly asked, 'Does Banes have an older brother?'

'No,' Rhys replied. 'What makes you ask?'

'Well,' Grant responded. 'If he does not have an older brother and his father was the Earl of Yarford and is now deceased, then is he not now the Earl?'

To Rhys, David so perfectly played the role of annoying little brother that it was difficult to think of him as the Earl. 'Yes. He would be.'

'Impressed as the boy is by dukes, you'd think he'd be telling everyone he has a title,' Grant said.

'You would think that.' So why did David introduce himself by name and not title? Did the boy do nothing right?

At least it made more sense that Helene travelled to Brussels. If David were killed watching the battle, as could happen to any spectator, what would happen to Helene? Some distant cousin would inherit David's title and estates and she would be forced to leave her home. Had her father made adequate provision for her in that case?

Rhys did not trust her father to have done so.

But why concern himself? His energies were better spent on his soldiers.

'By the way…' Grant broke into Rhys's thoughts '… I happened upon Lady Helene when I was handed the invitations. Her brother did refuse to escort her to the ball as he said he would.'

David was a disappointment at every turn.

'So,' Grant continued, 'I said we would escort her.'

Rhys looked over at him. 'We? I am not attending the ball.'

Grant returned his gaze. 'You are not attending the ball?'

Rhys shrugged. 'I have no desire to.'

'Indeed?' Grant spurred on ahead. 'I suppose I will have to escort her alone then.'

It was none of Rhys's concern who escorted Helene to the ball.

Still, a memory sprang to mind, of joyous village assemblies where he and Helene danced almost every dance together. He tried to tell himself it did not matter if this time she danced with Grant.

Rhys and Grant returned to the hotel and cleaned the dirt of the road off their clothes and boots, no easy feat.

Grant took the invitations to the ball out of his pocket and set them on a nearby table. 'Are you sure you won't attend the ball? Wellington and his staff will be there. Won't hurt you to be seen by them. You have the clothes for it too, do you not?'

Rhys had purchased the dress uniform required for formal occasions when he'd received his commission. The money for that uniform had come from Helene's father as well as the rest of it. His kit. His horse. His sword. Even his toothbrush.

'I have the clothes, but I'll not change my mind,' Rhys responded.

'No?' Grant said in a matter-of-fact tone. 'Seems cowardly of you.'

Rhys had no intention of responding to that comment.

Grant slapped his thighs and stood. 'I do not know about you, but I could use some Belgian beer and *frites* about now.'

'Name the place.' Rhys's throat was dry and his stomach empty.

Grant selected the tavern, the one with the best beer and best *frites* and mussels. It was where Rhys first saw Helene.

They started out the door and down the hallway when Rhys stopped. 'I should look in on Wilson, Helene's man-servant. Do you want to come with me? I will not stay long.'

'A sickroom?' Grant shook his head. 'I'll meet you at the tavern. I'll order for you.'

The two men parted and Rhys walked up the back stairs to the hallway where the servants slept. He hoped Helene would not be there.

He supposed he could believe that Helene had not known her father's true colours. It was not enough, though, to erase the wounds Rhys suffered. He'd never open his heart like that again.

He reached Wilson's room and knocked.

The door was opened by the very ebullient Mrs Jacobs. 'Captain Landon! How good to see you!'

'How are you today, Mrs Jacobs?' he asked.

'I am very well.' She stepped aside so he could enter. 'Your Lady Helene is not here at the moment. She and Louise are...out.' She said this last bit as if it was one very big secret.

Rhys was glad Helene was not here. Seeing her just tore open the wound. 'I came to visit Wilson.'

He heard a rustling in the cot. 'Is that you, Master Rhys?'

Rhys walked over and sat in the chair next to the bed. 'It is indeed, Wilson. How do you fare?'

The old servant sat up in bed. He was still pale and his voice weak, but he was no longer insensible. 'I suppose I am better. I remember very little of the last two days.'

The old man took his hand. 'It is so good to see you, my boy. We have missed you at Yarford.'

'Yes. I am in the army, as you can see.' Rhys wore his red coat.

The old man coughed, gripping Rhys's hand as he did so. Rhys waited until the spasm stopped.

Wilson spoke again. 'I hear that you and Lady Helene are together once more. Makes me happy, boy.' Wilson managed a smile.

Rhys wondered where that information came from. 'We are not together,' he said quietly. 'But we have worked together to see you have what you need.'

'And you brought my Louise to me. I know that.' Wilson gripped his hand again.

'That we did.'

Wilson looked worried. 'I do not know where Louise is right now.'

'She is with *mademoiselle*, Mr Wilson,' Mrs Jacobs called to him. 'They will return soon.' She grinned at Rhys. 'Will you wait for them with us, Captain?'

No! Not at all. 'I cannot stay.' He gripped Wilson's hand. 'I am expected elsewhere, but I wanted to look in on you.'

'You will come again?' Wilson asked.

'I will try.'

Mrs Jacobs walked Rhys to the door, even though it was not more than three steps away. She patted his arm. 'Do not fret, Captain,' she said. 'I have a feeling you will see Mr Wilson—and your Helene—again.'

As he reached for the door latch, the door opened. Just as Mrs Jacobs prophesied, there stood Helene. She looked lovely—she wore the same dress as the day before, but it looked different. Had she worn lace around the neckline before? He could not remember, but there was no doubt her beauty was enhanced by rosy cheeks and eyes spar-kling with excitement.

Rhys remembered a time when such a look of excite-ment on Helene's face would have meant the two of them had been up to some childish piece of mischief. No lon-ger. Her happiness had nothing to do with him.

Helene saw him and her eyes turned blank. 'Rhys.'

'Helene.' He nodded formally. Madame Desmet stood behind her. '*Madame*, good day to you.'

'And to you, Captain.' Madame Desmet looked bright-ened, as well.

'Forgive me, I was just leaving.' He bowed and was acutely aware of being inches from touching Helene when he brushed past her.

Mrs Jacobs grinned as she closed the door. 'Ooh, did you see his face, *mademoiselle*? He was like the fish who has just spied a fat worm. You will hook him soon enough!'

'Never mind Rhys.' Helene refused to let him dampen her spirits. She was determined to eke some enjoyment out of this ball, now that Louise and Mrs Jacobs made it impossible for her not to attend. 'We found a dress!'

Louise had taken her to the theatre where they'd searched through several trunks before Helene spied the most perfect dress—in the same gold colour as the im-practical lace shawl she had purchased earlier. They'd even found dancing slippers to match and some citrine jewellery. The jewellery was paste, but no matter. It looked real enough.

Louise, at Wilson's bedside, placed a kiss on his fore-head. 'Go to sleep, *ma chérie*,' she murmured to him. 'I will be here when you wake up.'

He nodded and closed his eyes.

Mrs Jacob picked up Louise's bag and in a loud whisper said, 'Come! Show me what you found. I am on pins and needles in anticipation.' She laughed, not too quietly. 'Pins and needles. Is that not a good joke?'

Helene could not help but smile. She was becoming very fond of this nurse.

The three women gathered in a corner of the room as far away from the napping patient as they could get, which was only a few feet away.

'You show her, Louise,' Helene said.

Louise lifted the largest package from her bag. She removed the tissue the dress was wrapped in and draped it over a chair.

The gown was simple design without the ribbons, lace and silk flowers that adorned the gowns so often worn at London balls, but it suited Helene more than any of the ones her mother had chosen for her. It was a gold silk dress underneath with a gold gauze overdress that caught the light from the window in Wilson's room. Cleverly twisted and pleated gauze elevated the bodice and the puffed sleeves from being ordinary to being worthy of a society ball.

'Oh, that is very pretty. Very pretty indeed.' Mrs Jacobs fingered the sleeves and bodice. 'I love how it shimmers in the light.'

'You can imagine how it looked on stage where the lamps can be very bright,' Louise said. 'It was quite effective.'

And Helene imagined the gown would be equally effective under the light of chandeliers.

She smiled. 'I even have a lace shawl that will match the dress perfectly. I purchased it this morning.'

Mrs Jacobs gave her an impulsive hug. 'You are going

to look so beautiful. All the men will be admiring you! Especially your captain.'

After their words last night, Helene could not even wish for it.

Chapter Twelve

The next day was overcast and grey, but Helene woke with a mood of optimism she had not felt in a long time. All because of a ball? She could not think herself so shallow, but life had been so bleak for so long that the prospect of music and dancing and wearing that beautiful gown was enough for her to look forward to.

As long as she kept Rhys out of her mind.

She rang for the maid and dressed quickly before heading straight to Wilson's room. Her preparation for the ball was to be a team effort. Mrs Jacobs and Louise were to bring items she might need. A papillote iron to curl her hair. A pot of rouge to tint her cheeks and lips. Extra pins for her hair and her dress. She could not have asked for two more enthusiastic lady's maids.

She spent most of the day in Wilson's room with them, while Louise altered the dress so that it fit her to perfection. Luckily Wilson was a great deal better and a good sport about being encompassed by this purely feminine business. She left them only to arrange for food or to run to the shops for whatever they forgot.

* * *

When the time came for her to dress for dinner, Wilson felt well enough to be left alone. He persuaded the ladies to attend to Helene in her own room, perhaps to gain a little peace for himself. At times, thinking of Rhys, Helene's spirits started to flag, but the ebullience of Mrs Jacobs and Louise always lifted her up again. Even if she did not enjoy the ball, she'd always fondly remember sharing this part of the day with Mrs Jacobs and Louise.

Helene sat at her dressing table as Louise pinned her hair up in a knot resembling a mass of curls high on her head and loose curls framing her face.

'After dinner, we will add ribbons,' Louise said.

Mrs Jacobs nodded. 'Yes. You must look very fancy indeed. The hair must complement the dress.'

Helene was fairly certain Mrs Jacobs had never been to a society ball, nor worn a ball gown, but she was beginning to enjoy the nurse's absolute certainty in her opinions. Would Helene have made it this far without Mrs Jacobs urging her on? If not for Mrs Jacobs, would she not have spent the past two days sitting in her hotel room, desolate about Rhys and worried about David?

For dinner before the ball Helene chose the other of her two day dresses, this one a dark green. It was a walking dress, not at all a dinner dress, but she added the finest of her new lace fichus to make it a fancy as she could. Her serviceable half-boots would not do at all, so she wore the gold slippers that matched her ball gown.

'Wear the earrings to dinner and add the necklace for the ball,' suggested Louise.

The earrings resembled two teardrops that dangled from her ears. 'Are you certain these are paste?' They were lovely enough to be real.

Louise laughed. 'Oh, they are paste. On stage they catch the light well enough.'

Mrs Jacobs put her hands on her waist. 'Well, I defy anyone to tell you they are not real.'

Helene smiled at her, an expert on jewels now. 'With that endorsement, I shall feel quite special in them.'

Mrs Jacobs beamed.

The clock on the mantelpiece struck seven.

Mrs Jacobs waved her hands. 'It is time. You must go now. Your Captain will be waiting for you!'

Helene wondered if that would be true.

Mrs Jacobs and Louise accompanied Helene down the stairway to the hall, where Captain Grantwell waited for her. Alone.

Helene turned to say goodbye to her friends before they reached the bottom of the stairs.

Mrs Jacobs looked as disappointed as Helene felt, see-ing only Grantwell, but she put on a resolute expression. 'Never you mind. Your Captain will show up. I will wager on it.'

'It does not matter,' Helene lied. She squeezed each of their hands. 'I will see you later!' When they would be helping her dress for the ball.

Grantwell stepped forward to meet Helene at the bot-tom of the stairs. He extended his arm to her. 'Good eve-ning, Lady Helene.'

She quickly scanned the hall again.

'He did not come,' Grant said.

She gave him a wan smile. 'I did not expect him.'

She took his arm and he led her to the dining room. Grantwell had been good company before, she told her-self. She could enjoy dinner.

The servant led them to a table set for three.

'There will only be two of us,' Grantwell told the man, who removed the extra setting, bowed and walked away. Grantwell turned to Helene. 'I took the liberty of ordering our food ahead of time. We will have more leisure to dine that way.'

She smiled again. 'How thoughtful of you.'

The servant returned and poured some wine.

Helene's smile fled as she glanced around the room, wondering if Rhys were seated with someone else.

Grant lifted the glass of wine to his lips. 'I am sorry about Rhys. I tried to convince him to come.'

She turned to him. 'I did not expect him to come.'

'I hoped he would.' Grantwell took a sip and did what she'd become used to of him. Made conversation. 'I am looking forward to the ball. Are you? I attended one society ball before Napoleon decided to escape Elba, but none for a couple of years before that.'

'A society ball?' She was puzzled for a moment. 'Are… are you perhaps related to Viscount Grantwell?'

He swallowed more wine. 'My brother.'

'I did not put it together before.' She was a bit embarrassed that she had not. 'I believe I met Viscount Grantwell during one London Season.'

'You met my brother?' He did not make this sound like a pleasant thing.

'It would have been three or four years ago,' she responded. 'I did not attend a Season last year or this.' This year she'd been nursing her parents or mourning their deaths. The year before she'd simply refused.

He gave a dry laugh. 'Did he court you?'

'A little perhaps, but he soon gave it up.'

He peered at her. 'You know, every time you call me Grantwell, I think of my brother. I do wish you would call me Grant.'

She smiled. 'Very well—Grant.'

The servant brought their first course. Waterzooi, a fish soup.

Grant went on. 'I assume you had a very good dowry. My brother would only consider a wife of elevated status and some wealth.'

What was she to say to that? 'I suppose it was good enough.'

'How was it my brother or someone like him did not win your hand?' he asked.

She lifted her wine glass and gazed over it to meet his eye. 'They were not Rhys.'

Rhys stood at the doorway scanning the dining room.

After Grant left for dinner, Rhys had paced a while, then impulsively changed into his finest regimentals. Why not attend the ball? See and be seen. He was a Captain in the East Essex Regiment and would outrank several of the junior officers who'd undoubtedly been invited. Rhys earned his right to stand next to them. He'd earned that right on the battlefield.

He could tolerate Helene for a few short hours. Besides, he wanted to tell both her and her brother to leave Brussels immediately. The battle was imminent. All the signs were there.

The dining room was crowded this Thursday evening. Most of the men seated in the room also wore their best uniforms. Sons of aristocrats, probably. Many had never seen a battle, as well. Rhys stood straighter. He had that advantage over them.

His gaze finally found Grant and Helene. Her back was to him, but, even from the back, he could see that her hair was arranged in curls and her dress had a nice piece of lace draped over the bodice. Not her ball gown, though. The ladies would change into ball gowns after they dined.

Helene and Grant appeared to be conversing happily. Rhys's approach would end that, certainly. Did he wish to spoil their dinner?

No. He must let her go. No matter what her father—and she—had done five years ago, Rhys had done well for himself. They were both where they belonged. Helene dined with the son of an aristocrat and anticipated a ball. Rhys had the army.

He turned on his heel and left. Rhys walked out of the hotel and on to the street. He told himself he would rather dine at one of the taverns he and Grant frequented in Brussels. Although he still had the invitation to the ball in his pocket, the idea of walking in to the Duke's house on Rue de la Blanchisserie lost its appeal.

After dinner Helene returned to her hotel room where her two makeshift lady's maids were eagerly awaiting her. She stripped down to her shift and stays and let Louise dab some perfume on her before carefully pinning a lace ribbon and gold chain through her hair.

Mrs Jacobs stood by with, as usual, much to say. 'I cannot believe your Captain did not show. What is the matter with him? He is a great disappointment to me at the moment, I tell you.'

Helene looked at Mrs Jacobs through her reflection in the mirror. 'I am determined not to allow Rhys to spoil my night.' Which was true. She'd spent most of the last five years accommodating herself to losing Rhys for ever. Encountering him here in Brussels changed nothing.

Mrs Jacobs folded her arms across her chest. 'I suppose Captain Grantwell is charming enough, but he is not your Captain.'

Rhys was not *her* Captain either.

'Be quiet and hold still,' Louise ordered. 'I am going to put a touch of rouge on your cheeks.' She turned Helene's face towards her.

'Do not overdo it,' cautioned Mrs Jacobs. 'We do not want her looking like *la putain*.'

'Certainly not!' Louise said. 'Just enough to put a bloom in her cheeks.' She dipped her finger in the rouge pot and lightly tinted Helene's lips. She turned Helene's face to Mrs Jacobs. 'What do you think?'

'Well done, Louise!' Mrs Jacobs replied. 'She is as pretty as she can be!'

Helene turned to the mirror. The colour on her cheeks and lips looked so natural she would have sworn Louise added nothing. Her complexion seemed to glow. 'You've made me look pretty,' she said.

The woman beamed in pleasure. 'I learned much at the theatre.' She picked up the gold dress from where it was draped over to the bed. 'Now the dress.'

Louise held the dress while Helene stepped into it.

'Make certain your feet are free,' Mrs Jacobs warned. 'You mustn't rip it now.'

Louise pulled up the dress and buttoned the buttons in the back.

'Let me see,' Mrs Jacobs cried. Both she and Louise surveyed Helene.

Louise smiled.

Mrs Jacobs clapped her hands. 'It fits perfectly!' She gestured to Helene. 'Look in the mirror, *mademoiselle*!'

Helene stepped back so she could see as much of herself as possible in the dressing room mirror. 'Oh, my!' She glanced from Louise to Mrs Jacobs and back to the mirror. 'It is perfection, Louise.'

'Not yet it isn't' Mrs Jacobs handed her the gloves,

which Louise helped her put on while Mrs Jacobs waited with the lace shawl over her arm. She placed the shawl around Helene's shoulders.

'No, let it slip to your elbows.' Louise helped her adjust it. 'There.'

Helene looked in the mirror again. She had never felt prettier. If only… No. She would not wish Rhys could see her. It was enough that *she* liked the way she looked.

'You are a dream,' Mrs Jacobs said, with a catch in her throat.

Helene gave the nurse a big hug and another one for Louise. 'I cannot thank you enough, both of you. I only wish you could come with me and share in all this excitement.'

Mrs Jacobs gave a hearty laugh. 'Oh, to see the faces of all *les nobles* if I were to walk in!'

Helene hugged her again. 'I do not care. I would welcome you.'

Louise pointed to the clock. 'You must go. It is time.'

She picked up her new lace reticule to carry with her. 'Come. See me to the hall. I promise I will stop by Wilson's room tomorrow to tell you all about it!'

Chapter Thirteen

The long lines of carriages, coaches and cabriolets, disgorging expensively dressed ladies and gentlemen in front of the property on Rue de la Blanchisserie, almost made Rhys turn around and seek the oblivion of some nameless tavern. Unfortunate that Grant had planted the idea of cowardice in Rhys's refusal to attend the ball. Now he'd feel a coward if he did not go in.

He nodded greetings to several people he did not know and took a place in line to enter, happening to be behind one of the four people he knew who would be attending.

David.

The young man seemed to be absorbing the whole scene. He turned finally and noticed Rhys. 'Rhys! Here you are! Where are Helene and Captain Grantwell?'

'They are coming separately,' Rhys said.

David blew out a breath. 'Whew! I am glad I am not caught in line with Helene. She has been plaguing me ever since she arrived in Brussels. She'd probably ring a peal over my head and not care who heard it.'

'I am certain you would deserve it,' Rhys said.

David made a face. 'You always did take her side.' His good humour quickly returned. 'Anyway, with any luck I will avoid her. I intend to enjoy myself. William said he will introduce me to General Maitland and to the Prince of Orange, who will be here. And I hope to say hello to the Duke of Wellington, as well. Perhaps I might introduce you to the Duke. Would you like that?'

'I would not wish to trouble him.' Wellington would surely be annoyed, Rhys was certain.

They reached a hall where footmen gathered ladies' cloaks and gentlemen's hats and inched their way to the ballroom.

The butler stood at the entrance to the ballroom, taking names and loudly announcing them to the receiving line and the room as a whole.

First David.

The man just leaned forward a little to hear the name, then bellowed, 'The Earl of Yarford.'

David lifted his head high as if everyone in the room would be watching him. No one seemed to notice.

Rhys was next. He gave his name.

'Captain Landon of the East Essex Regiment,' the butler called out.

He walked to the receiving line where the duchess and her three daughters greeted the guests. They, of course, knew David since he'd been a dinner guest and probably had spent as much time as he could in the family's presence.

David, to his credit, introduced Rhys. 'Duchess,' David said. 'May I present my friend, Captain Landon. Landon is from our village and I have known him my whole life.'

Rhys bowed. 'Your Grace.'

The Duchess extended her hand to be shook. 'A pleasure, I am sure, sir.'

The daughters, two of whom looked younger than David, greeted him with a little more warmth. The oldest daughter whisked David through quickly to make room for the long line of guests behind them.

Rhys followed.

David stood surveying the sumptuously decorated ball room. The room was not part of the main house, but somewhat separate, connected by an anteroom. Rhys could not guess its original purpose, but it was papered in a rose trellis design and transformed with red, black and gold drapery and fresh flowers into a garden-like setting. Nothing like the bare walls of the Assembly Rooms back at Yarford.

'Is it not grand?' David exclaimed.

'Very,' Rhys agreed.

David turned to him with a serious expression. 'By the way, Rhys, if you need to speak of me here, please do not call me David in front of anybody. Call me Yarford.'

'I am surprised you were not calling yourself Yarford before this.' Not that Rhys had any fondness for what had been Helene's father's title.

'Yes, well,' David muttered, 'I prefer to be called it here. It makes me important.'

Rhys suspected most people in this room would agree that a title made one important. And the reverse? If one did not have a title?

David's attention shifted. 'Oh, there is William. I must speak to him.' Off he went.

David's friend, the Duke of Richmond's son, still wore an eyepatch. Would he be ready if the French were on the march? Rhys wondered.

Rhys made his way through the room. He did not fool himself. He was looking for Grant…and Helene, telling himself that was because they were the only two other guests he could possibly know enough to speak to.

The room was an impressive sight, he admitted. Elegantly dressed ladies in gowns adorned with ribbons and flounces, jewels glittering at their necks and ears. Men mostly in uniforms of bright reds and blues, a few in black and green, all with gold braids shining under the chandeliers lit with dozens of candles. The room had the ground floor and a first floor with a balcony where an orchestra was tuning its instruments. The musical sounds mixed with a cacophony of voices, enough to make Rhys long for the relative quiet of the Brussels streets.

He did not need to stay, did he? There was nothing to say he could not retrieve his shako and walk back to the hotel. Or stop for a drink of whisky. At the moment it did not feel like a lack of cowardice to stay, but rather foolishness.

Through the din he heard the butler call, 'The Lady Helene Banes.'

He turned towards the door.

For a moment she was framed by the doorway, a vision sparkling in gold. Gold in her hair. Gold dress, shawl. Gold jewellery dangling from her ears and around her neck. He stared, feeling unable to breathe, unable to see anything but Helene. Rhys did not know what he'd expected to see when encountering Helene at the ball, but it was not this breath-robbing beauty. This breath-robbing *expensive* beauty who looked, not only as though she belonged here, but even more as though she deserved to own it all.

Grant was announced next and they made their way through the receiving line. Helene stood apart from Grant who was chatting with the Duchess's daughters. Helene turned to survey the room.

Her gaze locked with Rhys's.

He knew now what would decide if he stayed at the

ball or left. If after so obviously seeing him here she turned away, he would consider her her father's daughter and leave.

Rhys! Helene's heart leapt with joy at the sight of him.

He stood out from the crowd of other soldiers, ladies and gentlemen dressed in their finery. He stood tall, handsome, with a dignity all his own and the power she'd sensed in him even when he was a boy.

He'd come to the ball after all!

As quickly as her heart had soared, it plummeted. She did not know why he decided to attend the ball. Not to see her, perhaps. He'd refused to come for dinner, after all, so maybe he still wanted nothing to do with her. Was it not the height of vanity to think he had come to this prestigious ball solely to be with her? She must content herself with the hope that he would greet her cordially, that this might mean they could meet here as very old friends.

Just as easily that deep anger towards her could still smoulder inside Rhys, so that even her presence here would be anathema to him. She could not tell by his unsmiling expression.

She took a breath and straightened her spine. Well, if he wished to avoid her, all he need do was turn away. Then she would know her mistakes of five years ago were irreparable. If he did turn away, she would not seek him out; she would accept that she had destroyed in him even their once happy memories.

He stood as still as a statue, his eyes still upon her. They seemed to pull her forward and, before she knew it, she'd taken one step towards him, heedless of anything or anyone else in the room.

As if that first step had broken a spell ensnaring them

both, he crossed the room to her. Her heart raced at his approach.

'Rhys,' she managed to say when he reached her.

His eyes shone with admiration, but also with pain. 'You look beautiful, Helene.'

She smiled. How happy it would make Mrs Jacobs and Louise to hear that *her* Captain had given her such a compliment! 'I had a great deal of help.'

Grant left the receiving line and walked over. 'Ah, Rhys. Good to see you.' Grant spoke as if it was the most natural thing in the world to see Rhys at the ball, standing with her. 'If you both will pardon me, there is someone I must speak to.' He bowed.

And winked at Helene before he walked away. Her smile widened.

'Do you believe him?' Rhys asked.

She blinked. 'That there was someone he must speak to? Why would he say it if it was not so?'

Rhys's gaze followed Grant. 'To leave us alone.'

'Oh.' Did Rhys mean he'd wanted his friend to stay?

Rhys scanned the room, looking everywhere except at her. 'We may be standing in others' way. Would you care to walk a little?'

'Yes.' Her voice made her sound out of breath.

He offered his arm and she accepted it.

'I—I am glad you came, Rhys,' she said.

He shrugged. 'I almost did not. I cannot say I enjoy all this.' He gestured with his head. 'Only you, Grant, David and his friend Lennox know who I am.'

'Oh, David. I almost forgot about him.' She craned her neck. 'Have you seen him?'

'I walked in with him,' he responded. 'Or perhaps I should say I walked in with the Earl of Yarford as he precisely wishes to be known here.'

'He used his title?' For the first time, she believed.

'The title made him important, he said.'

How mindless of David to say such a thing to Rhys. Rhys's lack of a title was one of the arrows her father shot so cruelly at Rhys.

'I hope I see David so I might throttle him,' she said.

Rhys almost smiled. 'I believe he means to avoid you.'

'As he has tried to do ever since I arrived in Brussels.' She had no wish to talk about David, even though she was glad they were conversing amicably. Perhaps this was the best she could hope for.

As they strolled around the room, a few people took notice of them. Some officers nodded to Rhys; a few ladies greeted Helene by name and sent admiring glances towards her escort.

'You seem to belong in this company,' he commented in a low voice.

'I've had practice.' Three Seasons in London to be specific.

The air between them turned sour again. There was something about this ball that was different than the ones she'd attended in London, as if the air was crackling with tension instead of frivolity. As they strolled through the room, snippets of conversations reached their ears. The French. The French, she kept hearing. Rhys's muscles grew tense under her fingers. They passed a small group of officers. Rhys turned his head—at something he'd heard apparently—and he paused a moment before continuing.

'What is it, Rhys?' she asked.

'I am not certain.' He frowned. 'Men are talking.'

Talking about the French.

The discordant notes of the band tuning their instruments transformed into actual music and the dancing was announced. As much as Helene loved dancing—dancing with Rhys, that was—she hoped he would not ask her. The dance would separate them more and she did not wish to let go of him. They stood and watched the couples take their positions. The conversations around them became louder as the music played louder and the dancers' feet pounded the wooden floor.

'Let us find a quiet place,' Rhys said.

She brightened at the idea. 'Oh, yes.'

They walked back to the entrance where the flow of guests had dwindled. The duchess and her daughters had left the receiving line and her daughters were among the dancers on the floor. Rhys and Helene slipped out and found a door leading to the garden behind the building. A few other couples could be seen here and there in the garden, seeking some privacy. She and Rhys did not move far from the door. He seemed far away, though, lost in thought.

Helene's mind raced. Perhaps he did not wish her company after all. Had she misread his behaviour? Had Grant's abrupt departure once again forced Rhys to be obliged to attend her?

She gazed out at the garden. 'Rhys, do not feel you must be cemented to my side. I would not have you feel duty-bound to keep me company.'

He swivelled to her, his eyes flashing. 'Do you wish me to leave you?' he asked hotly. 'If you do, believe me I take no further offence.'

No *further* offence? Why was he so determined to misunderstand her? Why could he not set aside the hurt she'd done him just for a few minutes? She wanted to snap back at him, but she held her tongue until it was under better control. Instead she would be truthful. Unlike her father had been to her.

She softened her voice. 'No, I do not wish you to leave me. I value your company above all things. But I sense your discomfort and I accept that you might feel very differently about being with me.'

He glanced away again and it took him time to answer. 'Not that. Not you. Something is afoot. Something—everyone is on edge. I can feel it and I hear it in their voices.'

This was a new worry. 'Something about the French?'

'Yes, but I do not know what it is. I do not think anyone else knows either.' He rubbed his face. 'Something...' He turned back to her. 'Forgive my distraction. Perhaps we should return to the ballroom. I can help you look for David, if you wish to speak to him.'

David, again. She did not want to think of David. 'I believe I shall allow David to enjoy himself without my interference.' Be truthful, she told herself. 'Could we stay out here a little longer?'

'You do not wish to dance?' He made it sound like an accusation, but was he accusing her of not wanting to dance with him?

She was at sea. She did not know if he was pushing her away or daring her to come closer.

'You are dressed for dancing,' he added.

What a war raged inside Rhys. The soldier in him wanted to return to the ballroom to discover precisely what was causing the other military guests to be on edge. The wounded youth inside him wanted to still complain of how she and her father had deeply injured him. But he was also a man standing next to her, inhaling the allure of her perfume. That man merely desired to take her in his arms and again taste her lips as he had done so long ago. The lot of him was making a bungle of everything.

To his surprise, she smiled at him. 'Shall I tell you the story of my dress?'

'Your dress has a story?' He had no idea where she was leading him.

'Oh, yes.' She gave him a sideways glance. 'Did you think I packed a ball gown to bring with me to Brussels when I intended to be here only two days at the most?'

'I thought nothing.' He still did not know where this was leading.

'Men,' she scoffed, but her tone was light. 'You think gowns simply appear out of the mist.'

He was in no mood to be teased. 'So how did you come by the gown?'

She smiled again. 'Louise Desmet arranged for me to borrow it.'

'Madame Desmet owned such a gown?' Why would a woman, who lived as simply as Madame Desmet lived, have need of a ball gown?

'No, but, in a way, it is hers.' She smiled again as if ready to tell the answer to a riddle. 'She made the gown. She has been a seamstress for the theatre for many years. She took me there and we searched through their costumes until we found this dress. She altered it to fit me.'

'The dress is a theatre costume?' He would never have guessed such a thing.

Helene touched the earrings dangling from her ears. 'She borrowed these from the theatre, as well. They are paste.'

It seemed a great deal of effort to expend merely to attend this ball. Was it that important to her? As it was for David? And would have been for her father?

To his surprise, her eyes turned to mischief like they'd so often done when they were children. She leaned closer to him. 'Think of what these ladies would say if they knew I am wearing a dress, jewellery and shoes last worn by an actress!'

Unexpectedly his heart warmed to her. She seemed less like the Earl's daughter and more like the girl he'd once loved, amused by absurdities. 'How could they say anything but that you outshine them all?'

'Do I, Rhys?' Her gaze met his and he suddenly could not think of her as a girl.

It unsettled him. He lifted the edge of her gold shawl. 'And this came from the theatre, as well?'

She ran her hands over the intricately knotted lace. 'This? This lovely shawl, I fear, I purchased for myself, because I could not resist it.'

'You chose well,' he said and meant it. Even under the light from the lamp at the doorway, she sparkled.

Her eyes glittered with pleasure at his words.

He glanced away for a moment, unprepared for the emotions inside him. 'But you must have worn many beautiful gowns and shawls at the many balls you attended in London.' When he looked back, the pleasure in her eyes had faded.

She solemnly returned his gaze. 'I wore many fashionable dresses during my London Seasons, all made at the direction of my mother and never of my own choosing.' Her arms swept down her dress. 'I chose this actress's costume, this borrowed, *second-hand* dress, and I like it better than any the ones made by the *ton*'s most sought-after modiste.'

He let his eyes sweep over the full length of her. She had chosen *very* well.

She went on. 'And Mrs Jacobs and Louise Desmet were by far my favourite lady's maids. I have never before so enjoyed the preparation for a ball.'

Rhys could not help but smile. 'I'll wager Mrs Jacobs gave many instructions.'

She laughed and something like joy burst inside him. 'She did indeed.'

From inside the ballroom, Rhys faintly heard the next dance announced. 'They are announcing a waltz. Will you come back inside and dance with me?'

Her smile widened. 'Yes. Yes. I will dance the waltz with you, Rhys.'

He gave her his hand and they walked back to the ballroom in time to take their places on the dance floor. Rhys noticed Grant escorting the eldest of the duke's daughters on to the floor, as well.

The music started.

Rhys and Helene stood side by side, they clasped their left hands in front of them and their right hands behind, as they performed the four march steps. They then turned so that they faced each other, raising their left arms in an arc above their heads and holding each other's backs with the other hand. Then the waltz steps had them twirling with each other around the dance floor. The other couples faded from Rhys's view. He had eyes only for Helene, the most beautiful woman in the room. The music filled his ears and it seemed as if time suspended them in this dance. There was no anger and pain from the past; no thought of battle in the future. Only Helene in his arms, her face flushed, her lips parted, her eyes meeting his.

Chapter Fourteen

Helene's heart soared with every twirl. To waltz with Rhys, to be held in his arms, was a joy she thought she would never again experience. She must hold this moment in memory for all time.

The music stopped.

She and Rhys stood, their arms still holding each other, their gazes locked, while the other dancers started to walk off the dance floor.

Rhys finally spoke. 'Would you care for refreshment?'

She only cared that she be able to remain with him. 'Yes, that would be lovely.'

He held her hand as they walked off the dance floor to an area where servants were offering trays of wine. He handed a glass to Helene and took one for himself.

As they sipped, Rhys turned his attention away from her. That same tension she'd sensed in him when they'd walked outside returned.

'What is it?' she said.

'Wellington is here.' He gestured to a tall man dressed, not in regimentals, but plainly in black.

He had the prominent nose she'd so often read of in the newspapers and which was very exaggerated in the satiric prints displayed in shop windows. Grant stood not very far from the duke, who was conversing with the Duchess of Richmond and her daughter, Georgiana. Grant spied Rhys and Helene and walked over to them.

'What news?' Rhys asked him.

'Little more than we knew before,' his friend answered. 'Napoleon is on the march. The French attacked the Prussian advance forces on the Sambre. We are to be in readiness in the morning.'

'It is happening, then?' Helene asked.

'Very nearly,' Rhys said. He turned to her, seizing her arms. 'You must corral David.' He all but shook her. 'Insist he accompany you home right away. I will look out for Wilson. But you must leave Brussels.'

Leave? She trembled at the idea of a French attack and Rhys in the middle of it. Her principal aim had been to leave Brussels with David, but now…now she detested the idea. She wished above all things that she would not have to part from Rhys.

It was a futile wish. Napoleon had seen to it.

She nodded.

'We might as well stay at the ball,' Grant said. 'Wellington is staying.'

The incongruous sound of bagpipes startled them. Rhys put an arm around Helene as several Highlanders, dressed in kilts, marched in the room.

'These are the Gordon Highlanders,' Rhys told her.

Helene had read of them. Dressed in their red coats and kilts, they'd fought in many battles on the Peninsula.

As the bagpipes blared, the Highlanders demonstrated Scottish reels. They ended by placing their swords on the floor and dancing intricate steps around and between them.

After they marched out of the room, to the applause of the guests, supper was announced. Not everyone stayed for the supper. Some officers left the ball so there were many empty seats. The Duke of Wellington did not leave, however, and Helene could only think that meant matters were not as urgent as they could have been. No need yet to part from Rhys.

During the supper, a young officer dressed in riding boots and covered with the dust of the road, entered the room and passed a message to the Prince of Orange. The Prince, without even reading the message, gave it to the Duke of Wellington.

She noticed Rhys was watching this scene intently. When Wellington read the message and spoke quietly to several important-looking men at his table, Rhys said, 'Come. I mean to learn what was said.'

The Duke of Richmond led Wellington and others out of the supper room to another room nearby. Rhys, Grant and Helene followed.

Before closing the door, Wellington signalled Rhys to him. 'Captain, see no one enters this room while we are here.'

Rhys snapped to attention and stood in the doorway.

They all waited for what seemed a very long time but could only have been minutes. Finally, the door opened and the men inside rushed out.

Wellington took the time to speak to Rhys and Grant. 'We will sound the call to arms. Have your men ready to march at dawn. We'll meet the French at Quatre Bras.'

Helene did not know where Quatre Bras was. She only knew her time with Rhys was short. And her heart, so recently full of joy, again broke into little pieces.

Rhys, Grant and Helene made their way back to the ballroom. There was a crush of people at the entrance of the room, waiting to collect their cloaks and hats.

'We'll wait for the entrance to clear.' Rhys held on to Helene's arm. He was not ready to let go of her.

'I am going to push my way through,' Grant said. 'You see Helene back to the hotel. There should be a carriage waiting for her. I'll leave for the regiment as soon as I can change.'

Rhys ought to do the same. He glanced at Helene whose brow was creased with tension. How could he leave her like that? 'If—if I am delayed, see to my men, would you, Grant? I'll be there as soon as I can.' The regiment was to gather at the Parc de Bruxelles.

It was already near two in the morning. There were few hours left before dawn when his soldiers would march the less than ten miles to Quatre Bras, a crossroads he and Grant had noted when studying maps of the area.

While they stood waiting for the crowd to ease, he glimpsed David in the doorway.

'David!' Helene cried.

Her brother turned and saw her. 'I'll—I'll come see you tomorrow, Helene. I'm staying the night with William.' He disappeared in the throng of people, like the thoughtless wretch he was.

'Do you want me to go after him?' Rhys asked her.

'No.' She gripped his arm. 'Stay with me, Rhys. You'll never find him anyway. I doubt he'll get himself into trouble in the Duke and Duchess's house.'

Rhys gladly waited at her side until the crowd eased and he was finally able to retrieve his shako. When he and Helene walked out to the street, they found the throngs of people had simply moved out there. The street was jumbled with carriages and horses, all at a standstill. The call to arms rang through the streets.

'Which is your carriage?' he asked her.

She craned her neck. 'The driver wore yellow livery. I

do not see him.' She pulled on Rhys's arm. 'Let us walk, Rhys. It is not far. You cannot waste time waiting for a carriage.'

When they'd last walked the streets of Brussels, they'd not touched, nor spoken, having said so many upsetting words to each other already. This time he wrapped his arm around her and held her firmly while they made their way through the press of people waiting for carriages.

When they were finally through the worst of the crowd, he released her, but they walked swiftly.

Helene held on to his arm. 'Tell me what will happen, Rhys. What will happen tomorrow?'

'Quatre Bras is a crossroads that must be held. We'll face the French there, but I heard Wellington say we will likely not stop them there. He spoke of another place nearby. That is where the main battle will be.'

'Rhys!' He heard the stress in her voice. 'Men will be killed. You might be—'

He stopped and faced her. 'I have fought before, Helene. I am able to take care of myself.'

The truth was he'd have little control over whether he lived or died. No matter his skill in battle, death was one cannonball or musket shot or sword thrust away. In other battles he'd not given his own death much thought; his mind was more set on getting his men through. Tonight, though, his mortality weighed heavily on his mind. He'd just found Helene again. He did not want this to be his last night with her.

Memories raced through Rhys's mind as they resumed their swift pace. Of Helene and him as children playing for hours on end. Of his youth when he first noticed she was pretty and graceful—and shaped like a woman. How well he remembered those first stirrings of attraction towards her. Then, when only a little older, the thrill of planning to elope with her.

When they reached the hotel, it, too, was a frenzy of activity. Officers dashed past them or stood embracing weeping women. Rhys led Helene up the stairway to her room. When they reached her door, her hands trembled as she pulled the key from her reticule. He took it and turned it in the lock, opening the door.

They were at the moment of parting.

This was his last chance to protect her. 'When David comes tomorrow, do not let him go to the battle. Leave for England. Get away. I will see to Wilson—if I can. If I cannot, he has Madame Desmet. But you must get away.'

She grasped the fabric of his coat in her fingers. 'Rhys. Do not say the Allies will lose.'

He covered her hands with his own. 'We will win eventually, because we will fight until we do, but this will be a nasty business. Napoleon is a skilled general and his troops are seasoned soldiers.'

She lowered her head so he could not see her face and she pulled away. 'I know you must leave.'

He released her fingers.

Suddenly all her father's cruelty, all the pain of her rejection, meant nothing. This was Helene, his constant friend, the woman he loved, and he must part from her.

Helene slowly raised her head and her eyes glistened with tears. 'I wish…' She did not finish.

'What do you wish?' Rhys murmured.

She took a breath. 'I wish I had not listened to my father. I wish we would have eloped to Gretna Green. I wish we'd had our wedding night.'

It was as if the walls he'd erected inside him had cracked open and tumbled into rubble. They'd missed their chance to be together and he felt the depths of pain at their loss.

She took another breath, blinking away her tears and firmly setting her chin. 'So. Goodbye, Rhys.'

He could not stop looking directly into her eyes. He'd been stabbed a few times with a Frenchman's sword, but this pain was so much worse. 'I don't—' he began to say.

She wrapped her arms around his neck and clung to him. 'I don't want you to leave!'

He pressed her to him. She lifted her face and stood on tiptoe, reaching for him.

Rhys groaned and lowered his lips to hers.

She tasted warm and familiar and he was intensely aroused. It also felt as if he were home again where he belonged. With Helene.

They stood in the doorway. 'Come in with me, Rhys,' she rasped.

Her room was in near darkness. The only light came from glowing coals in the fireplace. He crossed the threshold with her and kicked the door closed, continuing to taste her lips, inhale her scent, feel her soft curves against his body. She let her lace shawl slip to the floor. His shako tumbled off his head. She pulled the earrings from her ears and unfastened the necklace, dropping them both on a nearby table. They still kissed.

Rhys wished for nothing between them. No uniform. No ball gown. He wanted to feel her skin against his. He wanted to plunge himself inside her—

He froze and carefully eased out of her embrace. She stared at him, eyes wild and confused.

'You matter to me, Helene.' His voice was even, more composed than the sensations and emotions raging through his body. 'I will not dishonour you.'

Her expression settled into a solemn resolve. 'What

do I care for dishonour? We might never see each other again. Do you think I wish to repeat the same mistake I made years ago? Send you off, because someone, somewhere might disapprove of our being together?'

'You do not understand,' he said earnestly. 'There might be a baby come of this.'

She still met his gaze. 'And would that not be the most blissful result? A baby. *Your* baby. A piece of you I could hold and love for ever.'

He hesitated. 'I cannot promise you I will return.' Because he could die.

Her eyes turned bleak. 'All the more reason.'

Lord knew he wanted her, had desired her since he'd been that foolish young man who thought all they needed to be together was this powerful love. But he also knew if he got her with child, her world could be cruel to her. And the baby.

He steeled himself. 'I cannot do this.'

She lowered her lashes. 'Very well. I understand your refusal. I suppose I deserve it.'

He closed the distance between them again and engulfed her in his arms. 'Do not say so. I do not refuse you. I need you, Helene. I will always care about you.' He rubbed a frustrated hand through his hair. 'I will not see you hurt, not even by me. I love you, Helene. I always have.'

'Oh, Rhys.' She melted in his arms and their lips devoured each other once more. When he freed her lips, she murmured, 'And I have always loved you. Always.'

He kissed her eyes, her ears, her neck. His fingers searched for the buttons on her dress.

She pulled away. 'I ask only one thing of you.'

He was at a loss. 'What?'

A mischievous smile widened on her face. 'Be very

careful with this dress. I must return it to Louise in one piece.'

He laughed aloud. 'Let me light a lamp so I might see to work the buttons.'

He found a taper on the mantel and lit a lamp. She turned her back to him. While he unbuttoned her dress, she took the chain and ribbon from her hair. Her luxurious mahogany curls tumbled to her shoulders. He helped her lift the dress over her head. She draped it over a chair.

'Now your coat,' she said, adding a laugh.

He kicked off his shoes while she worked the buttons of his red coat. She swept her hands over his chest to pull his coat off. She turned around so that he could untie and loosen her stays.

She looked over her shoulder at him 'Do you remember how we used to strip down to our underclothes to swim in the pond?'

He remembered. 'It is good we were never caught. I would have been forbidden to play with you.' They'd stopped when they were both old enough to think about the other without clothes.

She stepped out of her stays, slipped off her shoes, and took off her petticoat.

'Sit,' he said. 'I'll remove your stockings.'

She sat and extended one leg. Rhys slid his hands up her leg until reaching her garter. He untied it and let his fingers slip under her stocking to the smooth, warm skin of her leg. She leaned back and sighed and quickly extended her other leg to remove the other stocking.

Now she was dressed in nothing but her shift. He lifted her off the chair and carried her to the bed. She wrapped her arms around his neck and kissed him again.

Rhys stepped back, his senses on fire. 'Let me look at you.'

Her eyes smouldered as she gathered the fabric of her shift in her hands and pulled it over her head.

Rhys took a sharp intake of breath. He let his eyes feast on her, hesitant to touch her as if she were some piece of exquisite porcelain that could shatter if he dared. She, though, was made of much sterner stuff. She did not shrink from his blatant gaze.

Instead she lifted her chin. 'Your turn, Rhys.'

A smile tickled his lips. She used those very words when they were children taking turns daring each other to climb a tree higher or jump from rock to rock across a flowing stream.

He unbuttoned the fall of his trousers and pushed them down to his feet to kick them away. With a half-smile he lifted his foot on to the bed where she sat so naked and beautiful. She returned his smile and removed his stockings as he had hers. Her hands ran up his leg and each hair seemed to sing with the pleasure of it. By the time his legs were bare, he was nearly mad with need for her. He flung off his shirt and undid the buttons of his drawers, impatient to be rid of every stitch of clothing.

Naked at last, Rhys moved towards her, but she stopped him with a hand to his chest. 'Let me look, Rhys,' she said.

He felt her eyes on him as if she'd caressed him with her fingers.

'You—you are…' She hesitated. 'Rhys, you are so very handsome.'

Helene's views of naked men had come primarily from statues in gardens or London mansions. Rhys far outshone them. She knew enough about mating to expect his arousal, but she'd no idea that she could view it with such pleasure and anticipation.

He lifted her arm away and climbed on to the bed, laying her back against the pillows, kissing her again and tangling his limbs with hers. He ran his hand down the length of her neck to her breast and she writhed with the pleasure of it.

She was with Rhys at last with no barriers of clothes or harsh words between them. She ached with happiness and refused to think of anything but this moment with him.

His hand slid down to her abdomen and he pressed his fingers into her flesh. 'This may hurt you,' he warned.

She became impatient, but she did not know precisely for what. 'I do not care. I want this.'

'I will try to ready you.' He slipped his fingers lower to that most female part of her, the part that ached for him.

She arched her back under his touch and gasped when his fingers found entrance. He was so very gentle with her, but the sensations he created simply made her feel urgent, as though she would explode if—if—something. She did not know what. Something to come.

'Please, Rhys,' she begged. 'No more waiting.'

He rose above her and she opened her legs to him. He pushed into her a little at a time, as if she would break, but she knew her body was meant to welcome him. She lifted her hips, urging him on.

He gave one hard thrust and she cried out more at the pleasure of it than the pain.

He froze. 'Have I hurt you?'

She shook her head. 'No. No. Do not stop.'

Any reserve he might have been holding seemed released and he moved within her at a rhythmic pace which her body met with great gratitude. Sensation grew inside her, like a fireball growing hotter and hotter as his thrusts came quicker and deeper. She grasped his back, pressing her nails into his skin as the sensation built.

Suddenly sheer pleasure burst inside her. She cried out with the joy of it.

A second later he also cried out, pressing hard inside her, all his muscles taut, and grasping her firmly until he groaned and collapsed on top of her.

He slid to her side, but still held her.

They lay like that until Helene felt her body return to some semblance of normal. She rose a little to kiss him, her breasts pressing against his chest.

'Are you hurt?' he asked her.

She smiled at him. 'Not hurt. Intensely happy.'

Although the sounds of horses' hooves, men shouting, wagons rumbling and a bugle sounding, reached her ears from the street below. Her happiness would be fleeting. He must leave to go to war.

And he might never return.

Chapter Fifteen

Rhys made love to her twice more, dozing with her in his arms between times. When light began to seep through the windows and the sounds of the street outside grew louder, he forced himself to face his duty. He must dress for battle, retrieve his horse, and make speed to meet his regiment who might even now be gathering in the Parc de Bruxelles.

He gazed down at Helene, thinking she might be asleep, but her eyes were open and she returned his gaze.

'I must leave.' He sat up and rubbed his face. 'I need to change clothes. Gather my things.'

But instead of climbing out of bed, he moved atop her, leaning down for a long, yearning kiss. Reverently he caressed her soft skin and entered her once more, moving slowly, wishing to stop the clock ticking, trying to sear the moment into memory. He stroked her inside until his body overcame him and moved with her for that urgent release they shared together.

After, he held her, reluctant to let go.

'Rhys,' she whispered. 'You cannot stay.'

She pushed him away and he rose from the bed. There were no words he could manage to speak. Sounds from the streets reached them, the sounds of many voices, shouts, and rumblings. They'd been constant through the night and Rhys could no longer ignore them.

He looked out the window at columns of soldiers in the street marching to the Parc. 'I need to join my regiment.'

Helene, wrapped in bed linen, climbed off the bed and stood beside him to look down on the street packed with men.

'I must hurry.' He turned away from the window and began to dress.

While he put on his shirt and drawers, Helene quickly washed herself from the basin on the dresser. She donned her shift and wriggled into her corset. He buttoned his trousers and slipped on his shoes, stuffing his stockings in a pocket.

She presented her back to him. 'Help me dress. I want to stay with you.'

He helped her tie her stays and the laces of a dress she pulled from a drawer, the same dress she'd worn to dinner with Grant—had that only been the evening before? It felt as if his very world had changed since then.

She put on her stockings and tied her hair back in a ribbon while he shrugged into his coat, not bothering to button it.

'I'm ready,' she said, slipping on the dancing shoes she'd worn to the ball.

'Come.' He held her hand. They left her room and he led her down the hallway to where he shared the room with Grant.

'You were this close to my room the whole time?' she asked with a little laugh.

'And I did not tell you,' he admitted.

He unlocked the door and they entered. The rooms were in some disarray. It was evident Grant had made quick work of changing out of his evening clothes and into his battle uniform. Rhys needed to do the same.

Helene absently picked up clothes and straightened up the place while Rhys changed and prepared himself for the battle to come.

He slung his pack over his shoulder and faced her. She stepped into his arms one more time. Rhys held her, relished the scent of her, the softness of her, the memory of lying with her.

Again, it was she who moved away, her eyes shining with tears that she immediately blinked away. 'I'll walk downstairs with you.'

After he locked the door behind her, he handed her his key. 'Will you give this to the hall servant? Tell him to have our belongings packed up and stored. I'll arrange payment when I can.'

'I will.' She put the key in her pocket.

The hotel was not the bustle of frantic activity it had been only a few hours ago, but there were still people about, still couples saying goodbye. Helene walked with him all the way out the door of the hotel. The sky was even brighter than when he'd risen.

'I will say goodbye here. I need to get my horse and ride to the Parc.' Rhys must leave Helene again, to return to the army, with no certainty that he would ever see her again. 'Find David. Leave Brussels today.'

She faced him with such a brave look on her face that he took her in his arms again for one more kiss. He wrenched himself away.

'Goodbye, Rhys!' she called after him.

He turned and strode back to her, holding her by her shoulders and looking into her eyes. 'I never stopped loving you, Helene.' He released her again and hurried away.

He heard her voice call after him, 'I never will stop, Rhys!'

* * *

Helene watched Rhys hurrying away from her, nearly running through the people on the pavement and the soldiers marching down the street. She watched until she could only see a hint of red and the top of his tall black hat. A moment later he was gone.

She swallowed a sob.

No, she would not cry. It would not help him. She could do nothing to help him.

She walked towards the Parc and found a place to stand where she could survey the activity without being seen. The Parc was a sea of red-coated soldiers. She could make out the Highlanders, the same regiment of soldiers who'd danced at the ball, and another Scottish regiment dressed in kilts who were starting to fill the space between two other red-coated regiments. Was one of those Rhys's regiment? She fixed her eyes on them and watched until they started to march away. She quickly ran to the streets to watch them pass. The Highland regiment marched to the sound of bagpipes and the ground shook with the footsteps of so many men. First she spied Grant on horseback, riding next to the red coats. Finally she saw Rhys on a bay mare with a flash of white on its forehead. She watched him until he and his men marched out of sight.

All around her were men, horses and wagons heading to war. Some soldiers were still saying goodbye to tearful wives and children. One soldier embraced his wife again and again and took their baby in his arms, kissing the child one more time before handing the babe back to his wife, tears streaming down his cheeks. Helene's throat constricted and tears stung her eyes at the sight. She watched a woman riding next to an officer—his wife perhaps? She'd never imagined a wife could accompany her husband like that. How brave of her. Helene felt a pang of envy. If only she could have ridden next to Rhys!

Helene could not bear these heart-wrenching sights any longer. She wiped her tears with her fingers and made her way back to the door of the hotel.

Inside, the hall servant, who looked as if he'd not slept at all, was surrounded by guests, all demanding his assistance. No sense in talking with him now, especially since David was not here yet. It was too early. David had never risen this early and she doubted he would do so even today, after the late hours of the ball. He'd promised to meet her here, though. She must believe he would keep his word.

It was just dawn. She climbed the stairs but instead of going to her room, she went to Rhys's, letting herself in with his key. She would pack for Rhys and his friend. Who knew when the busy servants could do so?

She gathered everything she supposed to belong to Rhys or Grant. She picked up the coat Rhys had worn to the ball and held it to her nose, inhaling the scent of him, embracing the coat as if she were embracing Rhys himself. Tears pricked her eyes again, but she was still determined not to weep. She folded his coat and his other clothes and packed them in his chest. She picked up a handkerchief that was packed in the chest and rubbed it against her cheek.

She placed it in her pocket. A piece of him she would keep.

What she guessed to be Grant's belongings she packed in the other chest. After scouring the room to be certain she'd found everything, she closed the chests and left the room, locking it behind her. Downstairs the hall servant was still too busy, so she walked outside again. There were no more marching numbers of soldiers, only a few officers on horseback riding away. She walked to the Place Royale right next to the hotel and saw a few sentinels guarding military wagons. She was puzzled by a line of long tilted carts parked one after the other. Their drivers slept at their seats and the unharnessed horses grazed at some nearby grass.

She asked one of the sentinels, 'What are those wagons for?'

'To carry the wounded, ma'am,' the man replied.

His words were like a knife to her belly. There were so many carts. Would Rhys be among those placed in them? She stopped and said a prayer that he would survive unharmed.

She started back to the hotel door, suddenly feeling achingly alone. She wished David was here. He could never be counted upon to provide solace, but she would not feel so alone if he were with her.

Though it was still early, she decided to check on Wilson. Surely they would have been awakened by the call to arms, the sounds of the army on the march, the rumbling of wagons. She'd arrange for breakfast for Mrs Jacobs, Louise and Wilson. Louise would likely come soon to be at Wilson's side.

She entered the hotel and walked to the dining room, passing the guests still clustered around the hall servant. To her surprise there were diners in the dining room, including two officers seeming to take a leisurely breakfast with a young man and two young women. She ordered food and drink to be sent to Wilson's room and hurried there herself.

A distressed Mrs Jacobs opened the door to her knock. 'Oh, *mademoiselle*! Such commotion.'

Helene entered the room, surprised to see Wilson fully

dressed and seated on the side of the bed, equally surprised to see Louise, seated at his side.

'Wilson! You are up.' He made an effort to stand, but Helene signalled him to remain seated. 'You must be feeling better.'

'Much better, m'lady,' he said.

Mrs Jacobs broke in. 'We decided it best if Mr Wilson dressed today. Goodness! We do not know what will happen. What if the French are at the gates of the city?'

Helene was not certain Brussels had city gates. 'Things are not so bad, I assure you.' She turned to Louise. 'I did not expect you here so early. You must have seen the army on its march.'

'I stayed the night, Lady Helene,' Louise said. 'After you left, there were so many carriages going to the ball that I waited, but then Wilson did not want me walking home so late.'

'So, you've had no news of what is happening?' Helene asked.

'None at all, m'lady,' Wilson said.

'Let me tell you what I know, then,' Helene said. 'The French are marching towards Brussels, but they are still some distance away. The Allied army is readying to meet them. Wellington sent troops to a place called Quatre Bras today, but Rhys believes the major battle will take place later at another location.'

Mrs Jacobs's eyes brightened. '*Rhys?* You were with your Captain?'

Helene's throat tightened and tears again pricked her eyes. She could not speak, but simply nodded.

Louise rose and came over to her, folding her into a hug.

Helene had resolved not to cry, but her carefully constructed dam broke and tears spilled down her cheeks.

'There. There.' Louise patted her back.

Helene sobbed.

Mrs Jacobs joined them, engulfing them both. The two women held her until she gained control of herself again.

Helene reached in her pocket and took out Rhys's handkerchief, but she did not want to dampen it with her tears. She put it back again and wiped her face with her fingers.

Wilson, his expression full of concern, shuffled over and handed her his handkerchief. 'Come sit next to me, m'lady.' He walked her to the bed.

She had a fleeting memory of Wilson drying her tears when she was a little girl, sitting her next to him and listening to whatever tale of woe had upset her.

Louise sat on the other side of her.

'You are all so—' She broke into a sob again. 'You are all so kind.'

'Tell us what makes you cry,' Wilson used the same soothing voice she remembered as a child.

'Rhys might be killed,' she blurted out and the tears spilled again.

There was a knock at the door, which Mrs Jacobs answered. A servant handed Mrs Jacobs the tray of food and a pot of tea, then hurried away. Mrs Jacobs placed the tray on the table and fixed a cup of tea, handing it to Helene.

It helped.

There was another knock at the door. Another servant appeared. 'Is Lady Helene Banes here?' he asked.

Mrs Jacobs gestured to Helene. 'She is sitting right there. What is this?'

'A message for her.' He handed Mrs Jacobs a folded piece of paper, turned and left.

Mrs Jacobs closed the door and handed the paper to Helene.

She read it.

Dear Sister,
Am invited to stay with William. Cannot meet with
you today. Promise to be at the hotel tomorrow.
Yours, D—

Helene gave an angry cry.

'What is it, m'lady?' Wilson asked, worry furrowing his brow.

'David! He lied to me!' She crumpled the paper. 'He was to meet me here today. Rhys told us to leave for England today.' Rhys made her promise. 'David says he won't be here. Tomorrow, he says.'

Wilson's brows knitted. 'You wish to leave for England today?'

She clasped his hand. 'I know you are not well enough to travel, Wilson. I will leave you plenty of money to stay as long as you need and to pay for the trip home. Rhys will help you, if he can. You can come when you are ready.'

He looked her in the eye. 'I am staying, m'lady. I am not returning to Yarford. I am staying with Louise.' He exchanged a very loving look with her.

It moved Helene deeply. She squeezed Wilson's hand. 'Dear Wilson. I am so very happy for you both.' A part of her, though, grieved losing him.

Mrs Jacobs served the meal and they all ate without much conversation. Footsteps hurrying through the hallway made them all glance up at the door on occasion, as if someone might burst in on them with more alarming news.

Mrs Jacobs collected the dishes. She'd been uncharacteristically quiet.

'Is something amiss, Mrs Jacobs? Besides what we are all worrying about?'

The nurse wrung her hands. 'I—I need to go home to my husband. I need to stay with him. We do not know what will happen. What if the French return to Brussels? He cannot be alone.'

Would any of them be safe if the French came?

No. The Allies would stop them. They must.

Helene walked over to Mrs Jacobs and gave her a hug. 'Of course you must go home.'

'I will take care of Samuel,' Louise said. She glanced at him. 'He need not stay here any longer. I will take him to my house.'

These three dear people were leaving her, as well. Helene felt desolately lonely. She swallowed. 'We must arrange for a carriage, then. It is too far for him to walk.' She turned to Mrs Jacobs. 'You should leave for home as soon as you are able. Now if you like.'

Mrs Jacobs picked up the basket that she'd carried to and from her house. 'I have packed everything already.'

'Very good.' Helene bit her lip to keep it from trembling. She might never see Mrs Jacobs again. What would she have done without her? 'But walk with me to my room first. I have the money there to pay you.'

'May I come with you?' Louise asked. 'I can gather the ball gown and other things to take back to the theatre.'

Helene nodded. 'Of course. We can accompany Mrs Jacobs to the lobby and then arrange for the carriage at that time.'

Louise picked up her bag.

Both Wilson and Mrs Jacobs became emotional when the nurse said goodbye to him.

'I—I cannot thank you enough,' he said earnestly.

'Oh, now!' Mrs Jacobs put on a smile. 'You were no

trouble at all. I've had many worse patients in my time.' She took his hand in hers and patted it. 'Now you take good care of my friend Louise, Mr Wilson. If you do not, you will have to answer to me and I will make certain you need quite a bit more nursing care.'

He laughed. 'I will do so, ma'am. With pleasure.'

Helene smiled. Some of Mrs Jacobs's good spirits had returned, at least.

As soon as they left Wilson's room, Mrs Jacobs showed just how much she was restored to her old self. She leaned close to Helene. 'Now, *mademoiselle*. You must tell us all about the ball and about your Captain. He showed up, did he?'

Helene nodded. 'He did show up at the ball. And we danced the waltz together.'

'The waltz?' Mrs Jacobs clapped her hands.

'The waltz is a very romantic dance,' Louise added approvingly.

'And then what happened?' Mrs Jacobs pressed.

'We were together at the ball the whole time.' Helene talked about the decorations and the ladies' dresses and the food at the supper rather than speak about all that passed between her and Rhys. 'Then word came that the officers had to go to their regiments. The ball was over. Rhys walked me back to the hotel.'

Louise gave Mrs Jacobs a knowing look, but Helene did not comprehend its meaning.

They reached her room and, while Helene unlocked the door, Louise and Mrs Jacobs stood a little apart from her and talked together in hushed tones. She opened the door and they went inside.

Helene found her portmanteau and searched in its hidden compartment for her money. She handed some coins to Mrs Jacobs.

The nurse stared down at the number of coins in her hand. 'But this is too much, *mademoiselle*.'

Helene gave her another hug. 'It is not half as much as your help has been worth to me.'

The woman grinned and stuffed them into a pocket.

Helene glanced around the room. She'd left it in a telling piece of disorder. Her shawl was on the floor, the earrings and necklace where she'd dropped them on a table near the door. The chain and ribbon that had decorated her hair had been tossed on her dressing table. Most telling, though, was the bed and its very tangled bed linens. 'Let me collect the things for the theatre,' she said to Louise.

Helene picked up the jewellery.

Louise put a stilling hand on her arm. 'In a moment. Sit first, *s'il vous plaît*.' She led Helene to a chair.

Mrs Jacobs and Louise pulled up two other chairs to face her.

'Tell us,' Louise said in a soft, kind voice. 'Did Captain Landon spend the night with you?'

Helene felt her cheeks burn. She did not answer.

Mrs Jacobs leaned forward. '*Mademoiselle*, we understand being in love. We know of these things. Now if you need anything—you know—for the day after. We can help you.'

Helene looked from one to the other. 'I do not understand.'

'To prevent a baby,' Mrs Jacobs said.

Helene felt her face turn red again. 'Oh.' She took a breath. 'Thank you both, but—but if there is a baby—I will be happy.' She blinked away tears again. 'I will have a piece of him in case—in case I never see him again.'

The two other women teared up, as well, and the three of them wiped their tears together. Finally, Louise stood. 'Then we must not tarry. Mrs Jacobs needs to get home.'

Helene took off the dancing slippers and handed them to Louise. While Helene put on her half-boots, Louise folded the dress and put it in her bag. When all the items were collected, they left the room.

Outside the hotel's entrance they said goodbye to Mrs Jacobs.

'I will visit you, I promise,' Louise told the nurse. 'I know your direction. And you must visit me.'

Helene could make no such promise. When she left Brussels, she would not likely ever return. She hugged Mrs Jacobs one more time. 'I will never forget you,' Helene whispered.

The streets were eerily quiet still and, before Helene and Louise re-entered the hotel, Helene glimpsed the empty wagons again.

The ones that would carry the wounded from Quatre Bras.

Chapter Sixteen

For all the rush from the call to arms, the haste to get out of Brussels, the time, so far, had been spent in marching and waiting. Or as Rhys overheard one of his soldiers say, 'Hurry up and wait. That's the army for you.'

Instead of going directly to Quatre Bras, the regiment was ordered to Genappe where the soldiers rested under the shade of the trees to get some relief from the heat of the sun. They could hear the sound of guns, but in the distance. Still, the soldiers were ready to grab their muskets and march towards the sounds and do their duty.

Grant found Rhys and the two men sat in the shade of a tree. Their horses nibbled on grass nearby.

'Nearly two p.m. according to my timepiece,' Grant said, putting it back in his pocket. 'And whatever that is—' He paused until the faint boom of a gun reached their ears. 'It is not close by. I thought we would be hastening towards the crossroads at Quatre Bras.'

Rhys sat with his back against the tree trunk and his eyes closed. 'Wellington still isn't certain where the French army is headed. He's covering all roads.'

'Still,' said Grant, 'I would rather be in the thick of it than be waiting.'

'Would we not all prefer that?' Rhys responded.

He heard Grant shift his position. 'I know better than to ask for details, but how did you fare with Lady Helene?'

Rhys had been trying not to think of Helene, but his thoughts wanted only to drift to the memory of lying with her, making love to her. 'We set our differences aside. There is that, at least. It made parting…difficult. She should be leaving for England today. With her brother.'

'And?' Grant asked.

Rhys opened his eyes. 'And nothing.'

Grant regarded him. 'You made no plans?'

'We're facing a battle. That is not a time to make plans.' Rhys peered at him. 'Since when do you advocate planning a future with a woman?' He was baiting Grant who'd many times stressed how a woman cannot be trusted.

'I liked your Lady Helene,' Grant said, not rising to Rhys's bait. 'And so do you.'

What Rhys felt for Helene was more than liking her. He loved her.

So why had he not spoken even one word about the future to her?

Because he feared his luck might run out in this battle. Because now he cared enough to want to live?

They waited for over an hour at Genappe before the order came to march again. To Quatre Bras, where Wellington had told him they would meet the enemy. The sounds of guns intensified. Their drums beat a marching rhythm. They reached the top of a knoll and, for the first time, Rhys had a clear view of the enemy. His insides clenched and his muscles tensed. Fear rose, but so did excitement. There was nothing like a battle to make a man feel alive.

Thousands of French soldiers in formation filled the

field below. Strong and seasoned soldiers, if the intelligence was to be believed. Rhys smelled the odour of gunpowder and heard the pop of musket fire. They marched towards their enemy and the sound of its fire power. The men crossed a field of rye so high that Rhys would only see the tops of their shakos.

It was only three thirty.

They continued to advance, their companies moving in a line, two men deep. Cavalry could be seen on the other side of the road, riding towards the crossroads.

'Lancers!' shouted Rhys.

His men fired upon them, but General Pack, who commanded the brigade, furiously ordered the men to stop firing. 'They are ours,' Pack insisted.

General Pack was wrong. They were French lancers, as Rhys had said. The horsemen turned and galloped towards the battalion, on the attack.

There was no time for the men to form a square, so they were ordered to stand in line back to back. Rhys and the other officers rode up and down the line, reinforcing the orders and steadying the men. That he and the other officers were easy targets was not something he could even give a thought to. This was his job. This was how he got the best out of his men.

'Wait until the order to fire!' Rhys cried. 'Wait until they are close.'

The lancers were terrifying as their powerful horses galloped closer.

Finally, the colonel shouted the order, 'Present! Fire.'

Rhys repeated it, as did the other officers.

The line fired and few of the lancers escaped the volley. Horses crashed to the ground, their riders fell, injured, and were trampled by the horses behind them. One lancer escaped the carnage and rode straight for Rhys.

He lunged at Rhys with his lance, narrowly missing him. Rhys slashed at the Frenchman's back with his sword and the man fell to the ground. His horse ran on, riderless.

After the lancers passed, the regiment was able to form squares to repel the second onslaught, but many men had been lost. Rhys scanned the field, searching for Grant. He found him still mounted on his horse. Rhys caught Grant's eye. No need to speak. They were both grateful the other was alive.

The danger had not yet passed. The regiment fought on until short of ammunition. Just when Rhys feared the direst consequences, reinforcements joined their ranks and turned the advantage back to the Allies.

Musket fire continued until almost eleven that night when each side retreated to rest and tend the wounded. The fields were littered with dead and dying. Those who escaped unscathed were exhausted and thirsty. Rhys and Grant rested near the Vallée des Vaches stream, not bothering to find shelter. What was left of their men likewise spent the night wherever they happened to stand.

Helene spent the afternoon alone. Louise and Wilson left not more than an hour after Mrs Jacobs and after they were gone, Helene knew no one else, not even to speak to. She thought about Rhys all the day. Where was he? What was happening to him?

By the afternoon the distant booms of artillery fire reached Brussels. Helene left the hotel and walked the nearby streets, hoping for news. Some people had ridden out, trying to find the battle, but returned with conflicting accounts. One said the Allies had slaughtered the French, another that the Allies had been cut to pieces and were retreating in confusion. Of all Helene had read of the battles in Spain and France, she'd never read of British troops retreating in *confusion*.

She walked to the Rue de la Blanchisserie, to the Duke of Richmond's house to ask for David. Perhaps with the Duke's family as witness, he would not refuse to see her. Before she knocked at the door, she peeked in the other building where the ball had been held. Servants were busy taking down the drapery and carting away the flowers. Chairs and tables were pushed against the walls. The place where she and Rhys had danced now looked empty and forlorn.

She stepped out of that building and sounded the knocker at the front door. The butler cautiously opened it, fearing she was the French come to conquer Brussels, she supposed.

'I am Lady Helene Banes,' she told him. 'My brother is visiting Lord William. I should like to see him.'

The butler led her to a drawing room off the hall and it was not long before one of the Duke's daughters entered the room.

'Lady Helene, I am Georgiana, William's sister.' Her brown hair was still in the curls she'd worn at the ball. She had a pretty face, thin, with large, expressive brown eyes.

Helene curtsied. 'We met at the ball last night.' Georgiana sat next to the Duke of Wellington at supper.

'I remember. You wore a lovely gold dress.' The girl smiled. 'Would you care to sit? May we offer some refreshment?'

Helene had glimpsed the Duke and Duchess a few times during her London Seasons, but Lady Georgiana would have been too young for Helene to have known her then.

Helene knew she was intruding. 'I've no wish to trouble you. I need to speak to David.'

Georgiana's pretty brow furrowed. 'David is not here. He and William rode out this morning.'

'Rode out? In his evening clothes?' David had not returned to the hotel to change or, at least, the harried hall servant had not seen him.

'He borrowed clothes from William,' Georgiana explained. 'They went off to learn what they could of the battle.'

At that moment, the boom of a cannon made them both jump.

'I see.' Helene did not know whether to be furious at David or to fear for him. Foolish, reckless boy. 'If—when they return, would you please tell David I must see him?'

'I will,' she promised.

Georgiana walked Helene to the door and bid her goodbye.

The cannonade continued, distant but a reminder that David could be placing himself in danger. And what of Rhys? He and his friend Grant would be in the thick of it. Would one of those cannonballs strike him?

The streets were tense, as if the worries and fears of the people had filled the very air they all breathed. Helene had no one else to call upon. She certainly would not invade Wilson and Louise's newly found privacy, nor would she disturb Mrs Jacobs, even if she knew where the nurse lived. She walked by the lace shop, thinking she might drop in and at least browse through the lovely things. The shop was closed.

Helene laughed at herself. At Yarford she knew everyone on the estate and in the village. At the moment, here in Brussels, she knew no one.

She walked back to the hotel while the distant sounds of battle pounded at her heart.

* * *

The guns sounded all through the evening. Helene dared to walk through the Parc listening. She came upon the hotel guests she'd seen breakfasting with the two officers that morning.

She approached them. 'Pardon me. Have you heard any news of the battle?'

The one woman, who looked to be a few years older than Helene, was eager to share what she knew, which was not much.

'We heard that the French have won and are marching towards Brussels,' the woman said. 'We also heard that the Allies defeated the French, killing more men than one could imagine possible, but our friend Sir Neal Campbell heard from someone who'd been within sight of the battle, at least at five o'clock. He told us that there was fierce fighting. The infantry was facing the French without cavalry!'

The infantry. Rhys.

Helene must have looked alarmed because the woman put a hand on her arm. 'Oh, do not worry so. He said our men were fighting well.'

Helene hoped so. She said another prayer that Rhys be safe.

'I am Miss Charlotte Waldie,' the woman said. 'We only arrived in Brussels yesterday. Can you imagine such timing? Are you here alone?'

'I'm Helene Banes,' she responded. 'My brother came also, but he has gone off with his friend to find the battlefield.' She did not mention Rhys, afraid speaking his name would lead to a fit of weeping. 'So, I am alone at the moment.'

The young woman smiled. 'Then you must dine with us.'

Helene could not have been more grateful for the company. She learned Miss Waldie's companions were her brother and sister. They'd planned to travel throughout the Continent. Belgium was their first stop.

Helene left her new friends around ten, when the cannonade finally ceased. She crawled into bed, still in her dress, and hugged the pillow where Rhys had laid his head.

She woke to a rumbling outside so loud it shook the walls. She jumped from the bed and hurried to the window. Though it was dark she could see heavy military carriages speeding through the street. She peered at the mantel clock. Twelve thirty. She hurriedly tied back her hair and put on her shoes and left the room.

As she descended the stairs, she could see that many of the other guests had left their doors open, perhaps also in a rush to find out what was happening. When she reached the hall, it was in more chaos than she'd seen before.

'What is happening?' she asked one gentleman.

He answered her in French. 'The French are advancing on the city. Hear the artillery? You English should leave before it is too late.'

But the last news she'd heard was that the British had been fighting well.

Helene made her way to the door of the hotel and walked outside. All sorts of carriages and wagons were jammed up in front of the hotel and frantic people threw trunks atop them. Drivers barely waited for the occupants to take their seats before speeding off.

She spied her new friend, Charlotte, and her sister and brother. 'Are the French really approaching?'

Charlotte gave her a reassuring smile. 'All the military carriages are heading to the army, not retreating. Our friend, Major Wylie, just returned from the Place Royale where he heard officially that the French were repelled by the Allies. The city is perfectly safe, but rumours are rife.'

Helene breathed a sigh of relief.

Charlotte added, 'We are making arrangements to leave Brussels, however. There is more fighting to come. Perhaps you should do the same.'

It was what she'd promised Rhys. But she would not leave without David. He promised he would come to the hotel today.

Morning came after Helene had managed only a little sleep. She rose and straightened her dress and pinned up her hair. Eager for news, she put on her hat and gloves, wrapped her shawl around her shoulders and left her room to walk to the Place Royale. At least there she had a chance of hearing what was really happening.

She descended the stairs to find the hall was only a bit more orderly than the night before. The sense of panic was missing, but everywhere were piles of luggage and people asking how they might leave the city.

She made her way through the commotion to the door outside. The pavement was similarly filled with boxes and trunks and portmanteaux. Lines of carriages clogged the street.

Her new friend Charlotte stood nearby, saw her and called her over. 'Our coach is about to arrive, Helene. We're off to Antwerp. I am certain we could fit you in, if you would come with us.'

It would be what Rhys asked her to do.

'Thank you,' she responded. 'I wish you well, but I must wait for my brother.' Although Helene no longer believed her brother would come to her.

Charlotte's sister called to Charlotte, beckoning her to come to where a carriage was stopped down the street.

'I must go,' Charlotte said. 'Take care.'

Helene watched her climb in the carriage and stood long enough to wave to them as their carriage passed by.

The image of the officer's wife riding to battle next to her husband kept returning to Helene's mind. That was what she wished. To be with Rhys. To face what he faced. To know right this second if he was safe or…not.

But she could not let her thoughts drift on to that dreadful path.

She walked to the Place Royale, busy with people. They all seemed to be demanding information. What was being done to secure the city? Why was the City Guard not protecting Brussels? Would they merely give up the city if the French arrived?

Helene had no patience for such concerns. What she wanted to know was, had the battle cost many British lives? What was to be expected next? No. Her real questions were, was Rhys safe? Was he alive? Surely her heart would know if he were not alive.

And, of course, there was David. Had he been foolish, as she already knew? Had he at least tried to stay out of danger?

She returned to the hotel, suddenly hungry and longing for a cup of tea. As she headed to the dining room, the harried hall servant called to her, angering the several people making other demands of him. 'Lady Helene.' He raised his hand which held a piece of paper. 'A message for you.'

She hurried over and took the paper from his hand. She must remember to be generous in her vails to that poor man.

She waited until she was seated in the dining room, a pot of tea in front of her before unfolding the paper and reading its contents.

Dear Lady Helene,
I do have word of your brother. He and William re-
turned late last night but rode off again. Tomorrow
there is to be another battle, they'd heard.

I relayed your message and I am distressed to
tell you your brother said he had no intention of
meeting you at your hotel. He will do as he wishes,
he said. William is a military man and knows of
such matters.

I can only hope he can talk some sense into your
brother, who I am completely out of patience with.
With regret,
G.L.

Lady Georgiana merely confirmed Helene's fears.
David broke his word to her yet again.

The wretch.

She ate her breakfast as a plan leapt into her head. She
was done with her brother's irresponsibility. The battle
would not be far away, she'd heard. She'd go there herself, find David and bring him back. Then she could do
what Rhys asked her to do.

Leave Brussels.

Chapter Seventeen

Orders came in the morning for the regiments to withdraw to the area Rhys had heard Wellington mention the night of the ball. Waterloo. Rhys was glad to be away from Quatre Bras. It had been impossible to defend, but his men and the other men of the British regiments achieved the impossible once again.

Although at great cost. They left behind too many of their friends, dead or wounded. This was the worst of war.

As soon as his men cooked and ate their rations, Rhys informed them of the plan and praised them for a job well done the day before. They broke camp and marched. Wellington left enough men at Quatre Bras to fool the French into thinking the Allies meant to defend the crossroads again instead of moving to this more strategic location.

The men were still on the road past noon when the skies threatened.

Grant rode up to Rhys. 'Looks as though we are in for some wet weather.'

It looked as though Grant was making a very great understatement.

The length of the front that Wellington chose was about

two and a half miles long, stretching from a farm called Hougoumont to another named La Haye Sainte. Rhys's regiment was positioned behind one of the rises between the farms, closer to La Haye Sainte. Not long after their men were settled, the rains came. In the downpour, Rhys and Grant rode the entire length of the area, familiarising themselves with the terrain. Wellington had picked well. Wellington liked to protect his men on the downward slope of a hill where their numbers were hidden and they were safer from artillery fire. This terrain, though not very steep, would serve that purpose.

Evening came and the rain had been falling for some time when Rhys checked on his company again.

'Keep as dry and comfortable as you can, men,' he told them. His words were met with groans and laughter. 'I know. I know. Some reward for yesterday, is it not?' Rhys wore a cloak, but it was already soaked through.

Grant's and his batmen had found them reasonably dry accommodations in a small farm building not too far away. He left his men and wound his way through the other companies of the 44th to where some supply wagons and camp followers had settled. The wagons were covered with tarps, and the mix of hangers-on—wives and children, laundresses, prostitutes and sutlers selling their wares—were huddled under tents or other makeshift shelters. Some feet away, walking towards him, he saw a lone youth doggedly making his way past the encampment. The boy's boots stuck in the mud making progress difficult. He'd pause every so often to peruse the camp followers, then trudge onwards, head down. The boy was dressed in riding boots and a caped coat with a beaver hat on his head, too fine an outfit to be one of the hangers-on.

When the boy came close to Rhys, he raised his head and stopped abruptly.

As did Rhys.

Boy's clothes, but not a boy at all. 'Helene,' he rasped. 'What the devil—?'

Her shocked expression turned to one of relief. 'Rhys.'

He seized her arm. 'Come with me.'

He walked her away from the encampment to a place of relative privacy in the field behind them.

He turned to face her. 'What the devil are you doing here, Helene?'

Helene was too full of joy to see Rhys alive and unhurt to even form words. But she pulled herself together and shrugged out of his grip. 'I came to find David.'

'David?' His eyes flashed. 'You should be on a boat to Ramsgate by now.'

She supposed she deserved this angry tone of his, but, after the night they'd shared, could he not have been a little glad to see her?

She tried to keep her voice even. 'David did not keep his word. He did not show up at the hotel, so I came here. I thought I could find him and we could head back to Brussels and be back to the hotel before dark.'

'You thought you could find him? There are almost seventy thousand people here.'

'I thought he would be conspicuous without a uniform.' She glanced back at the encampment. 'I did not know there would be so many other people here. And he was with William Lennox. I thought that might make him easier to find.'

'With William Lennox?' Rhys scoffed. 'I credited that fellow with more sense.'

'I doubt David would listen to sense.' She wiped the raindrops from her face.

'You make no sense either, Helene.' He gestured to the sky. 'Did you really think David and Lennox would be camping out in this? If they are here, they are warm and dry in some inn nearby.'

She lifted her chin. 'Well, I did not know it would rain. Besides, I can ask for him at any inn I pass on my way back to Brussels. I am on my way back to my horse—if I can find her.'

Rhys took his hat off and rubbed a hand through his wet hair. 'You cannot get back to Brussels tonight. The roads will be clogged with supply wagons, no doubt most of which will be stuck in mud.'

What was she to do, then?

'Curse David,' Rhys grumbled.

They stared at each other while sheets of rain poured down on them. Rhys closed his eyes and when he opened them again, his expression softened.

'Come with me,' he said. 'To some place dry.' He took her arm again and practically pulled her along with him.

They walked and slid their way through a grassy field until they finally came to a small farm building, the sort that was meant to shelter field workers in bad weather or to store their equipment. Rhys opened the door for her and she went in.

It took a moment to get used to being in a dry place and for her eyes to adjust to the dim light. She saw three men. One seated, his back against the stone wall, two tending a fire in a small fireplace.

The two men at the fireplace stood at Rhys's entrance. 'Captain,' they said in unison.

The man who was seated did not greet him, but merely said, 'Who is this with you?'

Helene recognised him then. 'Hello, Grant.'

He sprang to his feet. 'Lady Helene?'

'Wha—?' one of the other men said.

'What the devil are you doing here?' Grant exclaimed.

'My exact words,' mumbled Rhys. He gestured to the other men. 'Helene, these fellows are Privates Rossiter and Smith, our batmen.' He turned to the men. 'Lady Helene and I grew up together.'

She supposed that was enough of an explanation. She nodded politely. 'How do you do.'

'Very well, miss.' Rossiter spoke as if she were in a drawing room dressed in a morning dress and not trousers and a caped coat. 'Water's boiling for tea, if you'll have some.'

'I would be very grateful,' she responded truthfully. She'd had nothing to drink in hours. 'But, please, everyone. I do not wish to be any trouble.'

'There are no chairs, Helene.' Rhys sounded apologetic.

At least he no longer sounded angry.

She tried to make light of matters. 'I'm perfectly dressed to sit on the ground.' She removed the caped coat, which was soaked through with rain and lowered herself to the dirt floor. She sat cross-legged.

Rhys sat next to her.

Grant returned to his place against the wall. 'You did not answer my question, Lady Helene. What the devil are you doing here?'

'I came to find David,' she explained. 'He promised to meet me at the hotel, but he lied. I meant to find him and make him return to Brussels with me.'

'You should have left for home without him,' Rhys said.

She turned to him. 'I could not do that.'

If she'd asked, anyone in their right mind would have told her not to come after David, but she was done with listening to what other people thought she should do— even if one of them was Rhys. She'd listened to her father, hadn't she? And that had ruined her life. Dressing as a boy, riding a horse, and finding her way to where the army was camped were all well within her capabilities, as her presence here showed. She'd misjudged the enormity of the task, though, and she had not anticipated a downpour of rain. Still, she was not sorry she'd tried.

She was only sorry she'd become a worry for Rhys. As happy and relieved as she was to see him, she knew her presence was not good for him.

Grant pointed to her and twirled his finger. 'Your clothes. Quite different than last I saw you.' Last he'd seen her was in her gold gown.

'What gave you the notion to dress in boy's clothes?' Rhys asked. 'Where did you find them anyway?'

'They're David's,' she replied. 'I took them from his room.'

Rhys eyed her suspiciously. 'I thought you said David did not come back to his room.'

'He didn't,' she agreed. 'That is how I knew his riding clothes would be there, because he would not have known to take them to the ball with him. No one knew what would happen that night. He borrowed clothes from William Lennox.'

Rhys frowned. 'How did you get in his hotel room?'

She lifted her chin. 'I picked the lock.'

Grant laughed. And sounds of smothered laughter came from the batmen who were at the other side of the room.

She gave Rhys a sly smile. 'You remember us learning how to pick locks with my hairpins, do you not?'

* * *

Rhys remembered.

They'd never done anything noteworthy with the lock-picking skill. It had been enough to know they could achieve access to wherever they were not supposed to go.

'Your tea, miss,' Smith handed her one of their tin cups. Unlike some of the officers, Grant and Rhys did not travel with complete sets of porcelain china. They'd learned in Spain to travel as lightly as possible.

Helene favoured the batman with a very grateful look. She immediately took a sip. She was very thirsty, he realised.

Rhys wanted to be furious at her. This was a very foolhardy escapade of hers. On the other hand, it all took pluck. Here was a side of Helene he'd almost forgotten when thoughts of anything else were driven from his mind the moment she'd turned into an alluring young woman. Here was the girl, his *friend*, who was up to any dare, any adventure. He had not realised how much he'd missed her.

But how the devil was he to keep her safe?

He shook his head at her. 'What made you think coming to where the army is preparing for battle was a good idea?'

'I never meant to cause you trouble, Rhys.' She sipped more tea. 'I meant only to find David and return to Brussels.'

'How could it be safer for you, a woman, to come here than it could be for your brother?' he pressed.

She countered, 'You'd said that the battle was dangerous. I meant us to leave before the battle.'

'Foolish of you, Helene.' Rhys's anger flared. 'Do you not know men before or after a battle can be very dangerous?' He had seen it too many times.

'That is why I am in disguise,' she explained.

'How did you get here?' Grant broke in. Trying to keep the peace, no doubt.

'I hired a horse,' she responded. 'And I followed some supply wagons.'

'Resourceful.' Grant nodded approvingly.

She had been resourceful. And daring. But the truth was he wanted her as far away as possible. British soldiers could be danger enough, but a French soldier coming upon an Englishwoman? Rhys knew what could happen. He wanted Helene safe and there was little he could do about it now. He could not even take her to an inn. Any inn, any building, would be packed with men trying to stay out of the rain. Men drinking. Men thinking this might be their last night alive.

As if to taunt him, a gush of water fell from the roof, splattering on the floor right next to her. She moved over as if it were nothing.

'Are you hungry, miss?' Rossiter called over. 'We have some bread and cheese.'

She swivelled around to face him. 'I would be very grateful for anything, Rossiter. I have not eaten since breakfast.'

'You might as well cook our beef, too,' Rhys said. 'While we still have dry wood.'

The roof was now leaking from many places. Smith found a bucket to place under the worst leak, but the building did not have enough containers to catch every drip.

The batmen prepared a simple meal and none of them mentioned to Helene that they were sharing their limited rations with her. After dinner, Rossiter and Smith pulled out a square piece of leather with concentric squares drawn on it and used it and some black and white game pieces made of wood to play Three Men's Morris.

Grant took out a bottle of brandy he'd somehow preserved and poured some for Rhys and himself. He lifted the bottle. 'Would you like some, Lady Helene?'

She offered her tin cup and the three sat together, sipping their brandy.

'Will you tell me of the battle yesterday?' she asked.

Rhys exchanged a glance with Grant. They both knew there were parts not to be spoken of.

Finally, Rhys spoke. 'It was hard fighting. The 44th lost four men and another fifty or so wounded. The French did not take the crossroads, though, so the objective was achieved.'

'I passed carts of wounded men when I rode here,' she said. 'Lots of them.'

Rhys took a sip of his brandy. 'It will be worse tomorrow.' He instantly regretted saying that to her. Why worry her more than he had already? 'But you will leave before it starts, Helene.'

She nodded sadly. 'I know I won't find David now.'

Grant gestured to their leaking roof. 'We won't have a battle unless this rain stops.'

'Those poor men outside,' Helene murmured.

Rhys liked that she thought of the men. Like always, the common soldier endured the worst.

'We'll try to stay as dry as possible tonight,' Rhys said.

'You should take off your coats and put them close to the fire to dry,' she said. 'Do not keep them on because of me.'

Rhys suspected they had been doing that very thing.

He must have looked sceptical, because she added, 'Come now, Rhys. When we were children, we stripped down to our underclothes to swim in the lake. You know I am not missish.'

Grant was first to stand and remove his coat. 'I do

not need a second invitation.' He took off his boots and stockings, as well.

Helene removed her coat and boots, and Rhys followed. He and Grant carried the clothes to the fireplace, interrupting Rossiter and Smith's game and their mugs of gin. 'You, too, men,' he said. 'Maybe you can devise some way to take best advantage of the fire.'

'I have just the thing.' Smith rose to his feet.

The privates drove spikes into the stone walls and strung a rope they'd packed from one side of the room to the other. When the clothes were hung on it, it also created a sort of barrier.

Grant picked up his blanket. 'I'm getting closer to the fire.' He walked through the clothes to the other side with Rossiter and Smith.

Helene remained seated on the ground. Rhys felt her eyes follow him as he gathered his blankets. He found a dry spot in the dark corner that afforded as much privacy as possible. He laid out one blanket on the dirt floor.

'Come here, Helene,' he said softly.

She rose and walked over to him.

'Best to get as much sleep as you can,' he murmured.

She stood close and suddenly he did not care if he was angry at her, did not care if she'd been foolhardy, all he cared about was that she was standing near. Without speaking, he wrapped his arms around her and held her close. She melted against him.

He lowered his head to be close to her ear. 'I thought I would never hold you again.'

She clasped him even tighter. 'I never expected to see you—' Her voice broke off.

He turned her face to his and he lowered his lips to hers. The memory of lying with her the night before came rushing back and he was consumed with a desire he could not slake.

No matter. No matter. He would be content that she was in his arms, that he would lie next to her for another night.

He eased her to the blanket that offered little warmth against the dirt floor. With any luck the ground beneath them would stay dry. That must be enough for this night. She nestled next to him and he covered them both with his second blanket.

She moved so that her lips were next to his ear. 'I wish this were last night.'

He did, as well, with every fibre of his being, but he feared his desire had dishonoured her. 'I am not sure—' he said.

She put her fingers on his lips. 'Do not tell me you regret last night. I will be furious with you if you do. I do not regret it. No—no matter what happens, I will never regret making love with you.'

He took her hand in his and kissed her fingers. 'I do not regret it.'

She nestled against him again. 'Good.'

He held her, laying his cheek against her soft hair. 'I meant what I said to you, Helene. I never stopped loving you.'

'Oh, Rhys.' She sighed. 'After I…rejected you, it took me very little time to realise that I'd made the wrong decision. I yearned to be with you.' She separated the slit in his shirt to place a kiss on his bare chest.

It was too late. The army was too much a part of him now. He'd thrived on the hardship that had tested his strength and resolve, but, no matter how scrappy Helene might be at the moment, she belonged in the world of gold gowns and glittering balls.

'I—I cannot promise—' he said.

She cut him off. 'I am asking nothing of you, Rhys.' She released a long breath. 'Except to live. You must live.'

Even that he could not promise.

Chapter Eighteen

Rhys heard stirring in the shack. He opened his eyes and spied daylight coming through cracks in the roof. He glanced over at Helene. Her hair had come loose during the night and curled around her shoulders. Her lips were slightly parted and her face was tranquil. She looked very much like that little girl who'd been his constant companion in his childhood. He eased himself away from her and rose, tucking the blanket around her.

He padded across the still damp floor, through the barrier of drying clothes. Rossiter and Smith were up and already had water on to boil. Grant sat up and rubbed his hair. None of them spoke.

Rhys felt his coat, which was still damp, but, at least not quite as bad as the night before. Rossiter held up his razor and Rhys walked over to shave at the small basin and mirror the private had rigged up. Rhys wiped his face after. He donned his coat, stockings and boots.

'I'm going out,' Rhys said. 'See what I can discover.'

As he headed towards the door, Helene stirred. 'Rhys?'

'Right here.' He walked over to her.

She sat up. 'What is that rumbling sound?'

Rhys had to stop to think about what she was hearing.

'Oh. That's the sound of the voices of seventy thousand men waking up.'

Her jaw dropped.

He leaned down and brushed the hair away from her face. 'I was about to go outside. Do you want to come with me?'

'Yes. Give me a moment.' She rose and quickly put on her stockings, boots and coat. She pinned her hair up on top of her head and placed her beaver hat over it.

'Good God, you look just like a boy.' Grant spoke as he emerged through the drying clothes. 'A very pretty boy, that is.'

She smiled. 'When we were young, I used to wish I was a boy.'

Grant grinned. 'I rather suspect Rhys is now glad you are not.'

Rhys opened the door. 'We'll be back. I just want to see what is going on.'

'Do not miss breakfast,' Smith called to him. 'We'll have some ham. And there's bread, as well.'

Rhys held the door for Helene to go out first, before he stepped outside. The sky was clear and the air smelled of the rye in the nearby fields, of wet grass, mud, and camp-fires. They walked to a hill and climbed to the top so they could see the regiments splayed out across the fields.

'What will happen today, Rhys?' Helene asked.

He responded. 'Napoleon must first wait for the ground to dry so he can move his artillery. He'll pound us with cannon fire first.' He pointed to La Haye Sainte at one end and Hougoumont at the other end. 'He'll try to take those farms, but Wellington will have us defend them to keep open the roads passing by them.'

'What about your regiment?' she asked.

He glanced down to where he knew his men had

camped for the night. He could see them stirring, getting ready for what lay ahead. 'Eventually the French will attack.' He would not tell her the French infantry far outnumbered the Allies, nor that many of the Allied regiments were filled with new and untested men, some who fled in panic at Quatre Bras. 'The British infantry are the finest in the world,' he assured her instead. 'We will either defeat them or we will hold them until the Prussians arrive to assist us.'

She turned away, so he was unable to see her reaction to his answer.

Finally, she spoke. 'Thank you for telling me.'

Suddenly the sound of musket fire filled the valley. She swivelled around. 'Where is that coming from? Has the attack started?'

'The men are merely clearing their muskets,' he told her.

He scanned the area again. Everything looked leisurely and unremarkable. Where the army had not trampled on it, the rye in the fields swayed in the breeze beneath a clear blue sky dotted with white clouds. An idyllic day.

He turned away from the scene and faced Helene. 'We should go back. Breakfast will be ready.'

He walked next to her, wanting to hold her hand or drape his arm over her shoulder, but he could not afford any hint that she was not the boy she was dressed up to be. Soon he would have to send her on her way. With luck she could pass unnoticed on the road back to Brussels.

They reached the farm building where Rossiter and Smith had breakfast ready, ham and bread and cheese and glasses of wine. She laughed when the bottle of wine was produced. When they finished, Rossiter helped Rhys put on his officer's sash, his sword and two pistols. Helene never took her eyes off him.

He met her gaze. 'Time to go.'

* * *

'I'm ready.' Helene smiled.

Rhys looked magnificent in his full uniform, but the sword and pistols reminded Helene of what he would be facing this day. She felt like pulling her hair and wailing out of fear that he might be hurt or killed. But she'd already caused him too much worry by being here. She refused to put any more on his plate. She'd merely be strong and assure him she would do precisely what he'd told her to do.

Leave.

Leave without knowing if he lived or died.

Rhys picked up his saddle while she said goodbye to Rossiter and Smith and thanked them for their kindness to her. She gave Grant a big hug goodbye, one that almost made tears fall. He, too, could die.

They all could die.

She scolded herself. How dare she assume these fine, strong, experienced soldiers would not emerge victorious? They'd survived the Peninsula, after all.

So she lifted her head and walked out of the farm building exuding confidence in them.

'I'll walk with you a little way,' Rhys told her. 'But I need to get my horse and join my company to await orders.'

'Why don't I walk with you to where your horse is stabled, then I will be on my way,' she suggested, wanting to stay with him until the last possible moment.

He agreed and led her to his horse, one of the few that had shelter during the rainy night. Although the groom was nowhere in sight, it was clear Rhys's horse had been fed and watered. Helene stood at the horse's head and stroked its neck while Rhys put on the saddle and bridle.

The smell of hay and horse brought back memories. 'Remember when we were finally old enough to ride my father's horses wherever we wished?' she asked Rhys.

He smiled at her. 'Most of my experience on horseback came from those days.' His father never had enough to afford keeping a horse for Rhys to ride.

She smiled back. 'We had many fine days.'

Her heart was breaking. Would those memories be all that they had?

He led the horse to the door of the stable.

She looked up at him. 'It is time, isn't it?'

He nodded.

She reached up and touched his face. 'You will make your country proud today.'

He enfolded her in his arms and held her so tight she could hardly take a breath. 'Go back to Brussels. Promise me.' His voice was urgent. 'I love you, Helene. You must stay safe.'

She pulled away enough to hold his face in her hands and make him look into her eyes. 'I will. I love you, too, but you must not worry about me. Do not give me another thought. I will be back in Brussels before noon.'

He leaned down and kissed her. As she tasted his lips, now so achingly familiar, she thought of the soldier she'd seen saying goodbye to his wife and baby. She knew that woman's heart had been breaking like hers broke now.

He abruptly pulled away and led his bay mare outside and mounted the horse. Helene reached up to grasp his hand one last time.

'Go with my love,' she said in a brave voice.

He merely nodded. He turned his horse and rode away.

Helene watched until he disappeared from sight. 'God, keep him safe,' she whispered. 'God, let him live.'

* * *

Rhys rode along the road to the ridge when he heard several horses behind him moving at a faster pace. He pulled his horse to the side of the road and waited for the riders to pass.

He saw instantly that it was the Duke of Wellington leading the cavalcade on his chestnut horse. He wore his typical battle wear—a dark blue coat, white neckcloth, white buckskin breeches, Hessian boots, and a cocked hat that further distinguished him from anyone else on the battlefield. In his entourage were his aides-de-camp, his generals, the Prince of Orange and other dignitaries, but it was not these important men that caught Rhys's eye.

At Wellington's side was his friend, the Duke of Richmond, who was not with the army, and with the Duke of Richmond was his son, William Lennox, eyepatch and all.

And David.

In such exalted company, Helene had never had a chance of finding David. Think how puffed up David must be at such an honour to ride with the Duke of Wellington. Rhys hoped the Duke of Richmond and the others who did not belong with the army would have the sense to observe the battle from a very safe distance. And he hoped David would have the sense to remain with them.

He waited for them all to pass. The last man in the group Rhys recognised as Quartermaster-General Sir William De Lancey. De Lancey glanced his way and acknowledged Rhys with a nod. Rhys followed behind them, but they quickly pulled ahead. It was time he joined his company. Wellington's arrival meant that orders would soon reach them.

As Rhys rode on, he glanced over towards La Belle Alliance. On the crest of the ridge he could just make out

lines of men. The French army. Rhys was glad Helene
would be well on her way to Brussels by now.

Suddenly a man on a white horse rode across the far
crest.

Napoleon.

Helene searched for her horse for more than two hours.
The mare had been moved from where she'd left it in the
care of a groom and he did not know where it wound up.
She'd searched everywhere horses had been kept, to no
avail. The day had become beastly hot and she wound
up carrying the caped coat and wishing she could just
leave it somewhere.

She was far from the road to Brussels, but she started
walking back to it. She was determined to keep her promise to Rhys so she'd have to return to Brussels on foot.
At least she was far behind the Allied lines. She could
not see the thousands of soldiers, but there were plenty
of people rushing here and there. Farriers shoeing horses,
servants tending to officers, women caring for children.

She made her way to a barn on one side of the battlefield but there were no horses there except the ones
hitched to a wagon full of crates. A man was moving the
crates from the wagon into the barn.

He beaconed her over. 'You! Lad! Come here a moment.'

She obeyed. 'Yes, sir?' She lowered her voice.

'Help me move these crates off the wagon.' He picked
up one and handed it to her before she had an opportunity
to refuse. She had just enough time to drop the coat she
held to take the crate into her arms. He picked up another
one and led her to corner of the barn. Inside were several
long tables. He directed her to place the crate atop others stacked in the corner. It was not a difficult task; the

crates were not too heavy, so she continued to help him until they'd moved them all inside the shelter.

'What is in these?' she asked.

'Lint, surgeon's tow, sponges, linen for bandages,' he responded. 'Thread, needles, plaster. You know. What we need for the wounded.'

For the wounded? There were so many boxes.

She turned to go.

'Wait,' the man said. 'Here's another wagon.'

Another wagon pulled up, this time carrying blankets and a large wooden chest. Helene helped him empty that wagon and its driver moved it quickly out of the way.

Helene was damp with perspiration. She wiped her face with her sleeve.

The man handed her a canteen. 'Have some water.'

She accepted it gratefully and drank her fill while he opened the chest and lifted out knives, scalpels and saws with plenty of spare blades. She finally understood. He was the surgeon.

She handed the canteen back to him. 'I should be going,' she said.

'Where to?' he asked.

'Back to Brussels.' She'd been delayed long enough.

'Brussels?' His brows rose. 'How will you get there? It's easily twelve miles.'

She shrugged. 'Walk, I suppose.'

'No.' He shook his head. 'Stay. Help me. My men are not here yet and I need help. If you stay, I'll let you ride to Brussels with the first wagon of wounded.'

She'd promised Rhys, though. The sun was high in the sky. Nearly noon, she guessed. She should be in Brussels.

A loud boom sounded. Helene jumped.

Cannon fire.

'It's started,' the surgeon said. 'Napoleon fired the first shot.'

In no time the boom was repeated over and over as more cannon shot their balls towards the waiting Allies, and the Allied guns returned fire.

Drums pounded. Trumpets blared. Shouts of *'Vive l'Empereur!'* could be heard even from this distance. It was terrifying and Helene froze, not knowing what to do.

The man's helpers arrived, but so did wounded soldiers, carried in by men in their regiment's band. One with his arm torn off. Another bleeding from his abdomen. Another dragging a shattered foot. The surgeon flew into action, barking orders to his helpers and to her.

'Do what you can to stop the bleeding,' he yelled. 'Send me the worst ones first.'

Helene shut off the part of her that wanted to weep for the men and did as he asked. As more wounded men poured in, she forgot about leaving for Brussels. She cut off trouser legs or removed coats so she could bind up bleeding wounds. She gave men sips of water or spirits while the worst of them screamed in pain. She watched the surgeon cut off limbs and throw them into a pile.

The cannonade continued relentlessly for at least an hour then it suddenly stopped. In its place came a distinctive drumbeat.

'What is happening now?' she asked.

'Infantry attack,' replied one of the injured men. 'That's the *pas de charge.* Supposed to scare us. Takes more than that—' He coughed up blood.

Would this infantry attack Rhys's regiment? Helene wondered. Where was Rhys now? What was happening to him?

She swallowed a sob. She could not think about Rhys right now. The wounded men needed her.

* * *

Rhys's regiment was held in reserve so he was free to ride through the battlefield, watching the attacks, learning what he could about the strengths and weaknesses of the French. He watched the French infantry march towards the Allied line in one massive column of men twenty-four ranks deep and one hundred and fifty wide. They were meant to frighten and they did indeed look like a formidable sight, but Rhys knew the formation's vulnerability. Hit the front ranks with a cannonball and the ball was likely to cut through the rest, like a game of skittles. The Allied guns were pouring shot into the valley and the approaching column.

It was all too much for a brigade of Belgian soldiers. They turned and ran, disappearing into the forest behind the ridge.

While rifles shot at the column from the hedges, Picton's Scottish infantry rose up at just the right moment, surprising the column with round after round of musket fire. A moment later a musket ball pierced Picton's temple. Picton fell against his horse, dead instantly.

But soon after the imposing French column had endured enough of cannon, musket and rifle fire. The French soldiers broke and ran. Rhys cheered when he saw the British cavalry chase them, a perfect rout.

He raised himself in his saddle as he saw a rider charging with the cavalry.

It was David.

David revelled in riding with the Duke of Wellington alongside the Duke of Richmond and William. After Wellington parted with them, David and William stayed with William's father to explore the whole of the battlefield. This was ten times better than watching from some distant hill, which was the best David had hoped for. He was right in the thick of things.

His heart soared when the cavalry began their charge. Two thousand horsemen. What a magnificent sight. The Guards regiments, the Royal dragoons, Scots Greys and Inniskilling dragoons charged towards the scattering French infantry. This was glory! This was not to be missed! David spurred his horse to join the charge.

William shouted at him. 'Come back! Come back!'

David did not heed him.

Nothing could be more exhilarating than galloping along with these flamboyantly uniformed cavalrymen. David relished the sight of the panicking Frenchmen— until he saw some beg for their lives only to be thrust through by a sabre. The dragoons at first looked dashing with their sabres shining under the bright sun, but those sabres drew blood and the French soldiers screamed in agony as they died.

David rode so far with the cavalry that he reached the enemy's guns, but by this time he wanted to go back. He did not wish to see the gunners being slaughtered. Or to see the grins on the faces of some of the cavalrymen caught up in blood lust. He wanted to be anywhere but where he was.

At last the horses began to tire and the cavalry turned back. David turned back with them.

Then came a terrifying sight. French cuirassiers and lancers, thousands of them, with their sparkling breastplates and brass helmets, galloping straight for them. In seconds they surrounded David and the British cavalry who were desperately trying to fight them off. Trembling with fear, David clung to his horse's neck and wailed in fear.

A cuirassier charged up to him, his eyes red and

bugged, his yellow teeth bared. The Frenchman raised his sword. David screamed as the sword came down on him, knocking him from his horse. He landed on the ground and rolled as horse's hooves trampled over him.

Pain enveloped him. And then everything went black.

Chapter Nineteen

Rhys witnessed the horror of the French cavalry decimating the British Guards and dragoons who were too caught up in their moment of success to hear the call to retreat. He had to turn away and ride back to his regiment knowing David was among them. He ought to have impressed even stronger on that foolish boy that the battle was no place for him. His stomach clenched. Would he have to deliver the news to Helene that her brother lost his life? Odds were not great for him to have survived.

By the time he reached his company, the artillery barrage resumed and his men all lay flat on the ground so they were not visible to the French observers on the opposite ridge. His men had not been involved in the first infantry attack, but more was coming. The air filled with smoke from the guns, the cries of the wounded and the scent of powder.

His men looked at him with impatience, as occasional cannonballs rolled and bounced into their ranks killing or maiming at random and they were ordered to do nothing to retaliate.

'Stay firm,' Rhys told them. 'Your time will come.'

It came sooner than he thought and in a manner he

could only describe as bizarre. Instead of an infantry attack, thousands of French cavalry appeared over the ridge. The Allied infantry immediately formed square, a formation largely impenetrable by cavalry. The front line of men crouched on to their knees and leaned their muskets, with bayonets attached, out. The second line and third lines fired volleys of musket balls. Cavalry horses would not charge the bayonets and the musket fire felled many a cavalry man. If any were able to fire into the square, the injured or dead were pulled inside and the ranks closed up the spot.

The cavalry charged again and again. Rhys, in the middle of the square, yelled his orders, 'Present! Fire! Close ranks!' until his voice was hoarse. When he could spare a second, he glanced over at Grant's company and was reassured to see his friend still mounted on his horse, barking the same orders.

The cavalry charges eventually ceased, and some of his men sank down into what had once been a field of rye to rest. Others carried the dead and wounded to the rear. Rhys figured it to be late afternoon, but time seemed to move differently in a battle. He took the chance to drink some water. Grant rode over and Rhys shared his canteen with him.

'Do you know the time?' Rhys asked.

Grant took his timepiece from a pocket. 'Five.' He put it back. 'How did you fare?'

Rhys rubbed his sweating face with his sleeve. 'Not too bad from the cavalry. The artillery weakened us, though.'

Grant nodded. 'Never took the French to be such fools. Using cavalry against squares.'

The ground was littered with the French casualties.

The French artillery resumed and Grant rode back to his company.

Rhys's men were hot and tired and the cavalry attack had shaken them.

'You got more of them than they got of us,' Rhys told the men. 'Stay firm. We'll get through this.'

But the cannon fire kept picking them off, weakening their numbers.

A second attack from the French infantry, though completely repulsed, weakened them further. The day was advancing and it looked to Rhys as though the Prussians were not going to come to their aid.

But finally word came that the Prussians were spotted. The tide of the battle turned and the men rallied. When Napoleon released his Imperial Guards, his best, most seasoned soldiers, the British regiments were more than ready for them. They cheered when these elite troops broke ranks and ran.

It was the end, Rhys realised. The Allies had won.

For Helene time passed not with minutes or hours, but with the numbers of wounded. As more men appeared needing help, more help also arrived. Other women came to render assistance and soldiers with relatively minor wounds. Helene's day was a blur of bandaging wounds, providing drink, holding the hands of the dying.

The surgeon—she still did not know his name—sawed off limb after limb, dug out countless musket balls, sewed up many wounds. The limbs piled up as did the number of dead. Blood pooled at their feet and Helene's boots were soaked through. She did what needed to be done, though, not allowing herself to think about it, or, God knew, not allowing herself any emotions. Especially picturing Rhys as one of the countless wounded. Or piled up dead. It was like being caught in a nightmare.

She'd long ago lost track of her brother's caped coat, and she could not remember when her hat had fallen to the ground and rolled away. She had not bothered to chase after it. Eventually her hair came loose of its pins. She tried to pin it back up, but only succeeded in lacing it with blood. She tried not to let her exhaustion stop her from tending to the endless numbers of wounded men. She simply did what was necessary.

The sun dipped lower in the sky, providing some relief from the heat, but the sounds of the battle continued, mingling with the cries and moans of the wounded. All of a sudden, a new sound reached her ears. She and everyone else looked up from what they were doing.

Cheers. Loud cheers. Too close to be the enemy. The cheers came from the Allies.

One of the wounded men tried to sit up. 'That's the end of it!' he cried. 'He's done it. Wellington's beat Napoleon!'

That did not stop the wounded from appearing, so Helene continued to work, until she thought she could not stay on her feet another minute. She took a small break to lean her weary muscles against the barn wall. The surgeon walked past her and turned back to give her a puzzled look.

He walked over to her. 'So, you are not a boy.'

She waved a hand. 'It is too much to explain.'

He put his blood-caked hand on her shoulder. 'You've done enough. Find the next wagon to Brussels and be on it. And know that you saved lives today.'

He walked briskly away. To lob off more arms and legs, she supposed.

She looked down on the ground and would have laughed if she'd been able. There was David's caped coat lying against the barn wall. She picked it up and carried it over to a wounded man whose uniform had been torn to pieces. She laid the coat over him.

Nearby men were being lifted into a wagon, but she had no energy to climb on it. She was not certain she could bear to see another bleeding wound, another shattered bone. Instead she decided to return to the farm building where she, Rhys, Grant and their batmen had spent the night. She did not suppose Rhys and the others would return there. She did not know what happened after a battle, but she knew it was shelter and all she wished was to lie down and sleep.

The sky was still light enough that she easily found the farm building, after walking past soldiers here and there, just sitting in the grass, too weary to pay her any mind. When she neared the building, she was as grateful as if she'd been on the threshold of Carlton House, the Prince Regent's London palace.

The door opened and Rhys stepped outside. He was in shirtsleeves and shook out his uniform coat. He turned as she approached and watched her as if witnessing an apparition.

'Rhys.' Her voice was no more than a whisper. When she came close enough, she reached out to touch him. 'Are you alive? Are you really alive?'

Her whole body began to shake and the day's worth of unshed tears burst from her. He took her in his arms and held her while she sobbed. She cried in relief and gratitude. He was alive! She cried for all the men who died and all who were wounded and maimed whose lives would never be the same again. She cried for herself, for all that she'd seen and heard that day that she would never be able to forget.

* * *

Rhys held her close while her body shook with sobs. 'Helene. Helene.'

He'd not entirely believed this was Helene in his arms. What had happened to her? She was covered in blood.

He looked down on her. 'Are you injured?'

She shook her head. 'Just. Tired.'

He wanted to ask why she was covered in blood, why was she not safely in Brussels, but he'd wait. She was in no condition to explain anything now.

He lifted her in his arms and carried her inside.

Grant immediately stood. 'What?'

'It's Helene.' Rhys called to the batmen, 'Bring her something to drink.'

Rossiter brought some water. Smith laid a blanket on the floor for her. Rhys lowered her to it. She sat and drank a whole tin cup of water.

She looked up at Rhys. 'S-sorry, Rhys. T-tried to leave. C-couldn't find my horse. The—the surgeon needed help...'

'Surgeon?' The blood now made sense.

Even her boots were stained with blood. He pulled them off her feet. Her stockings were red, too. Smith brought over a basin and rag. Rhys rinsed off her face and arms and hands. She let him minister to her as if she were a child's doll. She needed clean clothes to wear. Grant brought a clean shirt. That would have to do. The other men gave them privacy as Rhys peeled off her bloody clothes and dressed her in the clean shirt, which reached her knees. He handed the bloody clothes to Smith.

'I'll clean them,' Smith said.

Helene, no longer racked with weeping, lay down on the blanket. 'Just want to sleep now,' she murmured, but she reached for Rhys's hand. 'You are alive. You all are alive.' She closed her eyes.

Rhys placed his cloak, all folded up and now dry, under her head as a pillow. The rain seemed so long ago. He covered her with another blanket. She fell asleep instantly.

'Does she know about her brother?' Grant asked.

'I doubt it.' Rhys looked down at her. 'I'll have to tell her tomorrow.'

The next morning Helene woke to the scent of ham frying in a pan and tea steeping. For a moment she thought she was back at Yarford House and that her maid had brought breakfast to her room. Then her aching muscles felt the cold hard ground beneath her. She sat up.

It took another moment to realise she was in the farm building. She brushed a hand through her hair, but her fingers caught in its tangles and the memory of the day before came rushing back.

She gasped and buried her head in her hands.

Suddenly someone was next to her. She looked up. Rhys.

He lowered himself to the floor and stroked her face. 'You are awake. We have breakfast for you.'

She reached for an embrace. 'Rhys,' she murmured. 'You did not die. So many others…'

He held her. 'We are all alive and unhurt. Grant and Rossiter and Smith. We are all here.'

'Morning, miss!' Rossiter called.

The three men came into her view, all smiling.

'Good morning, Lady Helene,' Grant said.

She stood and hugged each of them. 'I am so glad to see you. So glad to see you.'

While tending the wounded, hearing their screams, holding hands of the dying, she'd not allowed herself to think of Rhys or these other dear men, but, now, seeing them, touching them, she knew the fear had been there all along. The fear of death.

'Are you ready for some breakfast, miss?' Smith grinned at her.

She returned his smile. 'I am famished!'

'Stay right as you are.' Smith gestured for her to sit. 'Rossiter and I will bring it to you.'

Rhys and Grant sat with her as the batmen readied their plates and brought tea.

She gazed at the tin cup before she took a sip, remembering it from before the battle, as if it were some relic from a distant time. She also remembered she'd broken her promise to Rhys.

She lifted her gaze to him. 'I tried to keep my promise to you. I tried to leave, but my horse disappeared—'

He lifted a hand. 'You told us last night.'

'Did I?' She blinked. 'I don't remember. I don't remember much after walking away from the...' She did not know what to call it. The place of death and dying?

'You were exhausted,' Rhys said.

'Asleep before your head hit the pillow,' Grant added, taking the plate Rossiter handed to him and placing it in front of her. 'How the devil did you get roped into helping with the wounded?'

She shrugged and took another sip of tea. 'The surgeon asked me. The wounded kept coming so I stayed.'

She caught Rhys's eye, seeing sympathy and pain there. She did not want them to feel sorry for her, though.

She straightened. 'I was glad to stay. There were others helping, but we were all needed.'

Rhys and Grant knew very well what Helene had endured. A surgeon's table, a makeshift hospital, endless numbers of wounded men with horrific wounds. Blood everywhere. Perhaps some day Helene would tell him of it, describe the pain and gore, and purge it from her memory.

Although he did not forget all he'd seen these last five years, in battle after battle.

Her brow furrowed and her voice shook. 'I never saw David. I hope he—' She didn't finish.

Rhys exchanged a glance with Grant. He looked down at his food, then raised his head and turned to Helene. 'I saw David.'

Her face brightened. 'You did?' Then worry returned. 'Where?'

'He was with the Duke of Richmond and his son.'

She let out a relieved breath.

'But—' How to tell her? '—but he got caught up in the cavalry charge and rode with them. They—they were attacked by French cavalry. I did not see David return.'

She paled and her voice shook. 'Then he could be dead?'

'Or wounded,' Grant said.

'He rode in a cavalry charge?' she asked in disbelief.

'He got caught up in the excitement.' It was the only explanation Rhys could think of.

She glanced away. 'Why would he do such a foolish thing?'

If only David had heeded Rhys's warnings.

She started to rise. 'I have to find him. 'How can I find him?'

Rhys leaned towards her and clasped her hand. 'You cannot find him. There are thousands still lying in the fields. It would be impossible.'

'I can't leave him there.' She stood. 'I must at least try to find him.'

Rhys jumped to his feet, as well. He held her by her

shoulders. 'You cannot go on to the battlefield. I cannot allow it.'

Her eyes flared in defiance. 'You cannot stop me! I am finished being told what I can and cannot do!'

Grant stood, as well. 'Lady Helene, the battlefield will be full of horrors. There are things you should not see—'

She cut him off. 'I have already seen countless things I should not have seen.' She tried to pull away.

Rhys continued to hold her. 'He might not be there. He might be among the wounded. He might even have come through unscathed. He could be anywhere. It is more important we get you back to Brussels.'

She wrenched away. 'I am going to look for him here. I'm not leaving until I have at least tried.'

Rhys wanted to argue with her, wanted to insist she do as he said, but was not he the one who'd wished she'd followed her heart instead of listening to her father?

No soldier wanted to return to the battlefield the day after a battle. It was a nightmare of a place, showing the true cost of men fighting over such things as land or power. The thought of her stepping into that scene made his stomach roil.

He tapped his fingers against his leg, not wanting to say what he was about to say. 'Very well, Helene. But I will search for David on the battlefield. I saw where he rode. I have the best chance of finding him.'

She straightened again. 'I will go with you.'

'No,' Grant chimed in. 'I will go with Rhys. You can, if you wish, look among the wounded who have not yet been transported. He might be among them.'

Neither Rhys nor Grant really believed that, though. They knew the cost of that cavalry charge.

'What say Smith and I help the lady look among the wounded?' Rossiter spoke up.

It was settled.

Rhys and Grant would return to the battlefield.

Rhys and Grant walked towards the fields where the battle had taken place. What they saw before them was worse than their worst imaginings. The field was covered with the bodies of men and horses. The men were stripped naked, most of them, the plunderers already having swept through, taking whatever could be of value. Even the corpses' teeth. Without clothing to distinguish one man from another, the task of finding David's body was made even more difficult.

Their progress through the part of the battlefield where the cavalry charge took place was slowed, because they discovered wounded men still lying on the field. They had to carry these wounded back to others who'd see to their care. Rhys and Grant persisted, however, not talking much, trying not to retch at the stench of sun beating down on the carnage. They managed to carry twenty men off the battlefield.

Finally they pushed to the place where Rhys thought the cuirassiers and lancers had met the British cavalry. They came upon a dying horse and put it swiftly out of its misery.

Walking a little further, Rhys stopped. 'Did you hear something?'

Grant listened. 'Whimpering?'

'Yes.' Rhys started forward again. 'That's what I thought, too.'

They walked around a pile of corpses lying next to a bush and found the source of the sound. A thin, naked figure sat, his back to them, crying like a baby.

Rhys approached the fellow whose face was black with

bruises. His cheeks were swollen and there was a cut above his eyebrow, but Rhys recognised him.

'David?'

David looked up at him, but without any sign of recognition. 'They took my clothes! And my leg hurts!'

There was a long, deep gash in David's leg, and his body was covered with bruises.

Grant reached Rhys's side. 'Good God.'

Rhys leaned closer to David. 'Do you see who I am? It is Rhys.'

'Oh, Rhys!' Tears rolled down David's cheeks. 'Look what they did to me!' He glanced around. 'I lost the Duke's horse.'

Rhys filled with pity for him. 'We're going to get you out of here.'

David looked up at him with a helpless expression. 'I cannot walk.'

'We'll carry you out, you dolt.' Grant's nerves were obviously frayed. He turned to Rhys. 'I cannot believe it. We found him.'

'Alive.' Rhys had had no hope at all of even finding David's body. He'd agreed to this search only to stop Helene from stepping foot into this nightmare. 'Let's get out of here.'

Rhys slung David over his shoulder like he had that night in Brussels when he'd come face to face with Helene.

David cried out, 'My leg!'

'We'll get you to the surgeons,' Rhys told him.

And to your sister.

Rhys and Grant found Helene at one of the field hospitals. She was talking to a man Rhys guessed was the surgeon because he wore an apron soaked in blood. Rossiter and Smith stood nearby chatting with some soldiers from the 28th.

'Rhys!' She rushed up to him as soon as she saw him. Her eyes widened when she realised he carried a naked man over his shoulder.

'Is it?' she said. 'Is he alive?'

The surgeon appeared. 'Here. Put him on a table.'

'It is David,' Rhys turned to answer her as he carried David to the table. 'He is alive.'

Grant spoke to the surgeon. 'He was conscious until a few minutes ago. I think he passed out because of pain to his leg.'

Helene came up to the table. She cradled David's head. 'Oh, David. Look at you.'

His eyes fluttered open for a second.

The surgeon, examining the gash in David's leg, beckoned some of his assistants. 'We need to clean this out and stitch it up.' He looked up at Helene. 'Your brother?'

'Yes.' She inclined her head towards Rhys and Grant. 'These are my…friends. Captains Landon and Grantwell.' She looked again towards the surgeon. 'This is Mr Goode, the surgeon I helped yesterday.'

'Captains.' Mr Goode nodded. 'You know you pulled off a miracle, finding him.' He didn't have to add *finding him alive*.

Rhys nodded to the surgeon. 'If he can travel, I'd like to take them both back to Brussels today.'

'We've been sending worse on to Brussels,' Mr Goode said.

Rhys turned to Helene. 'We have our horses. We'll ride you back today.'

She walked over to him and wrapped her arms around his neck. 'How can I ever thank you?' She turned to Grant. 'Both of you.'

Chapter Twenty

Brussels was a different city on their return. It was as if the field hospital had simply overflowed by twelve miles. Wounded soldiers were everywhere. In the Parc. On street corners. In shop doorways. Even in the Hotêl de Flandre where they were lying in the dining room and the hall.

Grant left almost immediately to march out with the regiment, but Rhys arranged leave to stay with Helene and help with David. Helene sent word to Louise and Wilson that David had been injured. When Louise saw the conditions of the hotel, she immediately insisted Helene, Rhys and David stay at her house. Mrs Jacobs, who cared for several of the injured, visited there often to change David's dressing and to see him through the inevitable fever from his wounds. Always full of news and gossip, Mrs Jacobs told them even the mansions of the town's wealthy were commandeered as hospitals. Everyone was pressed into service.

Louise put David in a cot in a little sitting room off her drawing room. Helene and Rhys shared her second bedchamber on the floor above.

Besides her nights with Rhys, Helene's favourite times were spent with Louise and Mrs Jacobs in the kitchen

where they treated her as a friend—and a very unedu-
cated friend indeed. They taught her how to make bread,
how to cook meat, how to clean and launder, things never
required of her before.

Her friends were also very watchful for signs she might
be carrying a baby, but Helene soon told them there would
be no baby. Helene tried to tell herself it was for the best,
but, in truth, she was deeply disappointed. Neither Louise
nor Mrs Jacobs had any children and Helene wondered
if they had yearned for a child with the men they loved.
Louise was past the age of childbearing, but at least she
and Wilson were to be married as soon as Brussels returned to normal.

This morning Helene, Louise and Mrs Jacobs sat
around the kitchen table drinking tea.

'Now it is not any of my business,' Mrs Jacobs said.
'But are you and your Captain planning to get married?'

'He has not asked me,' Helene admitted.

It puzzled Helene why Rhys had not spoken of marriage. She understood why he had not done so before the
battle—how could any promises be made at that uncertain time? But now the war was over. Napoleon had abdicated a second time.

Mrs Jacobs slapped her hand against the table. 'He
needs to marry you.' She shook her head sympathetically
at Helene. 'I know how it is when two young people are
in love, but he needs to be marrying you. I ought to give
him a piece of my mind.'

'Please do not!' Helene cried.

Mrs Jacobs crossed her arms over her chest. 'Well,
he'd better hurry or I just might.'

Helene tried to change the subject. 'How is your husband, Mrs Jacobs? Is he still feeling well?' Her dear Hulbert had recovered and was back to work.

'Fit as a fiddle.' Mrs Jacobs then shook a finger at Helene. 'Now what must we do to make your Captain come up to snuff?'

'Nothing!' cried Helene.

Helene was gloriously happy to be with Rhys every day, to be sharing his bed every night. It seemed that they'd put the past thoroughly behind them, but why did Rhys not speak of the future?

'Helene!' David's voice reached all the way into the kitchen.

Her brother took up the rest of Helene's time and she was very worried about him. At first, he was in a great deal of pain and the infection from his injury made him feverish, but now, after four weeks recuperating, he was more afflicted with nightmares and often woke in a panic.

'Helene!' he cried again.

She finished her cup of tea. 'I should go to him.'

Mrs Jacobs stood. 'I can see what the lad wants if you like.'

Helene motioned for her to sit again. 'No, I'll go. You have your other patients to see. Finish your tea first.'

She walked out of the kitchen, up the stairs and through the drawing room where she and Rhys had first spoken to Louise, to the small room behind it.

'Helene!' David's voice became more hysterical as she reached the threshold of the room.

'I am here.' She tried to sound calm, but she was alarmed at this mania he seemed unable to shake. 'What is it?'

David sat upright in bed, his body trembling, his eyes wide with fear. The swelling in his face had disappeared, but his bruises had turned various colours, now a sort of yellowish brown. 'I—I had a dream!'

She walked over to him and brushed his hair with her

fingers. 'It was only a dream.' She did not have to ask what of. She knew he'd returned to the field of the dead and dying. 'We should do something.' Something to distract him. 'Would you like to get up? Play a game of cards? I'll play cards with you if you get out of bed and come sit in the drawing room.'

It was not good for David to spend too much time in bed, even though he required a lot of sleep to recover. It was sleep, though, that brought the nightmares. Helene needed to get him home to Yarford, to familiar surroundings where he could feel safe again.

But home to Yarford meant leaving Rhys.

Rhys was, at this moment, out looking for transport to Ostend and passage to Ramsgate for her and David. It was no easy task. So many wounded men were travelling home to be cared for by loved ones. David was by no means healed, but Dr Goode, who looked in on him from time to time, pronounced him fit enough to travel.

Rhys, however, would be re-joining his regiment soon. Helene and David would be travelling alone. Helene could bear it if only she knew Rhys would eventually return to her.

David groaned as he turned to swing his legs over the side of the bed. 'Help me.'

She picked up his crutch and brought it to him.

He took the crutch and walked very unsteadily with it.

Rhys had gone to a great deal of trouble to find that crutch in a city where perhaps more than a thousand crutches were in demand. David had been afraid to walk with it and Rhys very patiently worked with him until he could manage well enough.

Helene followed close, in case David lost his balance or feared he would. He settled into a chair and she brought him a banyan to cover his nightclothes. He winced while she helped him put his arms through the sleeves. He'd been trampled on by horses and men and there were not many parts of his body that did not still hurt from it.

'What would you like to play?' Helene brought over the card table and placed it in front of him. She seated herself in a chair on the other side.

He stared past her. 'I don't care. Whatever you want.'

Piquet, the game they played together at home, would require more thinking than David was up to at the moment. 'Two-handed whist?' she suggested.

He shrugged.

There were times David would lose that distant look and return to his normal self—almost. Sometimes Helene merely needed to persist in pushing him to do normal things to make the old David return—almost.

She shuffled the cards.

From outside a man shouted and the sudden sound of a galloping horse reached their ears. David flinched and his arms flew up to protect his face.

Helene jumped from her chair and came to him. 'It is nothing, David. A horse going by, that's all. You are safe.'

She grasped his trembling hand until she felt him calm down.

'I want to go home,' he cried, sounding like a little boy. 'I want to go home.'

'Rhys is trying to arrange it,' she assured him. 'We'll go home as soon as he can find us passage.'

He glanced away from her and nodded.

She tapped on the cards she dealt him. 'Pick up your hand. Let's play.'

Helene returned to her chair and sorted her own cards. 'Would you like me to send word to William Lennox to call upon you again?'

Lennox and his sister Georgiana had called a few days before, but David refused to see them. Helene was sure he would perk up from such a visit, but he would not allow it.

'No!' David covered his face with his hands as if suddenly feeling shame. 'I lost the Duke's horse and William's clothes! How can I ever face him again?'

'I've already arranged payment,' she reminded him. 'They did not even ask for it. I think William was simply worried about you.'

'I do not want to see him,' David insisted.

Very well, Helene would not press him. It only distressed him more.

They played out the hand, which Helene easily won, because David forgot what suit was trump and put down the wrong cards.

She shuffled again. 'Another?'

He stared into space again. She wanted to shake him, as if that would restore him to himself.

The door opened on the ground floor and footsteps sounded on the stairs. Her heartbeat quickened and she looked towards the doorway, knowing who it would be. Rhys had returned.

'I am back.' His eyes smiled at her.

Sensation flared through her body at the mere sight of him. 'I am glad.'

'Let me go upstairs and brush some of the dirt from my clothes. I'll be right back down.' He turned and Helene could hear him taking the stairs to the second floor two at a time.

'Was that Rhys?' David asked, although Rhys had plainly been within his view.

'Yes.' What did David see when his thoughts took him away?

She dealt another hand.

Helene doubted David realised she and Rhys were lovers, that they shared the same bed every night. David had never been upstairs, so he would not know there were only two bedchambers up there, one for Louise and Wilson, one for her and Rhys, but mostly she thought David was caught too much in his own misery to notice the heat in every gaze she and Rhys shared. Or much of anything else, for that matter. Helene was desperate to shake David out of this miasma he was caught in. Bringing him home was the only way she knew to help him crawl out of it.

They played another hand of cards and she won again. David seemed not to care. He normally detested losing.

Rhys entered the room. He brushed his hand against hers as he sat in a nearby chair.

'Hello, David,' he said in a friendly voice. 'It is good to see you up. How are you feeling?'

David barely looked at Rhys. 'I am well.' His words were automatic.

Rhys shared a glance with Helene.

He took a breath before speaking again. 'There is a packet leaving in two days from Ostend.' A ship that would take them home. 'I booked you passage on it and I was able to hire a carriage to take you there. But you would leave tomorrow.'

Helene's heart sank. 'Tomorrow?'

His gaze met hers and she felt her pain mirrored there. 'So many people are trying to leave Brussels. I do not know when you'd have another chance to leave, so I seized the opportunity.'

She turned to her brother. 'David? Did you hear? Rhys said we could leave for home tomorrow.' A moment ago she'd been thinking it urgent to get David home, but not tomorrow.

'Home,' David repeated in a flat voice. 'I want to go home.'

'There is more.' Rhys turned to David. 'I also hired a valet to travel with you, David. A man of experience whose employer was an officer killed in the battle.'

David's expression turned pained at the mention of the battle.

Helene hurried to speak. 'A valet, David! He will be able to help you in ways I cannot.'

David turned his eyes to Rhys but did not appear to really see him. 'Thank you, Rhys.'

Her brother was not the only one struggling with emotions at the moment. Helene's were churning inside, as well. Her heart was pounding at the idea of parting from him. Tomorrow! Nothing was settled between them. How could she go back to Yarford House when Rhys would be so far away from her without knowing when—or if—they would be together again?

'Helene?' Rhys asked, his voice low.

She forced herself to meet his gaze. 'Yes.' Her voice shook. 'Thank you, Rhys. You have thought of everything.'

She placed her cards on the table and left the room, too unsettled to stay another minute.

Rhys put his head in his hands. Did Helene think he wanted them to leave so soon? It was tearing his guts out to part with her.

These four weeks were the most idyllic he could remember, spending each day with her like when they'd been young, making love with her each night. Only when he ventured out in the streets did reality shake him out of this reverie. The city was still filled with the wounded, still reeling from the aftermath of battle. There was more work to be done, even though Napoleon had abdicated. His regiment was heading to Paris, if not there already. Their job would be to ensure that the peace held. The French had so quickly welcomed Napoleon's return that no one knew how they would react to his final defeat.

Rhys's duty was to be with his regiment, to protect his men from the new dangers that could arise. He'd gone to the Allied headquarters at Place Royale and learned it was requested he re-join his regiment in two weeks' time.

His idyll with Helene was at an end.

'Rhys?' David's voice broke into Rhys's misery. 'Where is Helene?'

Rhys rubbed his face. 'She went upstairs.'

'I thought we were playing cards.'

At least the boy's eyes focused on him now, although there remained something distant about him. Rhys had seen such detachment before in soldiers after a battle, as if they had one foot in the present and one foot still caught in the battle's horror.

Rhys glanced away. 'Helene was upset. At the thought of leaving for home so soon, I expect.'

'Upset? At going home?'

Rhys thought it would be obvious, but David was not attending to much going on around him. 'Because Helene and I will have to say goodbye to each other,' he explained.

David still looked puzzled. 'Why would that upset her? I mean, I know you and Helene were friends, but that was a long time ago.'

Rhys peered at him. 'Do you not know of what happened between Helene and me? About why I left Yarford?'

David lifted his shoulders. 'You bought a commission in the army and left; that is all I know.'

David had been at Westminster School in London at

the time. Apparently, no one told him what happened while he was away.

The boy averted his gaze. 'I once wanted a commission in the army...' His voice trailed off.

Best to lead David away from those thoughts.

Rhys took a breath, deciding to tell David about him and Helene. 'Your sister and I were going to be married—to elope to Gretna Green.'

David turned back, eyes widened. 'Married? How could she marry you? Our father was an earl.'

And Rhys was the vicar's son. At least the old David was still inside him somewhere.

Perhaps Rhys would not tell him the whole story. 'Well, we did not marry and I did leave for the army, but being apart from each other was—' How to say it? '—difficult for each of us. Finding each other again has—has brought us happiness. That is why it will be upsetting to part again.'

David shook his head. 'But you can't marry. Helene is the daughter of an earl.'

Rhys gave him a disgusted look. 'The thing is, David, your father's title and my lack of one never made a bit of difference to Helene and me.'

David's brows knitted and his eyes flashed in worry. 'Are you going to marry her now? You can't! She needs to take me home! I need to go home.' He was quickly becoming overwrought.

Rhys lowered his voice. 'Do not worry, David. Helene will be taking you home.' Because Rhys could see no other option for them.

Rhys had spent a couple of hours walking the streets of Brussels thinking about his future with Helene, never mind all the time it filled his mind these last four weeks.

Rhys rose from his chair. 'Do you need anything, David?'

David had picked up the deck of cards and was absently shuffling it. 'No. Just to go home.'

Chapter Twenty-One

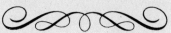

Helene sat on the bed in their bedchamber and stared out the window that looked on to the alley behind the house.

She and Rhys were to say goodbye tomorrow.

From the moment she saw him in the tavern that first night in Brussels, she knew this moment would come. But after these four weeks, it had become impossible for her to imagine being apart from him. How was she to bear another goodbye?

She thought of their first night together, after the Duchess of Richmond's ball. She'd thought then it would be their last time together. Saying goodbye to him then filled her with fear as well as grief, because he could have been killed in battle.

But she did find him again, on the eve of Waterloo. After another night in his arms, she'd had to face another wrenching goodbye. They'd not spoken of a future both those times, not with Napoleon so ready to snatch it away from them, not when her only prayer was that Rhys might live.

Helene knew what a soldier's death looked like from the countless maimed and bleeding soldiers who took their last breaths in her arms. She closed her eyes. Any one of them might have been Rhys.

It was an incredible gift that Rhys lived when all those thousands of men perished on the battlefield and in the hospitals. Goodness! They were still dying here in Brussels, from infection or other complications of their injuries. Rhys might have been one of them. He might have been lying among the bodies where he'd found David. If Rhys had died, then David would have died, too. No one would have known to look for him. God had been doubly good to her.

Perhaps it was too much to ask for what she wanted now. To stay with Rhys. To marry him. To spend the rest of her life with him.

At that moment Rhys entered the room. Helene could not bear to look at him, so she continued to stare out the window. He sat next to her on the bed, took her hand in his and raised it to his warm lips. The loving gesture pierced her heart and she fought to remain composed.

She turned and leaned her forehead against his. 'I'm better now. I—I simply was not prepared for the idea of leaving Brussels—leaving you—so soon.'

He lifted his head and stared directly into her eyes. 'I also found out I am expected back with my regiment within two weeks' time.'

There was no denying it, then. Parting was inevitable. Unless…

Rhys took both her hands in his. 'Helene, I have been remiss. I should have talked with you about the future, about what we should do. I fear you have long expected that of me.'

She placed a quick kiss on his lips. 'Rhys. Do you not remember? I said I would ask nothing of you but that you would live. I received my wish. You owe me nothing more.'

But she wanted so much more!

He tightened his grip. 'I owe you more. I vowed to myself that I would not repeat the errors of the past. Five years ago, I did not seek you out to explain why I had to leave. I will not repeat that mistake.'

Helene drew back, unsure she wanted to hear what he would say.

'Ethically I should marry you,' he began. 'I have compromised you, so marrying you would be the honourable thing to do—'

She cared nothing about that.

He glanced away as if a thought just occurred to him. 'Although if you are with child, I would do the honourable thing—'

'You *should.* You *would.*' His words wounded her. 'But you do not *want* to marry me.'

'It is not that.' He released her and ran a ragged hand though his hair. 'I love you, Helene. My heart wants to marry you, even more strongly than five years ago. But I am not that foolish young man any more.'

Foolish? He'd be foolish to marry her? Is that what he thought?

'I must use my head.' Now he seemed to be arguing with himself. He looked at her earnestly. 'My life, my livelihood, is with the army and my men, my superior officers, are expecting me in Paris.'

He wanted the army. Not her.

She lifted her chin. 'You could ask me to come with you.'

'And leave David?' He shook his head. 'I would not ask that of you. We both know he needs you now.'

'Then I could join you later,' she persisted.

'An Englishwoman travelling alone into France? You cannot.'

He would not escape this argument so easily. 'Perhaps Wilson and Louise would come with me.'

For a moment he seemed to be actually contemplating this possibility. But he shook his head again. 'No. We do not know what dangers we will find in Paris. Napoleon was instantly welcomed back. The people will not so welcome the British army in their midst.' He looked at her earnestly. 'Not only that. I do not know where I might be sent after Paris. If the peace holds, it will become even more difficult to advance to a higher rank. I may have to take posts that are far more unpleasant than Paris.'

These seemed like excuses to Helene. 'You know I can take unpleasantness, Rhys. I did so at Waterloo. There were many women at the battlefield—'

He stopped her. 'Those women, if married, were married to the soldiers. They live in terrible hardship. I will not have that for you.'

She continued undaunted. 'I know some officers take their wives with them. When the army was marching to Quatre Bras, I saw a wife riding next to her husband, an officer. She stayed by his side. Why can I not be like her?'

'Because the places I may have to go if I am to advance in rank—the West Indies, India—pose a great risk of disease and other dangers.' His tone remained resolute. 'Or if we married and you did not come with me, we'd spend years apart. I cannot want that for you either.'

'Other women manage that,' she told him, but she did not like the idea of years of separation either.

'Helene.' He looked directly into her eyes. 'I cannot support you on my captain's pay and I cannot guarantee I will advance in rank. You do not deserve to live in straitened circumstances—'

'I have some money from my mother.' Not much, though, actually. Her father had not provided for her beyond that inheritance. 'Besides, have I not shown you I am able to endure hardship?' She swept her arm around the room. 'Look how humbly I can live. I can even cook.'

'Yes,' he admitted. 'You are game for anything and I have always loved you for that, but what if we have children, which is very likely? How humbly would you wish them to live? How much hardship—and disease—are you willing for them to endure?'

Helene turned her face away. She had no counterargument for that.

He pressed on. 'If I left the army I would be as your father said—fit for nothing. I am trained as a soldier, Helene. Nothing else. I have no other options.' He made a helpless gesture. 'We are in no better a place than five years ago.'

That was not true. Helene felt changed from five years ago. She was ready to take chances, to leap into an unknown future. Surely they could surmount any obstacle as long as they were together.

She rose and walked to the window. The alley below looked bleak, as alleys often do.

She turned back to Rhys, squaring her shoulders and lifting her head high. 'I will not argue with you, Rhys. I wish only to point this out.' She paused to take a breath. 'If the issues that kept us apart five years ago are unchanged, as you say, so will be the fact that we are repeating the same mistake. We are parting.'

He stared back at her.

She suddenly could not stand to be in the room with him one moment more. She strode to the door. 'I need to be away from you for a while. I'll go downstairs and tell Louise and Wilson that David and I will be leaving tomorrow.'

She had thanked God that Rhys lived after the battle, but saying goodbye to him this time, as it had done before, killed any chance at her happiness.

Rhys saw little of Helene the rest of the day. She busied herself with packing or spending time with Louise or Wilson or David. Anyone but him. This would be their last night together and she wanted nothing to do with him.

If she only understood it had torn him apart to say those things to her, but her welfare was paramount in his mind. He would not risk her suffering again, not the way she'd suffered at Waterloo.

After a glum, uncomfortable dinner, the low spirits of which Rhys had no doubt were his fault, Wilson surprised him by inviting him out for beer at a nearby tavern while Helene and Louise served David dinner and cleaned up the kitchen.

As they walked out into the cool evening air, Wilson said, 'I am glad you accepted my invitation. It is difficult for me to know what is proper and not in my situation.'

'Proper?' Rhys did not follow at all.

Wilson smiled wryly. 'Am I servant or not? Am I acting out of place?'

Rhys laughed. 'I was never so high as to consider you *my* servant. You were, though, one of the few men around who would allow me to pester you.'

'You never pestered me, lad.' Wilson touched his shoulder.

Rhys smiled inside. Wilson called him lad, as he had done when Rhys was a boy.

When they entered the tavern they were met by the

familiar smells of hops, *frites* and men. There were almost as many men in the place as would be expected before the battle, and as great a variety of uniforms, but the men who wore them also wore bandages or carried crutches or wore that same vacant look that was often in David's eyes. Gone was the air of bravado that had been present before the battle. Now the atmosphere was subdued, weary, pained.

Rhys and Wilson found a table, sat and ordered tankards of beer.

When the maid placed the tankards on the table, Wilson took a sip and said to Rhys, 'I suppose Lady Helene is not happy to be leaving you.'

Rhys recognised that as an invitation to speak, but he'd spent too many years pushing his emotions down to be able to confide in anyone. He'd not even been able to share with Helene the desolation he felt inside at parting from her.

He asked Wilson instead, 'Tell me. Did you ever regret leaving Louise? Did you ever wish you would have stayed?'

'Regret?' Wilson looked pensive. He took another sip. 'Not regret. I was sorry about it, to be sure. Grieved for the loss. Missed her, but we did the right thing. She had a good life and so did I.'

This should have made Rhys feel better about his decision, but it did not.

'I take it you will not marry Lady Helene, then.' Wilson persisted.

'I cannot ask her to follow the drum,' Rhys replied. 'That's a hard life and I have nothing else to offer. Very little money, as well.'

Wilson nodded. 'Yes, lad. That was my situation, as well. Nothing to offer. No money.'

Rhys steered the conversation away from him and Helene and instead asked Wilson about other people at Yarford House and in the village. Rhys's parents never mentioned anything to do with Helene or her family in their letters, so there was much to catch up on.

When they walked back to Louise's house, Wilson talked about his and Louise's plan to marry. Wilson had saved his money and had enough to make their lives easy.

'That is what you should do, lad,' Wilson said. 'Save your money. When your fortunes change, come looking for her again. Might work out then, when it does not now.'

Wait twenty-five years like Wilson had? That prospect felt even worse.

Rhys loved Helene. It was shredding his insides to have to say goodbye to her, but he must stand firm. Above all else, no harm must come to her. No suffering. After the battle when she appeared in front of him covered in blood, he'd thought she'd been mortally injured. It shook him to the core. He would not risk that fear ever coming true.

Later that night Rhys helped David get ready for bed.

'I will be so glad to be home and in my own bed,' David said. 'I never want to see this place again. Or any of these people.'

'Wilson, Louise and Mrs Jacobs have been very good to you, David,' Rhys chided him.

'Oh, I know,' admitted David as Rhys helped him into a clean night shirt. 'They just remind me...' His voice trailed off and his face contorted in pain.

'Of the battle?' Rhys guessed.

David shook his head. 'Do not say the word. Do not speak of it! I hate thinking about it. It comes back. It all comes back!'

Rhys gave him a direct look. 'I know, David. I've been through many a battle.'

'Yes, but you wanted to be in the army,' he protested. 'You were supposed to be in battles. I was not.'

Rhys lowered his voice, as he helped David into the bed. 'You chose to be in the battle, too, David. I saw you join the charge. Accept the fact that it was your choice to come to Brussels, to witness the battle, to join the cavalry charge. What you experienced was the consequence of your decisions.'

David's eyes widened. 'You saw me?'

David seemed to miss the point, but Rhys answered him. 'I was too far away to stop you. Your friend Lennox told us he tried to stop you, but you didn't heed him.'

David glanced away. 'Odd. I did not remember that until now. My memory started with my horse galloping—' His breaths came fast. 'I wish I had never come here! I want to go home.'

Rhys put a hand on David's shoulder. 'Calm yourself, David. Get some sleep.'

David's voice became more strident. 'I hate to sleep! It all comes back when I sleep.'

Rhys firmed his grip. 'Listen to me. You survived a battle when thousands did not. That counts for something.'

'I was a coward!' David cried. 'I hid and played dead while they—while they—'

'You were clever,' Rhys said. 'You did what you had to do to survive.'

David peered at him uncertainly. 'Clever?'

Let him think on that a while. 'Tackle your nightmares like a man. Face them. Face the decisions you made and make amends.'

'Oh, yes.' David's voice turned sarcastic. 'Quite the easy thing for you to tell me to do.'

Rhys responded soberly, 'On the contrary. Facing the results of one's own decisions can be very, very difficult.' He patted David's shoulder. 'I'll say goodnight. Try to sleep. The travel tomorrow will be hard going for you.'

David relaxed against the pillows.

Rhys started to leave the room.

'Rhys?' David called him back.

He turned.

'Thank you for saving me.' His voice was small. 'And thank Grantwell, too. I do not think I ever said thank you.'

Rhys nodded approvingly. Perhaps David did have a chance to grow from a boy into a man. Rhys gave him a wave and turned to leave again.

'Rhys?' David called again.

'What?'

'Are you going to marry my sister?'

Not that question again. 'No, David.'

'Good!' The boy snuggled in the pillows again. 'Because I need her.'

Rhys's muscles tensed. David might be hopeless, after all.

Rhys started to walk away, but he whirled around to David and spoke through gritted teeth. 'Perhaps some day, David, you will be man enough to set aside what *you* need in order to consider what *your sister* needs.'

Rhys walked out.

When Rhys finally climbed the stairs to the bedchamber he shared with Helene, she was in a nightdress and was climbing into bed. She looked up at his entrance but did not speak.

'David is settled for the night,' he said.

She did not answer him.

He sat on a chair and pulled off his boots and stockings. He stood again and removed his coat. The other nights they'd shared together, undressing had been something they'd done in unison, like a dance with varied, but shared, steps. This night he undressed alone—at least down to his drawers. It appeared they would not lie naked in each other's arms this night.

It might be for the best. Each night they made love he risked getting her with child. As extraordinary an idea as that was, Rhys could not offer a son or daughter anything but hardship.

He washed, cleaned his teeth and felt as if they'd already said goodbye to each other, the distance between them seemed so vast. When he turned and finally faced her, though, she sat cross-legged on the bed, watching him.

He approached the bed, but she lay down and turned away.

This was agonising. No matter the risk, Rhys longed to hold her one more time, make love to her one more time before they must part.

He lay there, despairing, unable to even conceive of sleep, when she turned and spooned against him, her soft curves pressing into his back. He inhaled a long breath and savoured her closeness. He remained as still as possible, assuming she had moved to him in her sleep. He had no wish to wake her.

Her lips touched his bare back in a deliberate kiss. He rolled over. Moonlight from the window illuminated her lovely face. Her eyes were open.

She sat up and lifted her nightdress over her head, all the while her gaze continuing to pierce into him. Once naked, she stilled again and he basked in the sight of her. He could no more resist her than resist breathing. How could he ever let this night be their last? How could he allow her to leave him?

She eased him on his back, straddling him and joining their bodies together. They moved together, still silent, eyes still locked. His hands grasped her waist. They created a slow rhythm together, as if they'd both agreed not to hurry on this terrible final night together. Nothing compared to the exquisite pleasure of this dance with Helene. No other woman could come close.

Rhys wanted this joining between them to never stop, this connection, when bodies, minds and souls made them one. His body, though, his damned body—hers as well—betrayed him, intensifying his arousal, forcing them to move faster and faster…until…until…until the explosion of their climax made their joining complete—and very quickly separated them again.

Helene slid off him and, although he held her close, they were no longer one. They were apart again.

When Rhys's body recovered, he tried to recapture what he'd so recently possessed and lost. He rose above her as her body welcomed him again. This coupling, though, was more carnal, two bodies in need of each other, eager to get their fill while they were still able. When completed Rhys held her again and would not let her go. He fought sleep, wanting to remember each moment of the few hours he had left with Helene, but his body betrayed him again.

He almost instantly fell asleep.

Chapter Twenty-Two

When dawn broke Helene made love to Rhys again. This time was unlike any before and she knew it was because her emotions were high and raw. He was caught in the same mood and kissed her roughly. She returned his kiss in kind, her body instantly aroused and yearning for him. When he turned her on her back and entered her, it was with one hard thrust. Her fingernails raked his back as he moved, pushing deeper and harder than before. Still, the pain was in her heart; her body was glorying in his drive to their ultimate ecstasy. When her pleasure exploded inside her, she felt a momentary exhilaration, as if she'd proved once and for all that they belonged together. After he cried out in his own release and collapsed on top of her, she realised it was all illusion. Their bodies separated and he lifted himself off her.

She stared at him, her body trembling and he met her eye as he held himself away from her, giving them both room to breathe. Neither of them spoke but Helene sensed this was the last time she would see into his eyes, and he, hers.

He slowly moved to her side, and, as a clock struck

the hour to mark the time, she could mark this as the first moment of separation.

'I need to dress,' she said.

They might as well proceed with the day. Perhaps doing the ordinary things would make the day tolerable.

She climbed off the bed and walked naked to the pitcher and basin on the chest of drawers. She poured water into the basin and began to wash herself. When she washed away evidence of their lovemaking, the cloth came back red. At first she thought it was because they'd been rough, then her heart sank. All it meant was there would be no baby growing inside her, no precious consolation for parting from Rhys.

She glanced over at Rhys, but he was seated on the bed, his back turned to her. Should she tell him?

No. She could not see inflicting such pain if he'd grieve this loss as she did. If he met the news with relief, Helene did not think she could bear it. She took care of herself and put on her shift and positioned her corset.

She turned to him. 'Would you help me with my corset?'

'Of course.' He rose from the bed, gloriously naked.

She could not help but watch him, so muscular, so masculine as he moved towards her. When he came close, she turned her back so he could tie her laces. His warmth, his scent and the gentleness of his fingers made her body come alive again. She closed her eyes to help her remember this feeling; she would never feel it again. After he tied the laces, he wrapped his arms around her and held her close, his chin resting on her shoulder. How could she endure this? It hurt so much!

Rhys had to help her again when she needed her dress laced. While Rhys washed and shaved, she sat at the dressing table and arranged her hair. On other mornings he might have brushed her hair for her, a pleasure second only to lovemaking.

She was dressed before him. 'I'll see if Louise needs help with breakfast.'

She left the room. As she descended the stairs, she pictured her heart as that mended vase so carefully glued back together. One piece broke off again. Helene suspected the day would crack off the other pieces until nothing was left but jagged shards.

The carriage arrived at quarter past ten. David's new valet, Marston, came at the same time and Rhys introduced the man to everyone. Marston jumped right in to assist David, doing so with much deference and solicitude, as if David were not half his age and a world less experienced. He freed Helene to bid farewell to the people who had meant so much to her during these dramatic weeks.

Mrs Jacobs had come to see her off. After deluging Marston with detailed instructions for David's care, Mrs Jacobs burst into tears and embraced Helene.

'I will never see you again!' Mrs Jacobs wailed. 'I will never see my *mademoiselle* and her Captain!'

Helene feared that was true. She tried to blink away her own tears. She'd become very fond of Mrs Jacobs. 'Thank you, Mrs Jacobs. Thank you for everything you have done for me and Wilson and David. I will miss you terribly.' The nurse held her tight and was reluctant to let go.

Next goodbyes were with Louise and Wilson. She embraced Louise but could not speak through her tears which now fell in earnest.

'Write to us,' Louise managed to say, wiping her eyes.

Helene nodded. She turned to Wilson. Wilson, who had been a constant presence her whole life, someone she always could depend upon, someone incredibly dear to her.

She hugged him like she used to when she was a small girl and he comforted her for some hurt.

'I feel I am forsaking my duty to you, m'lady,' Wilson said, his voice rough.

'Nonsense,' she responded. 'It is your time to be happy. You have waited long enough for it.'

Rhys had supervised the loading of the luggage, Helene's portmanteau and David's trunk. That accomplished, he stood apart from the others.

He was her last goodbye.

She walked over to him and they faced each other. His expression was impassive and she wanted to flail at him. Did he not care? How could he let them part without a promise of being together again? She tried to tell herself she'd many times weathered this fear that they would never see each other again, surely she could do so one more time.

Helene mustered all her strength to remain composed. 'Goodbye, Rhys,' she whispered.

'Goodbye, Helene,' he responded.

Before the pain of this moment totally overwhelmed her, she turned away to walk to the carriage.

She took no more than two steps when Rhys seized her arm, spun her around and captured her in a fierce embrace. She melted into him.

'I am sorry, Helene,' Rhys rasped. 'I am so sorry.'

He loosened his grip on her and she reached up to touch his face. 'I'll never stop loving you, Rhys,' she whispered to him before pulling away and hurrying towards the carriage.

The drivers were on the box and David and the valet were seated inside the carriage. Wilson helped her to climb in and shut the door.

As the carriage drove off, Helene turned to look out

the back window. She watched Rhys standing in the road becoming smaller and smaller as the distance between them grew greater.

Until she could see him no longer.

The first hour of the trip found David restless and in a near panic.

'The sound of the horses,' he cried. 'I cannot take the sound of the horses.'

Helene tried to comfort him, but her own misery made it difficult to even speak.

Marston, in an un-valet-like manner, unexpectedly made conversation with David. 'The Captain said you got caught in the cavalry charge. Bad business, that.'

'Yes,' agreed David. 'Very bad.'

'Did you get as far as the French cannon?' Marston asked.

David nodded.

'Ah, the horses were blown by then.'

The valet sat on the rear-facing seat. David looked up at him as if seeing him for the first time. 'Were you at the battle?'

'I was,' Marston said. 'My officer was a cavalry man. With the Horse Guards. I was on a hill watching the whole thing.' He leaned towards David. 'You must be some sort of fellow to survive that charge.'

David just stared at him.

'How did you do it?' Marston asked.

To Helene's knowledge, David had never spoken of the battle. He became upset if the battle was even mentioned. Helene almost reached over to silence the valet, but to her surprise, David answered him. 'When I was knocked off my horse, I rolled away as far as I could and pretended to be dead.'

'Quite smart of you.' The valet's voice was admiring. 'But you got through the whole night, the Captain said.'

David blinked. 'I didn't want to remember this until Rhys—the Captain—talked to me. After the French cavalry left, I hid among the bodies. I could not walk. Night was frightening. They came and stripped off our clothes.'

'You played dead then, too?' Marston asked.

'I did not know what else to do.' David's voice turned small.

'You must have done right, because you made it out of there,' Marston responded.

Helene's astonishment must have shown on her face. The valet glanced at her and nodded, as if telling her he had her brother all figured out. He never implied any criticism of David for riding off with the cavalry. His tone was admiring or matter of fact. David was the calmest she'd seen him since Rhys rescued him.

Marston actually got David interested in how the entire battle proceeded. He must have witnessed it all. For Helene, it brought back the bleeding and dying men she'd cared for, so she stopped attending to the conversation.

But not listening to the valet only led her thoughts back to Rhys and thinking of Rhys only intensified her misery.

She tried to distract herself by looking out the window. They passed through Alost with its lovely churches and Gothic buildings, but those only reminded her of the buildings of Brussels she'd seen with Rhys.

The carriage continued for another hour or so before stopping at a coaching inn in Melle to change horses.

Marston was the first to climb out of the carriage. 'Let me help you, m'lord,' he said to David.

'Thank you, Marston,' David responded.

Helene climbed out after them.

The coachmen who had been conversing with the ostlers also climbed down. 'We'll be here at least half an hour, they say,' one told them.

'We could get some refreshment,' the valet suggested.

'An excellent idea,' David piped up.

'Shall I help you with your private needs first, m'lord?' Marston asked him diplomatically.

'Oh, yes.' David turned to Helene. 'We will meet you in the inn.'

After taking care of her own needs, Helene entered the inn and found the tavern. Marston stood and showed her where he and David were seated.

Helene sipped her tea and nibbled on a cinnamon biscuit, while Marston continued his masterful managing of the conversation with David. David was well in hand and Helene was not needed at all. It was a good thing. Helene was too overwhelmed with sadness to even think at the moment. She, only half listening, sipped her tea while the valet and her brother continued to talk.

'The thing is,' Marston was saying, 'you were helpless then. You didn't have any good choices.'

'I didn't!' David agreed.

'But now,' the valet went on, 'you are not helpless. In fact, who is it who can tell you what to do? You are the Earl now. You decide.'

'I am,' David said, as if realising it for the first time.

Helene smiled to herself. This stranger, this new servant, was able to get David to accept his role as Earl when she had repeatedly failed. Marston had pointed out the advantages. No one could tell David what to do. He would decide.

She started to raise her cup to her lips but stopped midway. Who really could tell her what to do? Not her father.

Not David, certainly. Not even Rhys. She was no longer helpless. She was of age. She could decide her own fate.

No one could tell her what to do. Not any more. *She* could decide.

She reached across the table and put her hand on David's arm.

He gave her an annoyed look. 'What is it, Helene?'

This time her own excitement made it hard for her to speak. 'I am not going with you.' She took a breath. 'I am not going on to Ostend with you. Or to England. Or to Yarford. I am going back to Brussels.'

'Back to Brussels!' David cried. 'Why?'

'To be with Rhys!' Though she did not know if he would even be there when she returned. If not, she'd find a way to travel to Paris and see him there. There was a risk he would not want her, but it was her risk to take.

'You can't go back to Brussels!' David whined like a little boy. 'I need you!'

'No, you don't, David,' Helene insisted. 'Marston can help you even in ways I cannot. You don't need me to travel home, and you don't need me at home.'

'Yes, I do!' he cried.

'Father trained you,' she said. 'You know what to do. But you don't even have to do it Father's way. You are the Earl now. You decide, like Marston said. I want to be with Rhys. I *need* to be with him.'

David lowered his head for a moment, then raised it again. 'You need to?' He glanced away as if thinking. 'Rhys said I should think about what you need.'

'He did?' She was surprised Rhys had talked with David about her.

'Rhys told me you were going to elope once.' His brows twisted. 'Are you going to marry him now?'

Her heart pounded. 'I don't know. But I need to find out.'

David gave her an exasperated look, more typical of the brother she knew. 'Oh, very well, then. I do not agree that you should marry him. An earl's daughter should not marry the vicar's son, but if that is what you *need* to do, we'll go to Yarford without you.'

She squeezed his hand and turned to Marston, a question in her gaze.

'I've no doubt we can get to Yarford without you.' Marston winked. 'The Earl knows the way.'

She smiled at him and rose from her chair. 'Would you ask the coachman to leave my portmanteau here?'

'As you wish, m'lady.' Marston bowed.

She gave David a kiss on the cheek. 'I'll write to you.'

Five years ago she'd done what her father wanted her to do, what she thought would be best for Rhys. This time she'd risk doing what she wanted to do, what she thought would be best for her.

She hurried off to find the innkeeper to arrange passage back to Brussels.

Once Helene left Brussels, Rhys saw no reason to delay re-joining his regiment. He'd packed his trunk and arranged to have it shipped to his regiment in Paris. Louise and Wilson begged him to stay one more day, to not hurry off, but Rhys suspected they were eager to be alone. They'd waited twenty-five years for it, after all. Besides, seeing the devotion between the older couple merely reminded Rhys of what he'd given up.

He'd been right, had he not? The army was no place for an earl's daughter. Her life would be nothing but hardship with him.

Rhys collected his horse from the stable and rode one last time through the streets of Brussels. A light rain started to fall. Rhys stopped briefly to put on his topcoat and to put some coins in the hand of a wounded soldier seated in a doorway. Other wounded men lay on the pavement or leaned against buildings, but in fewer numbers than even a week ago. Some might have recovered; others died. Or perhaps they merely found shelter from the rain. Had Helene tended any of these men? The enormity of their problems overwhelmed Rhys now; how much worse for Helene when, during the battle, their numbers must have seemed endless.

He approached the cathedral, which only brought more memories of Helene, so he urged his horse to go faster.

Rhys could have chosen two other routes out of Brussels, but he automatically chose the road that led to Waterloo and Quatre Bras. When he was still some distance from the battlefield, the putrid odour of death and rot reached his nostrils. Though a month after the battle, the stench lingered in the blood-soaked ground and the hastily dug mounds of buried men and horses. Several carriages waited at the side of the road by the battle site while their passengers, mostly English, toured the battlefield. Some were in groups led by a local man or an injured soldier; others walked the area alone, heads bowed to the ground, not in reverence, but in the hopes of finding a souvenir. Rhys passed by several urchins who were selling torn epaulets, bloody pieces of cloth, shards of scabbards or piles of musket balls. Visitors were eagerly buying whatever was for sale.

Rhys was glad Helene would not see this.

He closed his eyes. How long would it take for him to stop imagining the world through her eyes? As he rode the same path as he'd done the day of the battle, sadness engulfed him. He didn't need this reminder of her or of the battle. At a fork in the road there was a sign pointing to Nivelles. He could ride to Paris through Nivelles instead of Quatre Bras and avoid the agonising memories. He should have thought of that route in the first place.

From the outskirts of Nivelles, Rhys could see a huge white stone church towering above the other redbrick buildings. He found an inn where he could rest his horse and get something to eat.

Even this far from the battlefield, there were English in the tavern, waiting for their coaches to take them to see where Wellington defeated Napoleon. Rhys sat in a booth.

The tavern maid approached him. '*Bonjour, monsieur.* May I bring you some *tarte al d'jote*? It is our specialty.'

What the devil was *tarte al d'jote*? He was too tired to care. 'Very well. And some beer.'

He leaned against the back of the booth.

Every step of this journey so far felt laborious, as if he were straining against a tether that tried to pull him back. This was the right thing to do, was it not? To leave Helene?

He remembered five years ago, leaving Yarford, believing he'd never see her or the place he called home ever again. Then he'd been fuelled by anger and his anger made him glad to be away. This day he only felt regret.

The tavern maid brought his food. It looked as if *tarte al d'jote* was an egg dish.

She gestured towards his uniform coat. 'Were you in the battle?'

He nodded, not very interested in conversation.

But she went on. 'My cousin lives in Mont Saint Jean. She said it was pretty terrible.'

'It was,' he agreed.

She continued, 'They hid most of the day. Then after, *mon dieu*, so many wounded. They even came here.'

'Must have been very hard on everyone,' he said.

'I wish it had never happened.' She placed his beer in front of him. 'Don't you?'

Did he wish the battle never happened? He greatly regretted the catastrophic loss of life, but it had been the battle that brought Helene to Brussels and back to him, not to mention vanquishing Napoleon. There had been good in all that horrific hardship.

He looked up at the maid, but she did not wait for an answer. 'A lot of the soldiers who recuperated here said they wanted to quit the army after this. They said they didn't care what happened; they just never wanted to endure a battle again.'

Before Rhys could respond, she left to attend to another patron.

He took a drink of his beer.

Did he want to endure another battle? No, but he never wanted to endure another battle after surviving one. It was unlikely, though, that he—or anyone—would ever again experience the likes of the Battle of Waterloo.

Still, it had brought him Helene. The good with the terrible. They had each survived their particular hell of the battle. Against all odds. What could be worse? Good God, could leaving the army be worse than enduring Waterloo?

Apparently the soldiers the maid spoke of had not thought so.

Rhys faced other challenges now, other ways that could kill him. Certainly these challenges would not be as difficult as what he'd already endured. Would they be worse than leaving the army? He'd have some money from the sale of his commission. Helene had some money. How bad would it be, really, to leave the army?

He'd be jumping into the unknown, as he'd done when he left Yarford for the army.

He finished his beer and was suddenly hungry for this egg dish set before him.

Rhys had been thinking that the crucial issue was whether he could provide a good enough life for Helene and any children they might have, but maybe that was not the proper question. Maybe the proper question was, which was the bigger risk—facing the desolation of giving up a future with Helene or taking the chance that they could be happy together, no matter what they faced?

Her words returned to him... *We are repeating the same mistake...*

'Not this time, Helene,' he whispered to himself.

Rhys finished the last of his very satisfying meal and threw some coins on the table.

The maid came over and picked up the money. 'Anything else, sir?'

'May I see a map?' he asked. 'One showing the way to Ostend?'

The map showed he'd have to ride back to Brussels to reach the road to Ostend. He'd be on the same road as Helene's carriage, but several hours behind. He knew what inn Helene and David would stay in when reaching Ostend, though, and the packet they had passage on to England. He stood a good chance to catch up to her by then.

Make no mistake, though. He'd reach her even if he had to follow her all the way to Yarford.

Chapter Twenty-Three

Helene was only able to secure a seat on a coach to Brussels that would depart the next day, distressing, because she feared Rhys would leave Brussels before she could return there. Rhys had nothing in Brussels to hold him and he'd be eager to return to his regiment.

No matter. She'd travel to Paris alone if she must. She'd find the 44th Regiment and learn of Rhys's whereabouts from there.

She took a room in the inn for the night and, to pass the afternoon, strolled around Melle, visiting a few shops that sold silk, linen, lace and wool cloth from the manufacturers in Ghent. She purchased a linen handkerchief edged in lace as a remembrance of this place and the decision she'd made here. She put it in her pocket next to the handkerchief she'd taken from Rhys's trunk before the battle. At dusk she returned to the inn's tavern for dinner.

The inn was filled with other travellers like herself, but the tavern was nothing like the ones in Brussels where she and Wilson had searched for David—and found Rhys. Gone were the colourful uniforms and rowdy voices of the Allied soldiers that had filled those taverns, replaced by several English travellers and local people.

At the table next to Helene sat two English couples who, Helene could not help but overhear, had travelled to Belgium for the singular purpose of visiting the Waterloo battlefield. The battlefield had been cleaned up—meaning the corpses of thousands of men and horses had been removed—and had become a desirable destination for tourists, especially those coming in hopes of finding souvenirs left behind by the dead soldiers. Helene shuddered. She never wanted to see Waterloo again. She wanted nothing to remind her of the countless dead corpses that blanketed the fields between La Haye Sainte and Hougoumont.

The English couples' noisy conversation also stirred up vivid memories of the wounded men Helene had tended that awful day. She could again see their pain-contorted faces, hear their cries and smell blood, gunpowder and death. She lowered her head as the two couples went on and on about the glory of the battle and the greatness of the victory. They had apparently read much about the battle and spoke of the defence of Hougoumont, of the grand cavalry charge, of how the British troops stood fast when the French attacked, of the routing of Napoleon's elite Imperial Guard.

Helene could stand it no more.

'Stop!' she cried. She rose from her chair and pushed her way past them, hurrying to the door, eager to escape.

Suddenly she was directly facing a man who had just entered the tavern and was caught for a moment in the unexpected sight of him.

'Rhys?'

He closed the distance between them and, heedless of all the people watching them, enveloped her in his arms. 'Helene. Helene.'

She laughed and cried as she savoured the feel of his arms, the sound of his voice, the scent of him.

'I cannot believe it. Are you real?' She touched his face.

He released her but grasped her hand and pulled her out of the tavern and into the momentarily empty hall of the inn. 'I am real.'

She shook her head, still half in disbelief. 'Why are you here?'

He slid his hands to her shoulders. 'Merely to rest my horse and spend the night. I did not expect to find you here. I was riding to Ostend to find you. To tell you—'

She put her fingers on his lips. 'No. Do not tell me. I am so weary of people telling me what to think, what I must do. I have something to tell you. I sent David on with the wonderful Marston—he is a treasure, by the way—I sent them on so I could return to you. I have decided that I do not want to return to Yarford. I do not want a life of wealth and ease. I want to be with you. If that means danger, I do not care. If it means hardship, I do not care. I want to be with you.'

Rhys laughed and hugged her again, before holding her at arm's length once more. 'My turn.'

Words so familiar, spoken often when they'd been children.

'I came to tell you that I made a decision,' he said. 'I wonder I did not seriously consider it before. I will leave the army. I'll find something to do, some way to earn money, if our funds run low—'

'Leave the army?' she cried. 'Rhys, no! It means too much to you.'

'Not more than you mean to me,' he countered.

'But I do not mind coming with you wherever the army sends you,' she insisted. 'You are next going to Paris—is that not an exciting place to be? I would love to explore Paris with you.'

His expression turned serious. 'We do not know what it will be like for us in Paris.'

'We do not know what life would be like for us even if we returned to Yarford.' She threw up her hands. 'It will be a grand adventure!'

A grand adventure. Rhys and Helene had spent their childhood chasing grand adventures together, even if then the adventure only meant climbing a tree or learning how to pick a lock. Why not this adventure?

She was correct. Paris would be an exciting place to explore, and there was no one Rhys would rather explore Paris with than Helene. If the city was too dangerous, they'd not have to stay. He could make the decision to leave the army at any time. He'd been trying to sort out the rest of their lives, but there was no need to do that. He merely had to figure out the next step.

He gave her a direct look and still held her firmly in his grasp. 'Very well. I stay in the army and we go to Paris together. On one condition, though.'

She looked wary. 'What condition?'

'You must marry me.' He smiled. 'We stay together for ever. As husband and wife.'

Her expression turned indignant. 'You are telling me what I *must* do?'

This reaction startled him. 'I only meant—'

A grin grew on her face. 'It is a good thing marrying you is precisely what I *want* to do.'

Rhys laughed aloud as he took her in his arms again and swung her around.

His first friend—his closest friend—his best friend—would now be his wife.

And no one would ever again make them part.

Chapter Twenty-Four

Brussels, Belgium—June 1816

Like several regiments of the British army, the 44th Regiment of Foot, the East Essex Regiment, disbanded its second battalion in January of 1816, placing its officers and soldiers on half-pay. With the Continent in peace and Napoleon far away on the island of St Helena, there was little need for an army. Commissions were few in the regiments that did not disband, but the places these regiments were sent were less than ideal. Places like fever-ridden West Indies. Or Ireland, where the task was to police what felt like one's own countrymen. Or, at best, the isolated Mediterranean island of Malta.

Captain Rhys Landon and his wife, Lady Helene, had not sailed to Dover with the rest of the regiment. Instead they'd elected to take rooms in Brussels, where their funds were sufficient to live modestly and where they had friends.

They had another motive, as well. By January, Helene knew she was carrying a child. They worried that a rough passage over the Channel or further travel in

England might not be safe for her. That and the uncertainty of how they would live in England.

Their decision to settle in Brussels delighted Mrs Jacobs. She and Louise Wilson called upon Helene almost every day. This day Wilson had joined them. Wilson had brought a wooden cradle he'd made. After he and Rhys carried it up to the bedchamber, they'd gone off to a nearby tavern, while Louise, Mrs Jacobs and Helene sat drinking tea in the small drawing room.

Louise had brought a dress she'd sewn for Helene. She held it up to show her.

'I do not think you should have bothered with a new dress when I am due so soon,' Helene told her. She was uncertain precisely when she was due, but it must be soon.

'Your dresses are becoming too tight in the bodice,' Louise explained. 'Let us see if this one will fit better.'

The three women walked upstairs and had Helene try on this newest creation.

'This takes me back,' Mrs Jacobs exclaimed, as she handed pins to Louise. 'Were we not similarly engaged a year ago?'

Helene smiled. 'For my beautiful gold ball gown.' So much had happened since then. 'I must admit, I am able to breathe better in this dress.'

'Now remember, Madame Helene—' Madame Helene was the name Mrs Jacobs had settled on when *mademoiselle* would no longer suit '—Louise and I will come when it is your time, and I am prepared to be your baby nurse for as long as you wish it.'

Helene smiled at her. 'How could I forget?'

After her friends left, Helene washed their tea dishes in the scullery. She occasionally hired a maid of all work to help with the cleaning, but mostly she did not mind these daily chores. This was not the life she'd been brought up to expect, but it was one she much preferred.

Especially because she was with Rhys.

Their months in Paris had been idyllic, strolling along the Seine, exploring the glorious Notre Dame cathedral, dining at outdoor cafes. Helene would not have missed those days for the world. Paris after Waterloo had not at all been the atmosphere Rhys feared. The French people, if not welcoming the British army, were at least tolerant. They'd been very tired of war. But Helene had no wish to stay in Paris as some English expatriates chose to do. She much preferred Brussels where, in her mind, love abounded.

Rhys returned home. He entered the kitchen and gave her a hug from behind while her arms were plunged in dishwater.

'I collected the post,' he murmured as he dropped kisses on the tender skin of her neck.

'Mmm…' was all she could say.

He released her and pulled out two envelopes. 'A letter from Grant.'

'How nice!' she exclaimed.

'A letter from your brother.'

'Oh?'

David rarely wrote to her, although he was doing fairly well in Yarford. Marston stayed on as his valet and proved a steadying force for the young Earl. David was not yet old enough to take total control of his estates, but he seemed to have no difficulty asserting his will and having it accepted.

'Open David's first,' she said. 'My hands are wet.'

Rhys broke the seal and unfolded the page.

He paraphrased the letter. 'It is quite civil.' Sometimes David's letters were a bit irate when he was worked up about something. 'It is difficult to make out. He wishes your input on an estate matter. I can tell that. You should read it for yourself.'

She turned to look at him. 'David wants my opinion?'

He glanced at the page again. 'I am not certain. I think he wants you to agree with his opinion.'

She smiled. 'That does sound more likely. I'll read it later, when my hands and apron are dry and I have time to make out his hand.' She wiped a plate clean in the soapy water and rinsed it in clear water. 'And the letter from Grant?'

When the regiment disbanded, Grant returned to England. They'd not received a letter from him in a long time.

Rhys opened the letter and read to himself.

He gasped. 'I don't believe this!'

She turned around to face him. 'What is it? He is not ill, is he?'

'No. Not Grant. He is well.' Rhys shook his head. 'It is his brother.'

'The Viscount?'

'Yes.' He looked up at her. 'His brother was killed in a carriage accident. The Viscountess, too. They had no sons, so Grant is Viscount Grantwell now.'

'Oh, my.' She wiped her hands on her apron and came to his side.

He read further and looked over at her, all expression leaving his face. 'There is more.'

'What?' she asked, alarmed.

'Grant wants me to manage his estate for him. His brother left matters in disarray and the present estate manager seems to have been skimming funds.'

They stared at each other.

'Do you want to do that?' she asked finally.

Did she? she asked herself. Their lives had settled into

this comfortable routine—at least Helene's life had. Her days were busy with cooking, cleaning, shopping. Rhys was more at loose ends. Sometimes Helene wondered if he yearned to be back in the army, leading his men.

He perused the letter again as if to assure himself he'd read it correctly. 'What do I know about managing an estate? I do not know if I am even capable.'

She put her arm around his waist. 'Of course you are capable! Grant would not offer it to you if he thought otherwise.'

He turned to face her. 'Would you like to do this?'

She was so happy here in Brussels. 'I would miss Mrs Jacobs and Louise and Wilson.'

He nodded, but she thought the corners of his mouth turned down in disappointment.

On the other hand, they could always visit Brussels. 'There is much I miss about being on an English country estate, too, though.'

His expression brightened. 'You would consider it?'

She leaned her cheek against his arm. 'Of course I would.'

He frowned. 'I would not wish to disappoint Grant.'

She laughed. 'I am not sure of your meaning. Disappoint Grant by refusing?'

'By not doing the job well,' he said.

She reached up to touch his cheek. 'My love, you have led men in terrible circumstances. You found my brother in—' She swallowed. 'There is nothing you cannot do. And you will be with your friend.'

He still looked uncertain. 'The daughter of an earl married to an estate manager? Would that not be difficult for you?'

A return to England would certainly put her back in the society where status and titles mattered. 'Perhaps that will matter more to other people than to me. We will not know until we try. It will be another risk.'

The corners of his mouth turned up. 'Another grand adventure, you mean?'

She grinned. 'Another grand adventure!'

And nothing was set in stone. If this new life did not suit them, they could always embark on a different grand adventure.

She winced. A sudden pain took her mind in another direction entirely.

'I will agree on one condition,' she managed.

'What condition?' Rhys looked uncertain again.

She glanced down at her widening girth. 'I wish to wait until after the baby is born.' The pain recurred and she looked up at him in wonder and anxiety. 'Which I think might be very soon!'

His brows rose. 'Do you mean…?'

She nodded. The pain recurred.

He swept her into his arms and carried her to their stairs.

'Rhys, I can walk!' she protested.

He did not heed her. 'Is there time for me to summon Mrs Jacobs?'

'I think so.' Her water had not broken. 'And Louise.'

He lay her on their bed, but she immediately sat up. 'Wait!'

He turned back.

She slid off the bed, reached up and tilted his face towards hers. Their lips touched. 'I have a feeling this will be our grandest adventure of them all!'

He embraced her, holding her close as he had on other occasions of their parting. The morning after the Duchess of Richmond's ball. At the stables before the battle. At the carriage here in Brussels.

'I love you,' he said. 'I will be back soon with Mrs Jacobs.'

She climbed back in bed and he turned to go.

'Rhys!' She sat up and called him back again.

He stopped.

'Come back to me soon.'

'Always,' he said, and rushed out through the door.

* * * * *